White Mule

By *William Carlos Williams* (in print)

The Autobiography
The Build-up
Collected Earlier Poems
Collected Later Poems
The Farmers' Daughters
I Wanted to Write a Poem*
In the American Grain
Kora in Hell: Improvisations†
Many Loves and Other Plays
Paterson, Books 1-5
Pictures from Brueghel and Other Poems
The Selected Essays
The Selected Letters §
Selected Poems
Yes, Mrs. Williams §

Beacon Press
† *City Lights Books*
§ *Ivan Obolensky*

WHITE MULE

A NOVEL BY
WILLIAM CARLOS WILLIAMS

A NEW DIRECTIONS BOOK

Library of Congress Catalog card number: 37:11249

Chapters of *White Mule* were first published in the magazines
Pagany and *The Magazine*. Acknowledgment is made to the
editors of these publications for permission to reprint.

First published as New Directions Paperbook 226 in 1967.

Manufactured in the United States of America.

New Directions Books are published for James Laughlin
by New Directions Publishing Corporation,
333 Sixth Avenue, New York 10014.

To The Kids

Contents

Contents

White Mule

CHAPTER I

To Be

S HE ENTERED, as Venus from the sea, dripping. The air enclosed her, she felt it all over her, touching, waking her. If Venus did not cry aloud after release from the pressures of that sea-womb, feeling the new and lighter flood springing in her chest, flinging out her arms — this one did. Screwing up her tiny smeared face, she let out three convulsive yells — and lay still.

Stop that crying, said Mrs. D, you should be glad to get outa that hole.

It's a girl. What? A girl. But I wanted a boy. Look again. It's a girl, Mam. No! Take it away. I don't want it. All this trouble for another girl.

What is it? said Joe, at the door. A little girl. That's too bad. Is it all right? Yes, a bit small though. That's all right then. Don't you think you'd better cover it up so it won't catch cold? Ah, you go on out of here now and let me manage, said Mrs. D. This appealed to him as proper so he went. Are you all right, Mama? Oh, leave me alone, what kind of a man are you? As he didn't exactly know what she meant he thought it better to close the door. So he did.

In prehistoric ooze it lay while Mrs. D wound the white twine about its pale blue stem with kindly clumsy knuckles and blunt fingers with black nails and with the wiped-off scissors from the cord at her waist, cut it — while it was twisting and flinging up its toes and fingers into the way — free.

Alone it lay upon its back on the bed, sagging down in the middle, by the smeared triple mountain of its mother's disgusted thighs and toppled belly.

The clotted rags were gathered. Struggling blindly against the squeezing touches of the puffing Mrs. D, it was lifted into a nice woolen blanket and covered. It sucked its under lip and then let out two more yells.

Ah, the little love. Hear it, Mam, it's trying to talk.

La, la, la, la, la, la, la! it said with its tongue — in the black softness of the new pressures — and jerking up its hand, shoved its right thumb into its eye, starting with surprise and pain and yelling and rolling in its new agony. But finding the thumb again at random it sobbingly subsided into stillness.

Mrs. D lifted the cover and looked at it. It lay still. Her heart stopped. It's dead! She shook the . . .

With a violent start the little arms and legs flew up into a tightened knot, the face convulsed again — then as the nurse sighed, slowly the tautened limbs relaxed. It did not seem to breathe.

And now if you're all right I'll wash the baby. All right, said the new mother drowsily.

In that two ridges lap with wind cut off at the bend of the neck it lay, half dropping, regrasped — it was rubbed with warm oil that rested in a saucer on the stove while Mrs. D with her feet on the step of the oven rubbed and looked it all over, from the top of its head to the shiny soles of its little feet.

About five pounds is my guess. You poor little mite, to come into a world like this one. Roll over here and stop wriggling or you'll be on the floor. Open your legs now till I rub some of this oil in there. You'll open them glad enough one of these days — if you're not sorry for it. So, in all of them creases.

How it sticks. It's like lard. I wonder what they have that on them for. It's a hard thing to be born a girl. There you are now. Soon you'll be in your little bed and I wish I was the same this minute.

She rubbed the oil under the arm pits and carefully round the scrawny folds of its little neck pushing the wobbly head back and front. In behind the ears there was still that white grease of pre-birth. The matted hair, larded to the head, on the brow it lay buttered heavily while the whole back was caked with it, a yellow-white curd.

In the folds of the groin, the crotch where the genitals all bulging and angry red seemed presages of some future growth, she rubbed the warm oil, carefully — for she was a good woman — and thoroughly, cleaning her fingers on her apron. She parted the little parts looking and wondering at their smallness and perfection and shaking her head forebodingly.

The baby lay back at ease with closed eyes — lolling about as it was, lifted by a leg, an arm, and turned.

Mrs. D looked at the toes, counted them, admired the little perfect nails — and then taking each little hand, clenched tight at her approach, she smoothed it out and carefully anointed its small folds.

Into the little sleeping face she stared. The nose was flattened and askew, the mouth was still, the slits of the eyes were swollen closed — it seemed.

You're a homely little runt, God pardon you, she said — rubbing the spot in the top of the head. Better to leave that — I've heard you'd kill them if you pressed on that too hard. They say a bad nurse will stop a baby crying by pressing there — a cruel thing to do.

She looked again where further back upon the head

a soft round lump was sticking up like a jockey cap askew. That'll all go down, she said to herself wisely because it was not the first baby Mrs. D had tended, nor the fifth nor the tenth nor the twentieth even.

She got out the wash boiler and put warm water in it. In that she carefully laid the new-born child. It half floated, half asleep — opening its eyes a moment then closing them and resting on Mrs. D's left hand, spread out behind its neck.

She soaped it thoroughly. The father came into the kitchen where they were and asked her if she thought he could have a cup of coffee before he left for work — or should he go and get it at the corner. He shouldn't have asked her — suddenly it flashed upon his mind. It's getting close to six o'clock, he said. How is it? Is it all right?

He leaned to look. The little thing opened its eyes, blinked and closed them in the flare of the kerosene oil lamp close by in the gilded bracket on the wall. Then it smiled a crooked little smile — or so it seemed to him.

It's the light that hurts its eyes, he thought, and taking a dish towel he hung it on the cord that ran across the kitchen so as to cast a shadow on the baby's face.

Hold it, said Mrs. D, getting up to fill the kettle.

He held it gingerly in his two hands, looking curiously, shyly at that ancient little face of a baby. He sat down, resting it on his knees, and covered its still wet body. That little female body. The baby rested. Squirming in the tender grip of his guarding hands, it sighed and opened its eyes wide.

He stared. The left eye was rolled deep in toward

the nose; the other seemed to look straight at his own.
There seemed to be a spot of blood upon it. He looked
and a cold dread started through his arms. Cross eyed!
Maybe blind. But as he looked — the eyes seemed
straight. He was glad when Mrs. D relieved him —
but he kept his peace. Somehow this bit of moving,
unwelcome life had won him to itself forever. It was
so ugly and so lost.

The pains he had seemed to feel in his own body
while the child was being born, now relieved — it
seemed almost as if it had been he that had been the
mother. It was his baby girl. That's a funny feeling,
he thought.

He merely shook his head.

Coffee was cooking on the back of the stove. The
room was hot. He went into the front room. He
looked through the crack of the door into their bedroom where she lay. Then he sat on the edge of the
disheveled sofa where, in a blanket, he had slept that
night — and waited. He was a good waiter. Almost
time to go to work.

Mrs. D got the cornstarch from a box in the pantry.
She had to hunt for it among a disarray of pots and
cooking things and made a mental note to put some
order into the place before she left. Ah, these women
with good husbands, they have no sense at all. They
should thank God and get to work.

Now she took the baby once more on her lap, unwrapped it where it lay and powdered the shrivelling,
gummy two inch stem of the gummy cord, fished a
roll of Canton flannel from the basket at her feet and
putting one end upon the little pad of cotton on the
baby's middle wrapped the binder round it tightly,

round and round, pinning the end in place across the back. The child was hard there as a board now — but did not wake.

She looked and saw a red spot grow upon the fabric. Tie it again. Once more she unwrapped the belly band. Out she took the stump of the cord and this time she wound it twenty times about with twine while the tiny creature heaved and vermiculated with joy at its relief from the too tight belly band.

Wrapping an end of cotton rag about her little finger, Mrs. D forced that in between the little lips and scrubbed those tender gums. The baby made a grimace and drew back from this assault, working its whole body to draw back.

Hold still, said Mrs. D, bruising the tiny mouth with sedulous care — until the mite began to cough and strain to vomit. She stopped at last.

Dried, diapered and dressed in elephantine clothes that hid it crinkily; stockinged, booted and capped, tied under the chin — now Mrs. D walked with her new creation from the sweaty kitchen into the double light of dawn and lamps, through the hallway to the front room where the father sat, to show him.

Where are you going? For a walk?, he said.

Look at it in its first clothes, she answered him.

Yes, he said, it looks fine. But he wondered why they put the cap and shoes on it.

Turning back again, Mrs. D held the baby in her left arm and with her right hand turned the knob and came once more into the smells of the birth chamber. There it was dark and the lamp burned low. The mother was asleep.

She put out the lamp, opened the inner shutters. There was a dim light in the room.

Waking with a start — What is it? the mother said. Where am I? Is it over? Is the baby here?

It is, said Mrs. D, and dressed and ready to be sucked. Are you flooding any?

Is it a boy? said the mother.

It's a girl, I told you before. You're half asleep.

Another girl. Agh, I don't want girls. Take it away and let me rest. God pardon you for saying that. Where is it? Let me see it, said the mother, sitting up so that her great breasts hung outside her undershirt. Lay down, said Mrs. D. I'm all right. I could get up and do a washing. Where is it?

She took the little thing and turned it around to look at it. Where is its face? Take off that cap. What are these shoes on for? She took them off with a jerk. You miserable scrawny little brat, she thought, and disgust and anger fought inside her chest, she was not one to cry — except in a fury.

The baby lay still, its mouth stinging from its scrub, its belly half strangled, its legs forced apart by the great diaper — and slept, grunting now and then.

Take it away and let me sleep. Look at your breasts, said Mrs. D. And with that they began to put the baby to the breast. It wouldn't wake.

The poor miserable thing, repeated the mother. This will fix it. It's its own mother's milk it needs to make a fine baby of it, said Mrs. D. Maybe it does, said the mother, but I don't believe it. You'll see, said Mrs. D.

As they forced the great nipple into its little mouth, the baby yawned. They waited. It slept again. They tried again. It squirmed its head away. Hold your breast back from its nose. They did.

Mrs. D squeezed the baby's cheeks together between

her thumb and index finger. It drew back, opened its jaws and in they shoved the dripping nipple. The baby drew back. Then for a moment it sucked.

There she goes, said Mrs. D, and straightened up with a sigh, pressing her two hands against her hips and leaning back to ease the pain in her loins.

The mother stroked the silky hair, looked at the gently pulsing fontanelle, and holding her breast with the left hand to bring it to a point, straightened back upon the pillows and frowned.

The baby ceased to suck, squirming and twisting. The nipple lay idle in its mouth. It slept. Looking down, the mother noticed what had happened. It won't nurse, Mrs. D. Take it away. Mrs. D come here at once and take this thing, I'm in a dripping perspiration.

Mrs. D came. She insisted it should nurse. They tried. The baby waked with a start, gagging on the huge nipple. It pushed with its tongue. Mrs. D had it by the back of the neck pushing. She flattened out the nipple and pushed it in the mouth. Milk ran down the little throat, a watery kind of milk. The baby gagged purple and vomited.

Take it. Take it away. What's the matter with it? You're too rough with it.

If you'd hold it up properly, facing you and not away off at an angle as if — Mrs. D's professional pride was hurt. They tried again, earnestly, tense, uncomfortable, one cramped over where she sat with knees spread out, the other half kneeling, half on her elbows — till anger against the little rebellious spitting imp, anger and fatigue, overcame them.

Take it away, that's all, said the mother finally.

Reluctantly, red in the face, Mrs. D had no choice but to do what she was told. I'd like to spank it, she said, flicking its fingers with her own.

What! said the mother in such menacing tones that Mrs. D caught a fright and realized whom she was dealing with. She said no more.

But now, the baby began to rebel. First its face got red, its whole head suffused, it caught its breath and yelled in sobs and long shrill waves. It sobbed and forced its piercing little voice so small yet so disturbing in its penetrating puniness, mastering its whole surroundings till it seemed to madden them. It caught its breath and yelled in sobs and long shrill waves. It sobbed and squeezed its yell into their ears.

That's awful, said the mother, I can't have it in this room. I don't think it's any good. And she lay down upon her back exhausted.

Mrs. D with two red spots in her two cheeks and serious jaw and a headache took the yelling brat into the kitchen. Dose it up. What else?

She got the rancid castor oil and gave the baby some. It fought and spit. Letting it catch its breath, she fetched the fennel tea, already made upon the range, and sweetening it poured a portion into a bottle, sat down and rather roughly told the mite to take a drink. There, drat you. Sweet to unsweeten that unhappy belly. The baby sucked the fermentative warm stuff and liked it — and wet its diaper after.

Feeling the wet through her skirt and petticoat and drawers right on her thighs, Mrs. D leaped up and holding the thing out at arm's length, got fresh clothes and changed it.

Feeling the nice fresh diaper, cool and enticing, now

the baby grew red all over. Its face swelled, suffused with color. Gripping its tiny strength together, it tightened its belly band even more.

The little devil, said Mrs. D, to wait till it's a new diaper on.

And with this final effort, the blessed little thing freed itself as best it could — and it did very well — of a quarter pound of tarrish, prenatal slime — some of which ran down one leg and got upon its stocking.

That's right, said Mrs. D.

CHAPTER II

A Flower from the Park

Joe rose from the couch in the front room and went to the window, attracted perhaps by a sparrow which was twittering there. As he drew near, the bird darted off and he could see it alight on a tree which was just beginning to come into leaf below him.

April 18th, he thought, and added the year, 1893 — a springtime girl, like a leaf or a flower. Flora. He had seen that name often in his mind. No. He didn't think that a name one would call an American girl by. He didn't think she'd like it much after she grew up and was running around playing with the other girls. Florence, he said aloud. That's it.

Looking again out of the window he saw that it would be one of those rare April days, rare in this ountry, such as he had known in his childhood. Were they really so marvelous as he imagined them to have been? — with the daisies up, the sweet violets, the willow twigs golden. Run, shout! — the snow mountains of Silesia — there.

Somehow as he saw the knife of the lifting sun cutting the facades across 104th St. he felt happy. Free. Another little girl, his own. Maybe it would grow up to be better than it seemed now, stronger. Well, coffee. He could smell it and turned away from the window, looking at his watch. Half-past six. Mrs. D was busy in the other room. He drew a chair up to the kitchen table, got a cup, sugar, poured out the solid, shining stream, cut himself the bread, buttered it and munched and sipped his drink. He had forgotten the sugar. He added sugar.

The door to the dining room stood ajar. He heard a pan rattled. A door closed. Everything seemed very quiet now.

Now the coffee got him. Why it's Sunday, it flashed across his mind. I don't have to go to work today. Well, that's a good one. He had never forgotten a thing like that before in his life. That's funny. Well that's fine. He would go and tell Frieda, his wife's sister, that the baby was here.

Mrs. D came into the kitchen. How much do I owe you? he said to her. He wanted to pay her. I'm glad you got here on time.

What's your hurry? said Mrs. D. Am I fired? Then she laughed, seeing his face. I don't get paid till my job's done, she added.

You'd better take it while I've got it, he returned. But she shook her head and asked him if he'd finished his breakfast.

On his signifying that he had, Mrs. D remarked b way of conversation: That's a little divel you've got in there.

Yah, he grinned and left the room to get a cigar. Yes, he said to himself lighting the cigar, but as there was no one near him at the time, that was the end of it. So taking his hat and putting on his coat he went out, carefully closing the hall door behind him.

Four flights he descended on the winding stair, holding the cool banister in his right hand — soft on the carpet, hard on the tiles at each landing — out at the street door, down the gritty brownstone steps and out, out — alone, into the empty street. Turning to the left he walked idly off, smoking.

He bought a paper at the corner — the first one from the pile, paid for it without a word — five cents, folded it, pushed it into his pocket and walked on, pondering, under the elevated, on to the park.

The clatter of a robin startled him. Others answered all about. They were the first he had heard that year. The grass was soaked with dew, the benches were too wet to sit on. But the sun blazed in the washed air.

America, he thought as he sauntered, the United States of America — money. Without money, nothing. Money. Men who work should have enough money. In Berlin men worked. Here they had strikes — to get more money. A few worked. That's not the way. Everybody should work. Everybody should work the best that he knows how. He had served his time to teach them. He and Gompers and Hilyard. He had gotten up their journal for them — The Workers' Journal. Enough of that. He had seen men who did the work get it in the neck too often. He had been for the strikes. He had made speeches. He had arbitrated differences. Both sides had called for him. He had succeeded eminently in improving conditions. Guards had been put about dangerous machine parts, hours had been cut. But men should work — hard, well, honestly. And they should be paid for it, well paid. That was all. That was the basis of everything. He had settled the Buffalo printers' strike on that basis — work and pay, pay and work. Now he began to doubt that he understood aright what anybody wanted. Men should work and they should be paid.

But that's not it. A funny crowd. It's the Irish, he thought to himself, and the Sheenies. Those are the suckers who spoil everything. They don't like good work. Money, that's all, money. The men are like the bosses — they don't want it settled that way. He had quit. That's not honest work. This business of holding up the game to get a rake off from it affronted his philosophy, it was something foreign to his nature that he did not understand. And there was yet another side to it — I work and *they* get the money. I don't get it. And I know it.

Maybe that's the kind of fellow I am. His mind drifted back to his childhood, how the weight of it all had come upon his black, curly head when he was barely sixteen. Square piece of cloth, put your foot into it, a little oil — what kind of oil? he had forgotten — in the shoe, slip in the foot — and you could walk for hours without fatigue. Eyes like a bird he had had, grey like an eagle . . .

He watched the robins poise themselves, as if on wires, with head one side then pouncing forward with a lunge — grasp and tug at a worm, half in its hole.

That's why they wanted to make a professor of me, wanted to pay for my schooling, send me away to Berlin to learn. But he had to work, to get money quick — brother to the music conservatory, sisters to America, mother to keep.

If his father had not died — pneumonia, cold in the forest, head forester — *oberförster* — that's what he really would have loved to have been. Shoot straight, guns, walk for miles alone in the forest among the oaks — different from these trees — and balsams. There! What? A weasel. Slowly he raised his rifle, carefully. He could see its eye. It was watching him. Bang! through the head.

Americans want money . . . daughter . . . money . . . they don't *know* anything . . . to walk through the forest, seeing the pheasants get up, the small deer run — as he had seen them once, twelve of them — one, two, six at a time — poised in the air over a fallen tree, floating over it — grey, with coarse whitish hairs.

It was the same with printing — to do it well, to see it perfect, to have it come out best, to enjoy the work for that — and to make money. Not the machines. His delicate fingers in his pockets curled with distaste. There were other men for that. But to print, to shoot it in the eye, every time.

What is money? They should pay money for that. No, he never saw money, not real money for what he did. In America money was — like — work to him.

Money — in the press-work. That's where the money is. Must not forget that. There's nothing in composition. Get the work on the presses and let them go. Something the rest can't do. Something requiring accuracy and everlasting care. Serial numbers. Money orders. Do it like nobody else. Express money orders, numbered serially — requiring careful tabulation — no composition — put it on the machines — must invent small mechanical enumerator. Work the machines.

He smiled. I am an American after all. Not a grafter, though. I'll give them work if they'll pay a fair price for it. Work that is work. A good price.

Frieda had gone out. So early? Yes, about a half hour ago. That's funny. He turned home again. Must ask them for more money — tomorrow. Two girls. I wonder when they'll want the big girl home again. Money, money, money — whether you want to or not you've got to think about it.

As he was leaving the park he saw a bush in flower.

Happily, without a thought but for — a flower — he picked it and held it in his hand. It was a snowball. With it he walked unmolested home — thinking that soon now he would leave the city — go out to the suburbs, take a house, have a garden — and begin to live.

When all was quiet in the house, the mother asleep, the baby new-diapered, wide eyed, blinking but silent in its pillow-stuffed wicker basket, Mrs. D stretched out in a chair. The street bell rang. Mrs. D started and looked at the small clock on the mantel — 7 o'clock.

I couldn't sleep, said Frieda as she bounced in at the door. Is it . . . ?

It is, said Mrs. D shortly.

So I was right, I knew it — I had a dream. Is it a girl?

It is, said Mrs. D.

I knew it. Where is it, the darling little thing? And how is Gurlie? I'm the auntie you know, she said, introducing herself. And where is Joe?

Without waiting for an answer she darted through the first door at hand.

Shhh, said Mrs. D. But it was too late. A voice called out. Who's that? It's only me, said the visitor and she went into the hallowed room while Mrs. D drew off and sat down dully in her chair.

Where is it?

I don't know, said the mother.

Ah, there it is, the little lamb. Look, look! I see a little hand. The baby held its hand up like the limb of a tree — and slept.

Oh, oh, oh, oh, said Frieda and pulled the cover back a very, very little from the tiny face. The baby opened its eyes, blinked them and closed them violently. What are you doing? Leave it alone, said the mother. Oh, oh, oh, oh, said Frieda and put a finger cautiously upon the cheek.

Instantly the baby turned its head and began to reach as if to suck. Oh, the poor little thing, it's hungry, said Frieda, pityingly. Look, it wants to suck.

Leave it alone, said the mother. What made you come here this time of the morning anyway? But Frieda kissed her and told her she looked fine and that it was the dearest baby. But so little, she concluded. Lottie was not like that.

As the mother made no reply, she continued: Something told me. I felt that I must come. The poor little thing, have you given it something to eat? Shall I call the nurse?

No. Go home and don't bother me.

But now the baby had been roused and started grunting and rooting about. It began to whimper and Frieda picked it up — against the mother's repeated orders, as if she were in a trance unable to hear what was being said, and held it gingerly, awkwardly, so that its head hung back and it began to cry aloud. Mrs. D came hurriedly in — but without a word.

It's cruel, said Frieda. The poor thing is hungry. I was just going to give it to the mother. Ah . . .

Let it be hungry, perhaps it'll learn to nurse then. Let it cry. And the baby cried, fretfully.

Now the two women glared quickly at each other while for a brief moment Mrs. D tried bouncing the small thing to make it cease its noise.

At this moment in walked Joe and, smiling, looked at the group about the baby.

Ah, there you are, cried Frieda. Congratulations. The baby is hungry.

Well, give it something to eat then if it's hungry,

said he smiling. But Frieda turned at once to the
nurse and exclaimed: There, its father said you
should feed it.

Leave it to the nurse, said Joe, that's what she's
here for. Then, turning to his wife, he added: Well,
how is everything?

That's right, how's everything, replied she. Where
have you been? You leave me here and go off without
a word.

For goodness sakes, he answered, for he was in a
very good humor. Look what I brought you. And he
held up the flower he had plucked in the park. How is
the baby, really? He turned to Mrs. D. Is she all right?

Oh yes, how's the baby, said the mother. What
about me, though, you don't think of that.

Oh, you're all right, he smiled, you're strong as a
horse. He meant it to sound jocular and kindly but
it angered the woman in bed so that she turned on her
side and gave them all her back.

Mrs. D put the baby down — and motioned to them
to leave the room, which they did — as church bells
began to ring in the street beyond.

Gurlie hasn't any feeling for children, began
Frieda. No, said Joe, have you had your breakfast?
But the woman went on: Why is it always so, that
those that haven't any . . . If you want a baby so
much, broke in Joe, why don't you get married?
Frieda did not answer but walked to the window of
the front room where they had gone, while Joe took
his paper to read.

Her mind flew to those days in Christiana when she
had hesitated too long between two men — one light,
whom she had loved, and one serious, whom she admired — and lost both of them. Since then she had

travelled. She had travelled out of her own earnings. But it was a brilliant day outside and Frieda loved the sunshine.

Let me name it! she turned suddenly to Joe, but you must not tell Gurlie.

Sure, said he — for nothing.

Call it Frieda. All right, Frieda Florence. And he went on reading — the political situation: why in America such blind stupidity seemed always to be the power in the ascendancy. It's the majority, I suppose, he commented to himself. They like it.

There's the man, said Joe, looking up. What? said Frieda. There's the man for you, Grover Cleveland. Afraid of nobody. He had a child when he was a young man, before he was married. They wanted to bring it up in the first campaign. Go ahead, he said. What! said Frieda. That's the kind of a man we want. And he'll get it again. I mean the Presidency. No humbug, no tariff fence to protect the suckers so they can rob us. Let Europe in, it will drive the rotten goods off our market, make them give us good quality if they want our money. But he'll have a hard time with the politicians in Washington. Do you know what they ought to do with them? No, said Frieda. They ought to hang them up by the neck. Do away with them all, that's the only way to treat them. They're nothing but a pack of thieves. What's the government for if it isn't to put money in the pockets of the politicians? He's a smart fellow, he believes in hard work. But he won't last. They'll wreck the business of the whole country to get him if they have to. But he'll do a lot of good before they put him out. That's the man to vote for.

There it was again — America. It rose in his clear

mind as something beyond the grasp of reason, something mediaeval, ignorant, arrogant — at once rich
and cheap. A battle for something without value at
the cost of all that he knew of that was worth while.
What that worth was he saw as he had been trained to
see it, a material honesty, a logic of work and pay. But
his feelings, far subtler, remained bitterly confused.

Frieda's mind had wandered. She had not heard
more than the first few words of what he had said.
She stood at the window and dreamed children to herself. If only . . . but she would never marry now.
Yes, it would have to be another girl, she thought.
If it had only been mine! I would care for it, it would
see the world. At night I would talk with it, teach it
and it would love me. I am so lonely.

Now the baby began to cry again and a voice came
from the sick room: I wish someone would take that
thing away so I can sleep.

Frieda ran at once, almost dislocating her elbow
against the frame of the bedroom door, and brought
out the basket just as Mrs. D appeared tying on a clean
apron at the back.

Nu' ja, so you must bring that thing in here, said
the father. But he smiled just the same and got up to
look at it, holding the paper in his hand — but dubiously.

Making peace between themselves as women will,
Frieda and Mrs. D sat down together for a good talk
over the little girl which Mrs. D had put in her basket
across the arms of a chair turned to the wall. Sunday,
that day which in America, as in England perhaps,
seems without use, a machine that is broken, a departure from the stress of normal life but — as if by
reason of an illness. One goes to church and is hung

— or resists, cursing. It always irritated Joe, so long
as he believed in it. But he went, for all that, fairly
regularly.

Not today though. He didn't feel like going out
again. He turned back to his paper but found it dull.
He had smoked enough, not again till after dinner
— I wonder if we'll have any! he thought to himself.
He never wrote letters, there was enough trouble in
the family already without spreading the news any
further as to what had occurred. They might feel they
had to send presents or something. Foolishness. He
took a book from the case — Faust — and slid it in
again. He sat in a chair and would have broken his
habit and smoked anyway — save that he didn't feel
it would be right to cloud up the apartment.

Now in Silesia one could go out and be at once —
almost — among the little hills.

Joe, said his wife's voice from the next room. Yes,
he answered and went in.

She lay there half asleep, he was not sure whether
she had called or not. How this sort of thing wears a
woman down, so quickly too. She seemed old, the face
was spotted with brown marks, there were heavy lines
about the eyes — and there was the curious smell —
he had noticed it with the first. It made him feel that
he was of a different sex, a different race — and he
wanted to be kind. He could see her body in relief under the covers, look how she breathes — my wife. I
have done this. Man and wife. Paul and Virginia — I
guess not. Just the same it's over. That's good. Perhaps
she's fallen asleep again. He started to go out.

Stay here, she said, without opening her eyes. Sit
down.

I thought you wanted to sleep, he answered.

Where's the baby?

In there with Frieda and the nurse.

I didn't hear anything, I wondered where you were.

That's all right, he answered, go to sleep.

No. It's a girl again.

Ja, is there anything you want?

There was no answer so he continued: It's all right. Two girls are all right. They can keep each other company. But the mother was really keenly disappointed.

There must be a way to have a boy, she said. What is it? Ask somebody.

Ask somebody, he retorted with a laugh.

But that riled her and made her instantly unreasonable. Yes, ask. You never try to find out anything. Every day science is finding out new things. But you think all there is in the world is work, work, work.

He knew she was right — from her viewpoint — and he saw plainly enough that she was in bed, incapacitated, so he did not reply. But having begun to pity herself and her misfortune it was not long before — unable now to sleep — she went for her husband in good style: Well one thing sure — you'll have to make more money now.

I will, he consented.

You will, will you? How — if you don't ask for it? Tell them you've got to have more, that unless they give you more you will quit.

They'll tell me to quit, that's all.

Let them. And if they dare, start for yourself. What could they do without you? You are too careful, you have no daring, you must bluff!

Never, said he.

You must. In America bluff is everything. You say

that all the time. Then be a bluff, be a better bluff than they are. You know you are better than they are. You know you are the best trained printer in America today.

Yes, yes. Don't talk about that now. Don't excite yourself.

Yes, yes. Don't talk, don't ask, don't do anything. But you must. Work won't get you anywhere, it's the brains . . .

Who has the brains? he spoke up a little too quickly.

You have, she replied. But you are too timid. I could do it. But now is the time. You have two daughters now and I am not going to sit down and be a *hausfrau*. I am going to live and see the world and I must have money. And you are going to make it for me.

Don't talk about things you don't understand, he replied.

It's you that don't understand. You think you know everything you Dutchies. You have got to study people, like me.

What for, he said, to skin them?

No, to make use of them.

I don't need to, I've got too much to do, he answered.

Wait till I get up. If you think I'm going to stay here and have babies one after the other and nothing else you fool yourself. You tell those people you want more money or you quit. If you don't, I quit.

Don't get so excited. What's the matter with you?

You *do* it.

And he began to feel the force of her insistence more than he had ever felt it in his married life be-

fore. Watching her eyes flash, the very insensibility
of her fire somehow excited him in spite of himself.
It was something he did not understand but there it
was. Foolish or reasonable, there it was. He could understand that all right. And she was no longer carrying a baby. It came home to him through the contour
of the bedclothes. Soon she would be all right again.
It was his own wife. She had the brains of a chicken
— but that was his hard luck. He had married her,
hadn't he? That wasn't her fault. She didn't give herself the brains she had. He smiled at the folly but he
insensibly obeyed. What did he care? He felt admiration — a borrowed resentment against the world mo-
mentarily possessed him. Yes, she was right. He was
abler than the rest — with care; he saw it more and
more clearly every day. Give those bums something
to do and they botch it every time. Not one, scarcely,
can do the simplest thing without making a mess of
it. But they want the money! Oh yes, they want the
money. But he? Yes, she was right. He looked, must
look, to be afraid. But that was not it. It was only
that never, not once in his life, had he been in a position that permitted him to lose. He must always
have won, that was the thing that made it hard to
move.

Take it, she said, seeming to read his thoughts. You
are better than any of them, you have the brains.

He wondered, looking at her small, round head,
what good they were. But he caught the fire. You have
the brains, go out and fight them, continued his wife.
It is a free country. If you don't fight for it you will
get nothing — but to be called a fool. You owe it to
me to fight.

I'll think about it, he said, adding: Don't excite

yourself. It isn't good for you. And to let her be quiet — for he could already see plain signs of fatigue in her — he went out into the kitchen to play with the cat.

And the baby slept while about its head a drama that was its future had begun.

Gurlie in her bed felt tired after her few heated words with Joe. He was her man, he must learn; she had learned, he was too honest. In any case, Joe had supplied her with just what she needed for the moment. She was really fatigued by the talk and would soon rest again. The excitement of the birth effort had worn off completely now. If it had only been a boy. There had not been a horse on the farm she had not dared to ride, even as a child. Once, when she was no more than ten, she had climbed the mast of a schooner and looked down. No, she had not liked that. But she liked to climb, like a sailor, like a Viking. She had Viking blood in her, five centuries at least they could trace it, then a break — a slight break — and it ran back again into history. *Ein Blitzmädel* Joe would say of her sometimes when they were happy together. The Norse were the first to have a culture, no matter what was said of others. The women were free, admitted to the councils on the same footing as the men. They were not allowed to wear drawers, that was always amusing, because the country needed children. They were not allowed to wear closed drawers. That was to have children, many children. She had wanted boys, six boys — and she slept heavily.

Frieda had gone to tell her brother in Brooklyn the news. Joe stayed around — to be of service and not to leave Mrs. D alone in the house. He wondered when it would be time to bring the other daughter home again. Mrs. D in the kitchen was starting to get the lunch, peeling and slicing potatoes — she had scorned Frieda's offer to relieve her so that she could run home.

Now at last the house was quiet.

CHAPTER III

To Go on Being

M̄ONDAY MORNING they put the baby in the front room where it would be most out of the way. You'd think she'd been here for a month, said Mrs. D, with her little hands and the face of her and the little bit of hair she has all smoothed down to her head.

There Joe found her when he returned that evening from the office. He walked to the crib and looked in. The baby was turned from him to the left with fists placed one before the other before her nose. He recognized the gesture and smiled, nodding his head in assent.

Mrs. D came into the room so he asked her how things had gone that day. It's slept the whole time through, was the reply he got. Good, said Joe.

Tuesday Mrs. D brought the baby out to its basket as soon as Joe had left and laid it on its blue down pillow. Sleep again. But now she'd stir, wrinkle up her face, pucker it, then curl her lips and cry.

But mostly she lay sleeping — as before, but breathing air now almost imperceptibly until she'd wake and root around for food or squirm or yell. She sneezed.

The aunt, who was there again, jumped up.

That's nothing, said Mrs. D, they all do that. It's the air she ain't used to inside her nose tickles her. Leave her alone. She's all right.

It pressed and ached and gnawed. Sleep, the one refuge she sought only to return to it and to remain there. But she could not. That well where she had swum like so much weed two days ago had lost its charm.

The woman rescued her, lifting and wiping, loosing and binding, carrying her to food, warmth to her feet — to soften and allay — what else? but could not alter her condition.

Prickled by the light she moved her head from side to side, then started, flooded with urine to the armpits, to find herself flying, stiffened for a fall, only to land safely from the hold of Mrs. D upon some bed or table.

The little divil, I think she's made of it. That's the third time I've changed her hand running. She waits till I've a dry one on her and then she soaks it, said Mrs. D.

The baby yawned and blinked and wrinkled up its brows. A kitten or a pup would have been crawling on its belly. Not she. She was not able. Her mouth against the tit, unlike an animal, she sucked indifferently. Yet she sucked a little, her belly tightened, the nipple fell from her mouth — too soon.

I don't think you've much milk coming, said Mrs. D to the mother. Nonsense, replied she, I nursed the first one for a year. I can't help that, said Mrs. D, I don't like the way she fights it. Let her wake up first, said the mother, take a wet cloth to her face the next time. All right, said Mrs. D.

Meanwhile, the light got to her more and more.

But that night Joe came up to the crib again and seeing her quiet stood looking down. He had heard that if you look too hard at a sleeping baby you'll wake it. He wondered if that were true. Apparently not, for the infant didn't budge. So he touched its forehead with his index finger.

The baby slowly smiled, a crooked little grin. It pleased Joe marvelously. So when the smile had gone, he tried the trick again. No one else was in the room.

This time the baby opened its mouth and turned its head about as if searching for the breast. This wasn't so good. Joe felt a little panic at this twist of things and drew back.

Then it began to cry a little, then flung up its arms and yelled. He moved quickly away and tried to look innocent as Mrs. D came in.

Its harsh, small voice stilled a little as the woman slid her hand under it to feel its bottom. Finding this dry, she turned to Joe and, reminding him that he was the father and that she had work to do, went off.

He sat by the crib and joggled it. It did no good. It seemed some petty engine letting off steam, the thing drove its breath so furiously. The face grew purple. After ten minutes, Joe went back to the kitchen and told the woman she'd have to go and see to it.

She's got an awful temper, said Mrs. D. Let her cry it out, it won't hurt her.

But Joe wasn't going back. How can an infant that age have a temper, said he, stalling. You'd better go and take it up.

What! It shows you've never seen many babies, said Mrs. D, working at the sink. That baby's got a temper. They could hear it down the hallway yelling still, convulsively. In about two days you begin to notice a difference in them. They're no two of them alike.

What are you doing to my baby? they heard the mother calling.

And with that the thing stopped its noise as unaccountably as it had started. Mrs. D went on with her cooking and Joe went into the toilet — for a change.

In the front room it lay — still once more — its thumbs clenched into its fists, its eyes closed.

In the baby's comprehensive mind — unconscious thoughts were put — weaving the future out of the past — as it lay and sucked its lips.

Nothing lasted for long — since she had no strength to bear it — a flash — a sound! Then it focused in space somewhere — by chance, this thing that was disturbing her and fell as a bolt and stuck in her right ear — a boring pain.

The fight was on.

She rolled her head, screwed up her face, gasping and choking in her agony, her fists or fingers aimlessly striking across her brows.

It must have been about five A.M. on the fourth day. Mrs. D got up from where she had been lying asleep on the double bed beside the mother to go and see.

What's the trouble now, said the mother, why doesn't it go to sleep? It's been asleep all night, said Mrs. D seeing the gray dawn outside and lighting a candle, don't bother yourself now, I'll care for it. So she picked it up and took it to the kitchen at the back of the house to dry and change it. I'll be back in a minute, she added, for you to suck it — if you're awake, she said again to herself under her breath as she went down the corridor.

But the baby writhed and drew her nails about her eyes and nose until small bloody scratches marked her cheeks when Mrs. D had lit the kitchen lamp and closed the door and turned to look at her.

Look at you now, you miserable little brat, she said

to it. You've got yourself all scratched to bits. So she picked up the tiny reddish hands one at a time and looking closely at the nails bit them off — it would be bad luck to cut them — as well as she could, so the baby could no longer do herself a damage.

The infant cried again and pumped its bony knees up and down, knocking them together, crossing and recrossing its hands and wrists — that harsh, hoarse, grunting, barking, wheezing, scraping, frantic cry of an agonizing infant.

Shut up, you'll wake the whole house, she said to it again going to the stove in her bare feet to get warm water with which to wipe it. You'd think I was killing you the way you carry on.

But nothing would stop it. Mrs. D stopped her work instead and taking the thing up, unpinned, blanket and all, joggled it up and down on one arm while she shifted the kettle to the back of the range with the other.

When at last it sobbingly quieted, she laid it on the table once more and would have finished changing it. But no more it felt the hard surface than it began again — fairly frantic now.

She put the sweetened bottle in its mouth. It sucked eagerly, then as quickly threw back its head, opened its mouth and gurgling with half swallowed water, cried and choked again — until in alarm this time Mrs. D grabbed it quickly up and turning it over, jounced it in her hands once more until it could at least begin to breathe again.

Try once more. She looked carefully this time watching the twisting, tormented face. Then — while the baby, more from exhaustion than anything else, drowsed a moment, she went to the sink, found a piece of soap, took up a paring knife and began to whittle.

First she cut off the end of the soap cake a finger long. This she pared then sharpened, about an inch or two of it. Then wetting it at the faucet, she rubbed it with her fingers to take out the knife marks, smoothed it, and taking it in her hand, finally went to the baby, lifted up its flails of feet by their ankles no bigger than her finger and not half so strong, and gently pushed the soap plug into the little hole between the buttocks.

The baby startled, stiffened and the soap came out. Carefully Mrs. D inserted it again, well in this time, and held it there by pinching with her fingers. There, try and get by that, she said to the baby, yawning and pulling up a chair with her left hand to sit and wait.

The light was growing outside, a cat yowled bloodcurdlingly — a yowl that was matched instantly by another half a tone higher and with a fiercer accent. Then an explosion of wild spits and yells and the rattle of some fallen metal object.

That's why the garbage gets all out of the cans, said Mrs. D. You'd think they'd keep their damned animals in the house at night. There, that'll fix you, she added to the baby, that'll fix you, she said again with satisfaction.

The dawn was rapidly approaching now. Joe was up and in the bathroom shaving. You could hear the water and the hoarse sound of the closet flushed. Mrs. D took the baby, new diapered and half sleeping, back to the mother to be nursed.

But the infant would not.

Get out of here, said Gurlie finally, go on into the

kitchen and get breakfast. I can do this better alone. But Mrs. D could hear the battle going on as she worked. Joe heard it too.

What's the matter, he said to Mrs. D, coming into the kitchen.

What's the matter! said the latter pausing a minute to look at him. What's the matter? The baby's crying.

Joe lifted his eyes quietly a moment to hers then sat down to his coffee. Without opening his mouth again, he finished this — hesitated — arose, then went to stand briefly before his wife's door without entering, realized that she was busy, looked as though he was going to enter, then went back to the kitchen and, turning, said to Mrs. D, Yes, it's crying.

Well, there's nothing I can do, he added to the wall and stove. So he went and took up his hat from the rack in the front hallway and came back once more to say to Mrs. D, Tell her I've gone. Then he opened the door and went downstairs.

She'll be glad to hear that, said Mrs. D to herself after the door had closed. The baby was still crying distractedly. But Mrs. D, having already had two samples of the mother's temper during the past two days, made up her mind she wouldn't go in the room till she was called this time, so she went back and began to wash the breakfast dishes.

The baby cried all that day except when Mrs. D without a word to anyone gave it twenty drops of paregoric in a spoon of sweetened water. The baby slept three hours that time. But when Joe returned that night it was again crying in the front room where they'd placed it.

He came in, heard the sound, went toward it, saw the baby beating itself about the face with its hands and looking, heard no other sound in the place. Puzzled, he stood there wondering at the thing, troubled and amazed. He couldn't make it out.

Gurlie, he called out. No answer. That's funny. He went to the bedroom door, opened it, looked in. His wife was fast asleep, her face flushed, her hair disheveled. He went to the kitchen. No one. He went back to the infant. It looked sick to him, drawn, miserable. Its voice was cracked and sometimes it didn't sound at all when it cried. Where was Mrs. D?

Then he heard the stairs creak. And in she came, a paper bag in hand.

Jesus, is it still yelling, was the first thing the woman said between puffing breaths. There's been the devil here today. I never saw a thing like that for screaming in all the length of my life — I'm glad you're here to hear it.

And as she went through the room, Joe caught a strong whiff of her beery breath. He nodded and went over to watch the baby.

The thing's sick, he made up his mind. He put his hand on its face and the skin was dry and hot. And through his chest he felt a tight knot drawn. Sick. A tiny thing like that, you almost didn't dare to lift it in your hands it seemed so frail. It wouldn't live. He could see that from the first. It wouldn't live.

Mrs. D came into the room again, having doffed her draggled hat. And would you believe it if I told you its mother's sleeping? She looked at Joe but once again he lifted that quiet grey eye to hers and she didn't face it.

The child's sick, he said to her.

Sick? said Mrs. D.

Do you think we should get a doctor?

A what? said Mrs. D. A doctor? What for?

It doesn't look to me as if it will live, said Joe.

Live? That? It'll live to be a hundred, said Mrs. D with a slightly shaky roar of laughter. I never saw the like of it for strength — for its size. It's had us crazy.

What's that? said the voice from the bedroom. Joe went at once — slowly, to the door, then tapping on it gently, opened it and went in.

Well, how are you? he said cheerfully, attempting a broad smile. But this didn't go well with Gurlie.

Is that thing still crying? she said.

Well, you can hear it, can't you? said he.

I think the baby is sick, said Joe, seriously. Or maybe you haven't enough milk for it.

What! said the wife. Look at this. And she sat up abruptly, pulled aside her buttoned gown and showed him her breasts, taut with engorgement and the milk in them, the nipples erect. Look at this. I wish you had them. I'm soaked to the waist with them now. Not enough milk, did you say? And she took the nipples between her fingers so that a stream of milk spurted out, landing across the back of his hand as he sat there. He looked down at it but did not at once wipe it off.

Well, is it my fault? his wife went on. I have the milk for it, but it won't suck. And you come here and blame me.

Ach! who's talking of blame? If the child is sick, why don't you call a doctor?

What have we got the midwife for? That's her business. Don't you bring any doctor to this house. You must have money, the way you talk.

Well, said Joe then, settle it yourself. And he went out, lingering a moment at the door as Mrs. D passed him coming in with the baby to put it to the breast once more.

This time it took hold and the milk gushed so fast into its gullet that it choked it. It drew back and coughed, then cried, then when they put it back it merely yelled and turned its face aside. Joe shook his head and vanished.

For three days the house was an inferno. Each night when Joe returned he found the baby weaker, thinner, its scrawny face more shrunk and, worst of all, Gurlie's breasts suddenly were empty. The aunt had come to offer her assistance and advice. One blast from Gurlie and she had retired not to return again till the fall.

The baby cried and slept, surreptitiously drugged by heavy draughts of paragoric. Now it vomited from time to time, even when it did swallow a stomachful, or even half of that.

A vomiting baby always does well in the end, said Mrs. D, but that wasn't going so well either, latterly. So she looked around for someone to blame it on. Who else but Joe? Mrs. D couldn't see Joe. She felt now that when the baby cried somehow he was back of it — even though he was at the office all day. His awkward, sensitive hands — turned her sour. If I was your wife, she said to herself when she looked at him, I wouldn't be baking cakes for you when you come home, I'd have a nice big mud pie ready for you. And for the thousandth time she went to care for the baby who was still crying.

Tempers grew shorter as the days increased. It began to look really serious until finally Joe decided he'd put an end to it. Coming up the stairs one night and hearing the pitiful hoarse blast of the baby's torment still going on, he turned back and walked across a few blocks to where he had seen a doctor's sign one day on a residence near the park.

There it was — T. Wesley Colt, M.D. A different meaning it had now that he came for business — half relief, half distrust.

Joe mounted the brownstone steps, rang the bell and when a young woman came to the door, removed his hat and asked for the doctor.

The doctor is at supper. If you will come back at seven o'clock.

It's for the baby, said Joe earnestly.

A male voice sounded inside: Close that door. Then a man appeared, a young man. What's this? he said.

Are you the doctor? said Joe.

Yes, said the man, what is it?

A baby.

Been sick a week, I suppose, said the doctor.

Yes, just about, said Joe.

Then you come to me at this time, don't you know I'm eating supper?

Ya, said Joe, I suppose so. I'd like my supper too, and he was going out when the doctor stopped him. Where is it?

104th Street.

Poor pickings, thought the doctor, but — All right, wait a minute, he said.

Joe felt grateful to the young man as they walked over the few blocks and climbed the stairs to the flat which had been turned into some sort of a savage den for him in the last few days. He felt that now he had come armed, he felt he had a protector, he opened the door and invited Dr. Colt to precede him.

The doctor walked in.

Gurlie was furious when Joe went to her in the bedroom. Keep him out there, she said, I don't want to see him. So they took the wobbly headed mite into the kitchen and laid it on a blanket on the table.

Mrs. D was in the midst of preparing what supper there was to be that night. She too was skeptical and angry, looking down from her height of years and experience on this young man, this intruder, who seemed to threaten to dethrone her.

I guess this is the first she's fallen asleep in the last three days, said Mrs. D.

Strip it, said the doctor.

He thinks maybe a pin's sticking it, thought Mrs. D. But she did as she was told, fumbling and fussing. Let me see that diaper, said the doctor. It was spinach green. How many a day of these?

Every time you change it, said Mrs. D. She strains, doctor, till it's a pity to look at her — and the color is terrible.

How many times is that? said the doctor.

Mrs. D looked at him with a blank expression. Well, she said, did you think I counted them?

Oh, that many, said the doctor. For a week, I hear, is that right?

Mrs. D looked at Joe with murder in her eyes. Now, doctor — then she stopped. About a week, said Mrs. D.

And what have you given it?

We've tried everything, said Mrs. D. The last was a cup of water with a mite of bee's honey in it.

Maybe that's what's the matter with it, commented the doctor, half to himself. Is the cord off yet?

Yesterday, said Mrs. D as she finished undressing the infant.

Dry?

Not yet, I have a raisin on it, she added casually.

A raisin?

With the seeds out of it, Mrs. D continued.

Sugar cured, eh? replied the doctor.

My mother was a nurse for forty-five years before me, said Mrs. D. But the doctor was not listening.

Now the doctor picked the little thing up in his hands and turned it over. Its skin was hot and dry, it wrinkled under his fingers; there was no fat there. He shook his head, then asked: Where's the mother?

In the bedroom, doctor, said Joe, resting.

May I see her? Then sensing Joe's hesitation, he added: All I want to see is her breasts, if there's any milk in them.

Joe went to ask her if she'd see the doctor.

All right, let him come, said Gurlie. So he came, looked at her breasts which were flat now, said, Thank you, sorry to bother you, and went out while she stared at him unsmiling.

What does it weigh?

Weigh? said Mrs. D. Oh, about five pounds and half or so, I'd guess. It's lost a good bit in the last five days.

Haven't you some scales in the pantry?

I think I could find them, said Joe. So he went fumbling around among the pans until in a drawer he drew out a large pair of fish scales with a hook at the bottom. Dr. Colt tied the baby up in a diaper, knotted the four ends back and forth and lifted the weight up an inch off the table. All looked to see what the sliding point would rest at on the brass face of the crude instrument.

Five pounds and a half, said Mrs. D triumphantly. Didn't I say so?

That's bad, said the doctor, a little over five pounds,

about five and a quarter, as far as I can make out. The child's in poor condition. Dress it, he added after he had looked down its throat, felt of its belly, sounded its lungs and taken its temperature — 105 rectal. The child's sick — very sick.

Will you please wash this — in cold water, he added handing the thermometer to Mrs. D.

She took it gingerly, wondering how to work it. So that's one of them new temperature sticks, she thought to herself turning it over in her hand.

The doctor told them to give the baby barley water for three days, told Mrs. D how to prepare it — told them to sponge the baby, to syringe it — to bind up the mother's breasts. And went off saying he'd see it again two days later when they had had a chance to carry out his instructions.

Sure, and now go home and have your supper, my boy, said Mrs. D. You've earned your money — for Joe paid him at the door. How much? asked Mrs. D. Ah, what does he know, a young lad like that?

No use. The baby cried the same. Barley water, said the mother disgustedly. Barley water! to a starving baby? But Joe insisted so they tried the barley water and the infant would not take it. And when it did it vomited and purged as green as ever.

No more doctors, said the mother angrily. The fools, anybody can do that.

Well, said Joe, what are we going to do then?

To this Mrs. D responded that, if they would give her a free hand, she could manage it, but if they were going to take things out of her hands continually, what was she there for anyhow?

I'd like to know that myself, said Gurlie quickly.

The baby was two weeks old now and had lost a

pound or more. Each day after that when Joe came
home from the office he'd weigh it, hoping against
hope — until he gave it up — and gave the baby up
for lost. The doctor was taboo. Give it anything, at
last Joe said, get a can of condensed milk and give it
that. Children like sugar, give it some of that.

And kill it, said the mother. Joe felt the force of
that and had no answer.

The mother's breasts were entirely empty now, but
not knowing what else to do, they came back with the
baby to the breast as a last resort.

Or send it to Coney Island to the incubators, said
Joe finally.

Mrs. D had pumped some milk out of both breasts
and tried a spoon then a dropper — nothing doing.

They tried it till Gurlie was disgusted. One day she
was sitting with chest cramped over, cross-legged on
the bed, red faced, Mrs. D tapping her foot on the
floor, till it almost drove the mother crazy. She turned
on the nurse with a flash and damned her up and
down with such animal violence that she drove her
from the room in anger and surprise. Get out of here.
You're no good. It's all your fault, you dirty good for
nothing. Get out of here. What do we pay you for?

You haven't paid me a thing yet, said Mrs. D. But
seeing the fierce light in the other woman's eyes, she
quickly retired closing the door behind her and saying, Well, if she's not gone crazy with it, I'm a Jew.
And kept to the kitchen the rest of the afternoon till
Joe should come home for her to get her money. She
was through.

Gurlie sighed a sigh of relief, took up the baby and
put it to the breast again. It was thin, dry lipped, crying. As she touched it, it wrinkled up its wizened face

and squeezed out the maddening mechanical cry of a
starved child. Then it opened its mouth in an O and
stretched its skinny neck, as if seeking to suck. The
mother took it up for the ten thousandth time — she
thought — and pulled out her breast. It went eagerly
at the gross nipple but instead of sucking, it fumbled,
did not close its jaws but panted eagerly without
taking hold, rubbing its face back and forth on the
breast aimlessly, then screwing up its face again and
squawking feebly. It was infuriating to Gurlie.

She pinched up her breast once more, pushed it into
the mouth and, putting her finger under the tiny
thin-boned jaw closed that forcibly. The infant
screamed through its forcibly closed gums, struggling
and twisting to draw back and breathe. Gurlie persisted, her own chest bursting from the position she
was in.

Then suddenly she threw the baby from her. It
fell, of course, on the soft bed, bounced on its face and
screamed anew.

The woman threw back the covers and got up. She
was white with fury now. Leaving the child where it
was, she got a coat and putting it on, went out into
the other room, closing the door behind her and sat
by the window.

Gott in himmel! she raved, holding her hands to her
ears. Then she sat up cold as ice and looked at the
sharp details of the sky and street — at the approach
of evening. She felt big alone, she could have clutched
the whole world up in one fist and smashed it to
smithereens.

When Joe came in, she was still there. She turned
with a hard look at him but he was not in a mood for it
this time.

Where's the baby?

I don't know, she said. On the bed, I guess.

He went into the bedroom and finding it un-
covered, turned back the edge of the quilt over it,
seeing it was asleep.

What's happened today?

I don't know.

Where's the woman?

I don't know — and with that his wife arose and
went into the bedroom and closed the door.

Joe went to the kitchen and found Mrs. D with
two empty beer bottles on the table before her —
but she was not drunk. I'm leaving, said Mrs. D,
I'm through digging out anybody's dirty place for
them.

How much do I owe you? said Joe.

Two dollars a day, for fourteen days, that's twenty-
eight dollars, said Mrs. D.

Here you are, said Joe, handing her the money.
Count it before you put it in your pocket.

I'd be honest enough to return it if you give me
more than is coming to me, said Mrs. D. And with this
she took off her apron and began to look around for
her bag in which to pack her things.

When she had gone, Joe went back to the bedroom.
There was no supper ready. I'm going down to get
some delicatessen, he said. What's happened to the
baby?

Gurlie, dull and indifferent, had not touched it
where it lay. There it is, she said.

Nurse any better?

No.

Joe looked and the thing stirred a little without
waking. Then he went out and returned with a can

of condensed milk among other things he had bought. It was still sleeping.

He took up the can, read the directions, and opened it, ladled out a teaspoonful of the contents awkwardly, measured out the water, filled a bottle and, handing it to Gurlie, told her to put it in the baby's mouth. This she did indifferently. The thing sucked eagerly. Finished the bottle. Gaped for more. He went back to the kitchen and filled the bottle again. It emptied that. The third bottle it refused after a few sucks as its head rolled aside slowly with milk oozing from the corner of its mouth and, with a comical distorted look of contentment on its face, fell asleep again.

On the coverlet where the child's head had lain the whole afternoon there was a yellow drying spot. The abscess in its ear had broken.

The battle between the pigmy and the giants was now over. The child was fed with condensed milk and began to thrive, not perfectly, but at least it fed and grew.

Now it was time for the sister to return home. Five years of age. Where is my baby brother? she asked at once. I wanna see him. But when she saw the baby and was told it was a little baby girlie like herself, The nasty thing, she said and, before anyone could stop her, she slapped it with all her strength right in the face.

CHAPTER IV

To Start Again Once More

It was the middle of May. The nightmare of the baby's birth and later illness was already fading into the past. Gott sei dank! said Joe to himself as he walked slowly up 104th St. to the elevated station — as slowly as he might, that is, without endangering his arrival down town on time at the office. He left the house always at 6:30. In his pocket he carried the shop keys. It was a matter of pride with him to be there every working day at least half an hour before everyone else, to have things ready for the men to start the presses on the minute of eight. That's business, he would say to himself and — he might have added — that's a man's business, that's what I get paid for. But he got mighty little for it, generally speaking. And besides, had you put it up to his bosses, nobody asked him to get there that early. That was entirely his own doing.

After five days rain this was one of those cool moist mornings in May when the country calls to the instincts with a voice of leaves and of flowers. Joe knew he was a working man, he had to be, that's all he asked them to expect of him. But very deep inside him moved another man — under water, under earth — among the worms and fishes, among the plant roots — an impalpable atmosphere through which he strode freely without necessity for food or drink, without breathing and with unthrobbing heart. How could a man exist there otherwise?

Life's a nice thing to keep, if you can keep it, he was saying to himself as he saw, without knowing what they were, a swarm of flying ants, which had emerged from a crack in the pavement and were fluttering now in the early sunshine above their scurrying fellows. Their iridescent wings caught the subtly exultant fancy of the walking man. That was the mood of the day for him. But it made him think of fishing. He shook his head in stern self-denial however as he imagined moths and bugs of all sorts falling into the streams and trout rising with a flash to take them. Sunday maybe, he'd go out on the Erie and look around, maybe put a line in his pocket — Sunday.

What the hell to do with the baby though — there you are. No, not this year. She was beginning to pick up a little now. You almost forgot she was in the house sometimes. The light of early sun flooded into his eyes as he mounted the L steps. He paid his nickel. Again the light. The rumble of the train came growing out of the light. The light dimmed and mounted again as he entered the car and sat at an east window among laborers and serving women. Today he could see light, it had to do with all that is awake early and moves and grows stronger. It is a nice thing to keep, if you can keep it well and happy. A man must keep on, he must keep on working and then, finally, he will see the light. He will come out of poverty and be able to keep everyone happy. What is lovelier than a place in the country with small children playing in the grass, or picking flowers — that is wild flowers and peonies. That's the trouble, they always want to take things, anything — everything. They have to be taught not to take the things that are planted in the gardens — they are children. They want to take things that don't belong to them. That's the Unions. Revolutionists. All the same.

That's what she is, a little socialist! He smiled to himself. She's right too. Take everything you can get. Let somebody else plant it and tend to it. Just take it.

He looked around, smiling a little to himself, at the backs and faces of the sleepy figures in the train with him before the jerky background of the Ninth Avenue houses. Fools! He bit his teeth together disgustedly. Children, I suppose, he said then, babies, that have to have their arses wiped for them while they try in every way to smear themselves from head to foot while you are doing it. That's a funny thing the way a baby tries to spoil everything you do for it. They hate clothes. When they get their clothes off, they're happy. Then they kick like frogs. They kick and if you don't watch yourself they'll kick themselves right out of your hands. That's stupid.

If you want to feed them, they try to knock it out of your grip. She's a smart one, though. I think she's going to have blue eyes. When you come near her, she stops crying. She seems to be listening. She lies still, listening. Then if you pick her up, she's happy. But if you go away again, after a minute she starts crying. She ought to be out in the park these days. But I won't push the carriage. That's a woman's job. I'll work, I'll provide, I'll be responsible for everything you want of me — but I'll be damned if I'll push a baby carriage. That's the place for a baby — out in the country.

Hello, Frank. Hello, Mr. Stecher, said the night watchman to him at the entrance to the building. Nice morning, eh? Yah, a nice day to go fishing. But I guess you're going to have a big time round here

in the next couple of weeks from all they say. Do
you think you'll get the contract again this year?
Sure, said Joe, why not? Makes a little extra work
for me, that's all replied the old man. Well, you're
paid for it, aren't you? Yes, I guess so — rotten pay,
said the watchman. Do you expect any trouble from
the A. F. — American Federation of Labor — this
year? Do *you?* was Joe's answer. To which the old
man said nothing.

Letting himself into the empty offices and shop,
the stillness of the presses, the dull, cold smell of it,
Joe did however think of the old man's words. Yes,
it was a battleground all right, his battleground —
the bosses on one side and labor on the other — he
in the middle. And he didn't know which end of the
mess was most to be distrusted. Of late — well, he
didn't know. Work, that's all he had to do for the
time being.

He picked up several torn sheets of paper as he
walked down the aisle between the presses — mutter-
ing to himself as he did so — and put them in the
waste basket in his own particular corner over by
the west windows as far as possible from the main
offices. These were partitioned off with oak and
opaque glass at the other end of the floor. But here
they had given him a small desk — as manager — and
here he had his own safe, his own files which he
himself cared for without other assistance.

For the twentieth time he took out the six sheets
of carefully written foolscap and laid them before
him, the writing and the numerals on it, a minute,
delicate tracery as if it had been engraved — a work
of art, really. But the art was not really in the writing,
that was just the show of it. The meat as well as the

art was in the accuracy of the figures. All estimates
originated from that corner — nothing was done,
nothing accepted, without that. And for this he was
paid twenty-five hundred a year without vacation. Big
money. Yes? he ran over the figures again rapidly,
changed nothing, put the papers back into the safe,
closed that and the first of the press hands began to
arrive.

They wandered over to the lockers one by one and
began to take off their collars, roll their sleeves and
put on overalls.

I suppose we're gonna get the God damn Government Contract again this year, said Carmody, one of
the pressmen.

Why not? came back from one of the others near
him. You ought to be glad you got a job to keep you
from starvin' — the way you did last winter.

I suppose they'll be havin' a cop standin' behind us
next when we're workin' and send us all home in the
Black Maria for safe keepin'. You can tell what's up
when you see old parrot feet sittin' at his stall that
way this time of the morning.

Aw go wash your drawers, said another of the men
near him. Your old woman's sinkers is killin' you.

Christ, you guys has got a lot of wakin' up to do,
youse guys — if you think you'll ever get a break
around this place — as long as that tamale is sittin'
over there in the corner — pointing to Joe at his
desk.

Aw shut up, said the one who had first answered
him.

A fine labor leader he must a bin. Who the hell
do you think he's workin' for? Youse? He paused a
moment. That's what happens when they come up

from the ranks, they turn on you and work the hell out of you for old time's sake. I got that little Dutchman's number a long time ago. You wait and see.

As Joe pressed the electric buzzer that sounded all through the plant, the men began to move over to the machines.

Come on, boys, get to work, said Joe, his watch in his hand, eight o'clock.

Right, Mr. Stecher — and in a few moments the presses groaned, slapped, grated a little and were off, so that from that time on for the rest of the day — save at the noon hour — you had to speak at a yell everywhere on the floor to be heard.

Later in the morning Joe took his arithmetic in to Mr. Wynnewood at the main office. He knocked first, though he had been told it wasn't necessary.

Come in, said the boss's voice on the inside. Then when the door had opened: Oh, good morning, Joe, he added, and how's the new kid getting along these days?

Fine, sir.

Good, I'm glad that's off your mind. What do you know about this, Lester? said he heartily to a young man sitting near him, Joe's got another daughter. That's fine, Mr. Stecher, said the Junior partner. Meanwhile Joe was glad Gurlie wasn't there. Thank God Gurlie isn't here, thought he, or she'd make me strike him for a raise.

Probably all were thinking much the same thing for the moment, for there was an awkward pause. Then Mr. Wynnewood cleared his throat and resumed: Let's see the figures.

Joe handed them to him. He glanced them over.

Hm, that's what it amounts to, eh? About the same as last year, isn't it?

Twelve hundred less, said Joe.

Pay roll?

Yes, said Joe.

Do you want me to check them over? said the one he had called Lester to the old man.

Christ, no, said this one laughing. What the hell would you know about it? Or me either — for that matter. Isn't that right, Joe?

Stecher smiled, his boyish grey eyes twinkling gaily but he said nothing. It was at these moments when he was completely cryptic that the true quality of the man most made itself felt. He closed himself in behind that quiet smile and a complete mystery took place before the onlooker. Old man Wynnewood knew that smile, knew what it meant, knew there was nothing more to be said — and knew besides that it was all to the good as far as the Wynnewood Crossman Co. was concerned, there wasn't an abler printer than Joe Stecher in New York City. But the old man wasn't entirely satisfied with his manager for all that, though there were never any words between them, thanks to Joe's unfailing reticence.

Joe's too honest, the old man would say sometimes. Christ, you can't carry on a business that way.

How much do we make on it this time, Joe? said he to his manager who was still standing there waiting.

10%, that's what you wanted, isn't it?

Think we'll underbid them?

Joe smiled. Can't see how anybody could honestly bid less and do the work at a profit, was his answer.

All right, thanks, Joe. When are the bids opened?

Monday, the 23rd. 10 A.M. at the Post Office in Washington.

Thanks, I'll go down myself this year. Look over your pressmen and weed out anyone you don't want. Fire 'em, that's all. We don't want any breakdown this time once we get going.

When Joe had left the office Mr. W took up the figures again. Take a look at this, Lester, he said to the younger man, Just take a look. You won't see anything like this again as long as you're in the printing business in this unchristly hole of a country. Look at it. And what the hell good is it? Do you think I'm gonna send those figures in? Like hell I am. And he knows I ain't gonna send them in either. Those are our figures, that's what it costs us to do the job and I tell you one thing, those figures are right to a split nickel.

Well, what's the dope then?

What's the dope? Can we do business on a lousy 10% margin? On a government contract? When we go down there and those bids are opened we're gonna be close to the top bidder and every bid under ours is gonna be thrown out — that's the way we work it, that's your father's job. I'm tellin' you. Every bid under the bid of Wynnewood-Crossman Co. goes in the waste basket. Come on, get your hat. We're going up to the club.

It was hot in the shop that day. Word got around that the old man was out to skin the hide off the loafers and the machines banged and clattered all day without a let-up. Joe walked up and down the aisles a couple of times, checked on a few proofs here and there but aside from that it was just a day like any other. When the men were going out, he happened to be over near the door looking over the addresses on some mail that was stacked to go out in the morning.

As Carmody passed by him, Joe looked up and fixed the man with his eye for the flick of a second. Good night. Good night, said the pressman. Finally when everyone had gone, Joe went quickly, expertly, among the machines to see that the rollers were properly lifted and everything tidy, took another final look around, then locked up the place and started out for home as usual.

Sunset — out of the elevated windows between the houses toward the North River. He always sat on the west side of the car going home so that he could look up from his paper and see the sun setting over Jersey — where he wanted to live some day — in the country.

Götterdämmerung, he said to himself unaccountably as he caught sight again of the red blur. A fine day today though, he added. A fine May day.

When he arrived home Gurlie was giving the baby a bath before putting it to bed. Joe forgot all about supper in his amusement. He took off his coat, took Lottie, the older girl, on his knee and sat at one side to watch his wife go through the simple ceremony. He felt like that today.

There were no frills to it when Gurlie did anything. But she was in one of her gay humors tonight so everybody felt happy.

Look at the thing, she said, having stripped the baby and laid it on a blanket over the tubs. The darlin', I wouldn't give you a cent for it. That comes from your side of the family. Anybody could see that.

Yah, said Joe, it's a smart kid.

You think you're clever, said Gurlie, laughing,

when you say a thing like that. Well, you are a smart little Dutchie, or I wouldn't have married you. You can bet on that, bejabbers. Gurlie was fond of imitating the Irish when she felt in a good humor.

Look out, said Joe, as his wife grabbed up the baby in one hand as she attempted to lift the half full tub out of the sink with the other. You'll drop it.

Drop it, me eye, answered the mother sturdily. You've got a smart head, but I'm the one — in this family — yah?

Well, be careful of the baby, said Joe, Never mind anything else.

The older girl came close so that when the baby was slopped into the tub it splashed out some water which wet her shoes. With that she moved further away toward the window.

Now the baby was in the water, it folded up its little legs and shot them out like a bull frog until the mother almost dropped it entirely. She let out a yell of laughter. What, she said, look at it! look at it!

Go on, wash it, said Joe. Don't stand there playing with it.

Look at it, said Gurlie, it's stronger than you think. I think it could swim. In some places they put little babies like that in the water and they swim.

Well, don't you try it with this one.

Say, who's washing this baby, you or me?

Look out! said Joe. You'll drown it.

That's what it needs, replied his wife mockingly.

So Gurlie ably and quickly made a few passes with a cloth up and down the baby's back and belly, here, there and around, and she was through. She picked the child out of the water.

Do you call that a bath? said Joe.

Mind your own business, said his wife nonchalantly rubbing the baby vigorously with a towel. Give me those clothes. You're one of those important blokes that has to tell everybody how to do everything. Well, you can boss your printers and the rest of the men down there, but you can't boss a woman — you can't boss me.

For some reason — tonight this sort of thing only made Joe feel warmer inside — and made him chuckle and laugh — it relieved him and made him love her the more — whereas when he was tired some days — he nearly wanted to kill her.

But today was a happy day — any way you looked at it.

Yah, you're right, he said. How's supper?

Oh you get out of here. And she shook her wet hand in his face.

He jumped. The child at the window laughed outright and coming forward wanted to throw water too. But her mother waved her off with a sweep of the hand.

That's enough foolishness, said Joe going.

Good riddance, she answered. But he stayed to watch her nevertheless.

The infant, drugged by the warm bath, drowsy, lay back perfectly contented and smiling. She put it into its crib as if she had been putting down a cat, tossed the covers over it and taking up the bottle, felt if it was warm enough, pushed it into the baby's mouth — as it lay on its back with its head turned to one side — balanced it on a folded diaper and said to Joe who was watching her: Come on now, leave it alone. Go sit down. Get out of the way.

But he merely stepped back and let her pass, turning again to look at the baby whose little hands were pressed hard together as it sucked so that the fingers seemed quite bloodless.

Come on get your supper, Gurlie called to him from the other room, if you're so hungry.

He could smell it already and it smelled good. He went at once. She served it. Lamb stew with string beans. Delicious. Down in his heart he loved this wife of his like nothing else in the world. She was beyond him — everything which he was not. Fine! he commented generously — when he felt that way.

One thing I'll say for you, he said, as he sat in his shirt sleeves and unfolded his napkin. You are a fine cook.

All Scandinavians are, she came back at him swiftly. If you give us money enough to do it with.

CHAPTER V

The Boundaries of Thought

THE BABY, still scarcely more than six pounds in weight, lay upon Gurlie's hands across her lap as she sat at the front window looking out. It pumped its legs, waved its arms as she held it listlessly. Then it puckered its face and once again coughed and wheezed out its cries of cat, fowl or whatever other straining barnyard thing no one could say. So hard it forced itself it farted at the other end in its effort and its voice finally whistled in its throat.

Gurlie's look came back from the street to stare at the struggling infant — not bewilderedly but absently with some amazement but no recognition in it. Then she stood up, comforted the baby gently for a moment against her breast and — though it was still crying — placed it in its crib and walked away. She closed the door behind her, walked to the other end of the house and sat at the back window, there to continue looking out. It was mid afternoon, the small back yards were full of new washed clothes.

Well, said Joe coming in later on — at the usual time, how have things been today?

We've got to get out of this place by the first of July, was her answer. We have a lease, said Joe. Well, do you want the baby to die because of your lease? She'll die here, stay home and take care of her yourself then.

God damn it, said Joe, flaming into a sudden wild fury, get the hell out of here then, if that's all the good you are. His face had gone suddenly ashy white, his eyes seemed to or actually did sink into his head, from which they looked out as beasts from their caves. What the hell good are you here anyway? He shouted, he stormed, he took hold of a book and dashed it to the floor.

His wife cowered away from him, laughing but backing up. She stopped and straightened finally, just stood and tried to get in a word.

Shush! Shush! What's the matter with you? You act like a fool. I didn't say anything.

What! he shouted at her — beginning to cool in spite of himself — forcing himself now suddenly to appear angrier than he was. What? you didn't say anything? Do you know what it would cost us to pay rent here and in some other god damned stinking hole in this . . .

Hey you! She broke in. The neighbors will think you are crazy.

I don't give a good god damn . . . Do you know what I make? I've told you a hundred times. Fifty dollars a week. What's the good of talking to you? But we have to live on that. We have to sleep, eat, dress, travel, amuse ourselves on that — that's all we have. We can't afford any more. Do you understand that? Can you get that much through your thick head? We can't, we can't.

I don't care what you do. What do I care? I tell you we've got to move. We've got to. Do you understand *that?* Or else the baby will die. It can't live here, I can't take it out into the street every minute. It has no air, it's dying from these rooms. I'm dying. We're all dying here.

You don't look it, said Joe.

We've got to go somewhere where there is more fresh air, somewhere near the river — or anywhere. That's up to you.

We can't afford it.

Well, get more money then. Tell them you've got to have it. Tell them if they don't give it to you you'll quit.

Sure, sneered Joe, that's a bright idea! Ha, ha, ha! Then we won't have anything at all. We can sit on the gutter then, can't we? And eat out of garbage cans.

You make me sick, answered his wife. Are you afraid? Is that what it is? Afraid to ask them? Afraid to quit if they won't give it to you? Let them fire you. That isn't what scares me! I'll sit on the curb if I have to, I'm not ashamed. You'd be ashamed to. That's what's the matter with you. We've got to have the money and you're afraid to make them give it to you. Let me go down there.

That always sobered Joe, for he did have a fear that she would, actually, go to the shop some day and make a scene. He cooled down now rapidly — and began to use his head. The color began to come back into his cheeks — he felt a little ill, nauseated over his violent temper — but steadily now he was breathing easier and his heart thumped less violently.

Go wash your face and hands and come in to supper, said his wife to him at last. And he went silently as she bade him. How about some beer? Yes, said Gurlie, but you ought to be hit over the head with it instead of drinking it.

This made him laugh, a good chuckling laugh and by the time he came to sit at the table he was again in reasonably good humor. Where's Lottie? he asked. Oh yes, he answered himself, remembering that she had been sent away to a relative for the time being. You get so excited, commented Gurlie, that you don't even know what you're talking about.

Yah, he answered, eating carefully. Open a bottle for me. Gurlie had to do everything at the table — and she did it with a swing and plunge, as if brushing some petty obstacle out of her way, which was always impressive. There it is, quick! But it foamed over on the cloth before he could get his glass to it.

There, he scolded.

What's that? she replied definitively, giving the spot a swipe with her finger. When do we move?

Before July first is what you said, didn't you? Go ahead and find a place. Hire a palace on Fifth Avenue. We can't pay for it, what do we care? Go ahead, see what you can find.

But do you think we can sublet this one? she asked somewhat disturbed — not having thought of that previously.

Why bother, he answered, we have lots of money.

But after supper when he was sitting in the front room reading his paper he called to her. What do you want? she replied. Here, he said and pointed to the paper in his hand where he had placed a check against a two line ad among the apartments-to-let column. This is over near the East River, near the Astoria ferry.

Do you mean it? she said. But what about this place?

Leave that to me.

To you? She hesitated a moment looking at him, then came over and began to stroke his hair somewhat roughly.

No, he said, go away, get out . . . but he liked it just the same. Gurlie called him her smart little

Dutchie in a lisping, babyish voice which he could never quite fathom and finally went back to the kitchen where he could hear her singing a few unmusical yodeling notes.

But the next morning, though nothing was said of it at breakfast — nothing whatever — as soon as Joe had gone down the stairs on his way to the office Gurlie took the baby up to the woman in the flat above her and set out on her strong, straight legs, walking — across Central Park — toward the East Side.

Immediately she was out of the house her spirit veritably leaped with the release — a drunkenness shot through her — the impersonal joy of people used to the country who have been cooped and tormented by city exigencies. It was a clear, hot day. She did not linger however but hurried on to her destination.

With the piece torn from the newspaper in her hand she went on until she stood before the house itself and looked up. The revulsion she felt at the sombre, rather respectable building with its fire escapes and grey brick facade struck her motionless for a moment. But finally she shrugged her shoulders and went in.

Not on your life would she take *that* apartment! She gave it one sniff. What else have you? So the janitress showed her one on the third floor, seven rooms, newly trimmed and papered which she knew at once was too expensive for her, but . . .

No, she said, and walked out. And for two hours thereafter she walked the streets looking at other places until her mind was made up. She went back to the one place which she knew now she must have, looked it over once more, told the woman to hold it

until the next day and took the 86th St. horse car to
the West Side once more.

Joe argued, lost his temper a few times but finally
— and within no more than a week — the family
found itself established in the new location. It was
really a very pleasant place, quiet, cool, with good
rooms, in a respectable German neighborhood. But,
of course, it was too big.

Gurlie solved that at once, though only in part, by
having her mother, who had been living in Brooklyn,
come to live with her.

The old lady took one look at the baby whom she
had not seen more than once or twice in its short existence and said at once that she prayed God would
take it. She shook her head and over and over again
said the same thing.

And that was one of the things that helped to save
its life — for that made Gurlie mad. Every day she
took the child out now in its little carriage. She too
prayed, that the baby should be saved and she worked
hard to give it the air and sunlight which her instinct
told her it must have. How she did walk — she and
the baby. The park and the river were her resorts.
She travelled the ferry time and time again, over to
Astoria and back, and then one day a German woman
with a big husky child on her arm stopped to look at
the puny infant.

What are you feeding it? Gurlie told her. Good!
said the woman. Give it all it wants though — whenever it yells. From that time things went better.

But Gurlie grew tired of walking and one night
announced a servant.

CHAPTER VI

Summer Days

How much does a little thing like that really know? said Joe half to himself one evening. It doesn't look as if it ever would know anything, said his wife sitting nearby. It's a smart kid, Joe went on. All it does is cry, broke in the grandmother, the poor thing.

Vinie took it out every day and walked by the hour with it always in the park — with her slow gangling gait, looking around over her shoulder whenever she'd hear some outcry of the playing children there, or sitting lazily watching the smart carriages go by on the drive. But she liked the baby and considered her job minding it a pleasant and amusing one.

That's the worstest lookin' baby I ever *did* see, she would say to herself putting it in the carriage or taking it out as it wobbled and slid about in her able hands, the po'est baby I *ever* had to do with — as if she had ever had to do with any white baby before — which she certainly hadn't. But she was a natural mother for all her lack of years. And she'd give black looks to anyone who happened to look into the carriage, some old lady who would perhaps exclaim at the baby's appearance.

It was from the beginning the baby's very scrawniness which seemed to fascinate her. It wasn't that she was sorry for it. She was charmed by its curiousness, its unlikeness to anything familiar to her in her brief experience of living. It tickled her to see it naked, she'd grin all over and shake her head from side to side: Well, if you ain't the worst! But Gurlie kept pretty close watch on the little nigger — for a time, so Vinie could only stand by and watch while the baby's toilette was being made, her hands on her hips, her head on one side, her face intent on watching every movement of her white mistress. Can I . . . won't you let me dress her this mornin', Mrs. Stecher?

No, said Gurlie.

But one day the third week, a hot day, Gurlie had to take her mother over to Brooklyn, so after several words in Norwegian between the two women, Gurlie came to Vinie and said they were going to leave the baby alone with her — that it was asleep and maybe it would sleep till she came back. But if it did wake — and so forth and so forth. To which Vinie nodded solemnly: Yas'm. Yas'm.

It was awfully hot in the apartment. Vinie watched from the front window as the ladies emerged from the door downstairs, looked up and then, seeing her, walked slowly down the street and finally disappeared. There she continued to lean listlessly in the baking sun for half an hour, kneeling on the floor and looking up and down, leaning way out to try and look into the apartment next door — which she couldn't quite do. So she pulled her head in and after getting a drink of water at the tap in the kitchen, soaking her face and head there, letting the water run up and down her arms, she shook her hands more or less dry and went in to see if the baby was still asleep. And there she sat down and looked at it till it opened its eyes to hers. That made her goggle and look around instinctively to see if she were being watched. Then she picked the baby up, took it over to the big bed and saying to herself, out loud, that it was an awful hot day, she started to take off the baby's clothes. What you doin'? she said to herself. What you doin' takin' off that baby's clothes? Didn' I tell you never to do that? Didn' I tell you? But she kept on steadily, carefully undressing the baby for all that. It grinned its crooked little grin at her as she lifted and turned it — which encouraged her to work rapidly. Her heart was beating with excitement.

Carefully she spread a soft cotton blanket on the big bed and upon it lay the completely naked baby — carefully, skilfully. There, she said at last, tha's the way. There you is. There you sho'ly is. You ain't got nothin' on you. You ain't got nothin' on you at all. Nothin'. Tha's what you like. Tha's yo' summer dress, tha's yo' summer dress. Vinie gived you that. How you like it?

For a fact the baby liked it immensely in that hot room, if actions mean anything, for it lay completely relaxed on its back, its head moving slowly about as if it were viewing the room though its eyes didn't seem to focus on anything — or if so just for a moment and then wandered on.

What you seein'? asked Vinie watching it intently. Can you see Vinie? Hea! here, she moved her own face so as to get it into the baby's line of vision, but without result. Tha's a funny baby, she said now. You is a real funny baby, she changed her manner, talking direct to the little mite. You ain't even a cat. How big *is* you?

With that, she put her elbow down on the bed by the baby's feet and then lay her forearm down beside the baby, her finger tips coming just to the mite's rounded crown. Half an arm, she said, tha's how big you is, half an arm.

The baby was playing up to the girl's gentle voice and easy manner to perfection. With half closed eyes, it moved first a finger then an arm as if talking some mysterious sign language. Vinie couldn't contain her curiosity. She got right onto the bed beside the baby and started carefully to look it over. For no reason at all her look began at the belly button. Now will you tell me what in the world is that to do for? she wondered to herself. She took her finger and gently pushed at the small rosette of skin where the umbilical cord had grown, then put her hand up to her own belly feeling there also. She looked deeper into the little umbilical pit, spreading the skin apart and saw there a little accumulation of cotton dust which with great care she picked out upon her sharp finger nails. The baby did not move but seemed to enjoy the play.

But all at once the infant voided freely, the little amber puddle rolling over the blanket as if it had been quicksilver — without sinking in. Vinie jumped and in a flash was back with a diaper. It had not got on the coverlet — luckily. Man alive! she breathed, is I lucky!

The whiteness of the baby's body caused her to look and look again. She pinched the flesh of the belly gently up between her fingers, shaking her head again and again. So flabby was the skin that it remained that way, pinched up, for several moments after she had withdrawn her hand. You sho' is po', was her only comment.

Its little ribs seemed to slide back and forth under the skin as the infant breathed, irregularly. Now it would take half a dozen rapid, fluttering inhalations. Then it would stop, it seemed, no sign of life there, then the fluttering. Its hands were open but the minute Vinie went to look at them they closed vigorously shut so that she hardly dared to spread the fingers out. But she did, finally, and there, in the little sweaty palms, were the same dust flakes she had found elsewhere. The feet squirmed and drew back suddenly from her hands, sharply with a snap. But somehow the baby did not cry. Vinie was slow and gentle.

You ain't got no legs at all, said the girl sympathetically. No more than a frog. But the little feet wiggled and twisted away each time she put her hand upon them. And your arms is worse. But when the baby got a grip on the colored girl's strong index fingers with each of its tiny fists, Vinie could almost lift it from the bed.

The diminutive pimples of the breasts next caught her eye, she gently rubbed them with her finger tips as the baby squirmed and stretched. Tickles, huh? she said. Tha's right. All under the opaque white skin she could make out the blue veins. Blue blood, like you Mammy say.

Rather uncertainly she looked now at the miniature middle parts but got to laughing, sniggering, before she had gone very far. And with a deprecatory — You's a girl all right. You ain't no boy. A white girl, they ain't no difference — don't seem to be — she turned to the baby's ears and nose and face with evident relief.

By chance her finger fell into the fontanelle whose lack of bone made her pull back her hand suddenly. That was one too many for her.

The time was getting on. Hurriedly she began dressing the baby which, when finally she had clothed it as it had been before, she put it back in its crib, then giving it its bottle as she knew how to do, she left it

and lay down on her own bed where Gurlie found
her fast asleep — the baby crying — when she returned at six, all excitement and bustle to begin to get
supper ready.

The grandma went in to the baby and picked it up
instantly, found it soaked, and spoke sharply to the
mother in Norwegian while Vinie stood with wide
eyes feeling doom descending upon her. But it didn't.

Agh, nonsense, replied Gurlie in English to the
older woman, leave it alone. Take the baby out of
here, I've got to get supper. She was satisfied with
Vinie who only cost her two dollars a week and
couldn't bother to get another girl. The grandmother
took the baby and went away still talking.

Sure, if you pick the baby up every time it opens
its trap, said Joe later in the evening, it will get to
like it. Wouldn't you? To this the grandmother objected that it would rupture itself if it were left to
cry. How many babies have you known that ruptured
themselves crying? asked Joe. None, because we pick
them up when common sense tells us to in my country.
Then what are you talking about? was his reply. Anyhow the baby, who began crying again at that time,
was picked up and he went out of the room.

How long is the old lady going to live with us? he
asked his wife later in the evening. But she didn't
take it amiss as he thought she might — for he was
half joking. She herself had not been so well satisfied
with the new menage since it had been growing on
her in the past few weeks. Seizing the situation as it
stood, she told her husband she would like nothing
better than her mother out of it — any time they
could find a place for her — the sooner the better.

Turn out the light — hard, he replied. I've smelt

gas around this place ever since we moved into it. Did that damned little nigger come in yet?

Oh, go to sleep, said his wife. Good night, she added leaning over him. Go on away, he answered her, it's too hot tonight for that sort of thing. But he kissed her just the same.

Mornings Gurlie bathed the baby with her own hands — like that! A blanket on the table, as the mother laid the infant down, brusquely, feeling the hard under surface, it tilted back its head, stiffened, and over-balanced by the weight of its own occiput, rolled half to one side, felt itself falling and in a sudden fright threw out all its limbs, rigid, and instinctively caught its breath then let out a convulsive yell. Then in the effort rolled wildly to the other side, careened and kicked out stiff again, yelling, shaking and growing red with the effort.

It's all right, said Gurlie in her usual collected manner, drawing the water.

All right? said her mother hurrying to pick it up. It's terrified. That's no way to treat a baby.

Oh, said Gurlie, I'm watching it.

Yes, you're watching it. It could kick itself onto the floor. I pray God may take it — you'll never raise it this way. You let it lie there. You let that ignorant child mind it. You are not a mother to it. You should hold it in your arms.

I do, said Gurlie.

When? replied her mother. A baby needs to be held. Look at the back of its head, all the hair is worn off. That's how much you mother it.

Vinie had noticed that too.

Look at it, flying in all directions. It doesn't know what to do. Babies should be swaddled to hold their

legs straight, to make them feel firm. But I am old
fashioned, I know nothing. Nothing but a diaper that
is too big for it — a big wad of cloth pushing its poor
little legs out like a frog. You don't even know how to
put on a diaper. But you won't listen to me. Its legs
need to be comfortable and firmly held. And it should
not be left to cry.

Well, pick it up then when it cries. It knows how
to get what it wants. Ever since you came here it cries
and you pick it up. Now you've taught it that.

Sure, Joe would say at such a time, I told you. It's
a smart kid.

And Vinie, witness sometimes to all this, Vinie too
would say: Lady, you sho' knows what you want —
amazed, amused, when the baby would be convulsed
with crying, her sensitive mouth opening in imitation
of the baby's who would be mad through.

But most mornings, the weather being fine, when
the baby would begin its whining yell, Gurlie would
call to Vinie to drop whatever she was doing and take
it out — into the park. And she had never to speak
twice.

We got that fixed, said Vinie to the baby, taking it
downstairs. When you wants to take yo' ride, you
yélls. And I's here to take you. And *does* you *know* it?

Once in the park the morning ramble would begin
once more. The baby drowsy or else its eyes wide open,
staring, or so it seemed, at the joggling fringe at the
edge of the hood which the mother would tell Vinie
to pull down to keep the sun out of the baby's eyes.

How you gonna see that a way? Vinie would say to
the baby, later on. And back she would push the hood,
though if the baby squinted and blinked too much
she was careful to turn round and walk away from the

sun until she could find a shady bench to sit on and watch the squirrels or the others like herself with children there.

If the baby yelped she'd look at it, change it or joggle it awhile, then if it went on yelling she'd sit and look at it intently, watching how its little mouth would go into a square, showing the gums and the curled back tongue, stiffened, unmoving as the surprising sound issued from that hollow throat. Vinie would try to look far down to see if she could see where all that noise came from. The whole posture, lips and tongue, might have been a flower so unaffectedly did the little colored girl look at it sometimes. Its eyes would pucker closed. If it got its cap cockeyed over one eye, even down over its nose, she'd push it back and say: You sho' can cry. You sho' can cry when you gets set to it. Then she'd be attracted by some other happening and appear to forget the baby. Till it would stop. Then she'd straighten it, get up maybe and walk a little further.

These summer days were doing the infant a world of good. But what would the fall and winter bring later? It was hard to say.

But as the thing seemed to know when to cry so that the grandmother would rescue it, so in the end it learned not to cry when in the park with Vinie. Mostly as July wore on it would rest quietly in the carriage when outdoors, or miraculously cease crying as soon as Vinie spoke to it.

It lay in the sun moving its hands, tentatively fumbling with them in spasmodic jerks along the cotton quilt, then wildly gripping — the air — or whatever came against them — locking its fingers into the loose fabric and holding on like grim death.

Leggo, Vinie would say. Leggo a that. Take yo' fingers away.

Then the baby would swing the other hand up and grab blindly with that also. Her face would be all excitement at such times, her whole body would draw itself up and she'd try to cram the object, no matter what it was, toward her mouth.

I'll fix you one of these days, you wait and see, said Vinie, if you suck that blanket that way. Look at yo' mouth, all red slobber. Leggo! I'll put some pepper on yo' fingers. You see if I don't.

CHAPTER VII

Conflict

O SCAR!

Gott, Gurlie! You're getting good looking. Joe must be making money.

Come in. Where in the world did you come from? What's happened to bring you here?

Thanks. Chicago. Nothing. Give us a kiss.

He made to kiss her on the lips but she turned her cheek. Go long wid you.

How are you anyway? he said then.

Fine. But what brings you here, insisted Gurlie.

My feet, old Gal. And the train, straight through the country. Where is everybody? Where's Lottie? And the baby! Hey Lottie.

There was a small commotion of a chair and little feet at the other end of the corridor. Shhh! said Gurlie. Lottie's in the kitchen and the baby's sleeping. Come in here. And she pushed the curtains back from the big door to the front room.

Oh, sleeping! said the man in a whisper. But when he had got into the parlor he spoke out again. Ump um! I should say! Joe *is* making money.

Don't be silly, said Gurlie. Rents are very cheap down here.

Ha, ha! Quit your kidding, he answered her.

Sit down here, said Gurlie, and don't make so much noise with your big voice.

Oh, is that so? said Oscar. But he sat down easily and carefully for all that. Do you think it will hold me?

But that wasn't the kind of question Gurlie bothered to answer. He took out his pipe and began to load it up but stopped and put it back in his pocket after a moment.

Were you fired? said Gurlie standing before him with her arms akimbo.

No, said the man, I quit.

Yes, you didn't, replied his sister-in-law looking down at him. Did they close down?

Be yourself, Sis. I got tired of hefting their beef. Wanted a little air. Life. The big city. You know. Got a place here to put me up in?

For how long?

About a year maybe? And he roared out his amused laugh at the look which came over her face. Go on, find Lottie for me. And wake the baby. Tell her her old German uncle from the wicked west is here with a horse and wagon for her. What you worrying about?

But Gurlie didn't move.

I've got my card, haven't I? I can get a dozen jobs any time I want 'em. That's what the Union does for you.

Didn't you even bring a satchel? asked Gurlie.

Sure. I left it down at the room.

Oh, said Gurlie, brightening. What's that? pointing to a big paper bundle he had dropped into a chair. Presents?

As they turned, at a little sound, they saw a serious black-curl-surrounded face looking at them from the edge of the curtains.

You don't mean that's Lottie? said the man getting up slowly. Gott in himmel! Why she was just a baby. And he went over and raised the little tot in his hands as though she were a kitten. She grinned sheepishly down at him without a kick or quiver. Then smiled from ear to ear. Lottie! said the man. Don't you know me?

How could she? said the mother. After almost two years.

Leave her to me, said Oscar.

So Gurlie went out, saying she would make him some coffee.

I drink this! said the little girl showing a small bottle unobserved by the others up to that time clasped firmly about the neck in her hand. What? said Oscar. Let's see that. Why that's medicine. Hey, you Gurlie! What's this? . . . But the cork was still firmly in place and so no harm had been done. Gurlie went back to the kitchen. Then the child held out one foot, the shoe unbuttoned — and looked down at it.

Oscar picked her up and placed her upon his left thigh with her two feet sticking out in front of her and did up her buttons: And there you are.

The child looked up at him and smiled. Where do you sleep? she said.

Where do I sleep? Well, by God, Lottie, that's a good one. Why, on my head, of course. Where do you sleep, old girl? Tell me that. But the child just kept looking up fascinated at him where she sat sidewise on his lap. Can I stay here? And so they talked together while Gurlie was making the coffee in the kitchen.

And now I'm going to show you something nice, said the man. But first standing with the little girl between his hands he began raising her up as if he were going to toss her into the air: Ein, Zwei. And a half! and he didn't toss her after all. Then again. Ein, Zwei. And this time at Drei he gave her a full toss so that she flew up, her arms spread wide, her legs out, high into the air, looking down at him still, unafraid, into his eyes — and he caught her under the armpits, easily breaking her fall. And again. And again. Until she began to laugh drunkenly and he saying: Whoops! Whoops!, every time and, There she goes!

Well, what's this? suddenly broke in a voice from the doorway, and there stood a tall, thin woman in street clothes and a hat, looking in from beside the curtains. Oscar, put the child down. Both stood there looking at the woman. Then they heard Gurlie coming.

My! how did you get in?

Well, if you leave your front door open . . .

Silly, we always leave it open, said Gurlie. Don't you know who this is? This is Oscar, Joe's brother. You've often heard us speak of him. This is my sister Hilda.

Oh you mean? I'm very pleased to meet you, said Hilda coming forward.

Same here, said Oscar taking her hand.

Ouch! said Hilda. Ha, ha, said Oscar, did I squeeze it too tight? Ooo! said Hilda again, what hands!

Gurlie brought out a little table and they had coffee and cakes. Lottie sat on the man's knee and ate what she pleased in spite of the protests of the women. She even had some coffee.

Tell you what we'll do, said Oscar at last. I'm feeling good. Let's have a party tonight.

What sort of a party? said Gurlie.

Let's give Joe a surprise. Will you cook it if I bring it in? Bring what in? said Gurlie. Everything. What time is it now? Four o'clock. In half an hour. *Auf Wiedersehen!* And he was on his way, kissing Lottie in departing and bending his head again at the curtains as he went through. She ran to the window to see him go running down the front steps.

And that is Joe's brother! said Hilda catching her breath after the cyclone had departed.

Yes, said Gurlie. Now I'll have to work.

Is that the one . . . ?

Yes. Here, help me take out these things.

What did he do? persisted the thin auntie. He ran off with the general's wife? Gurlie laughed heartily. His captain's wife, said she, not the general's. Oh, said Hilda, and so he had to come to America. That is very romantic.

A lazy, good-for-nothing, replied Gurlie, coming like this in the middle of the afternoon to disturb everybody.

Joe should have some of his light heartedness, began Hilda. But Gurlie broke in on her. See here! she said, don't you say anything against my husband.

Why I never said anything against Joe, replied the thin auntie.

Yes, you did, came back Gurlie. That one can run away with a married woman. And you think that's fine, you think that's wonderful. Foolish people like you. But his brother had to work, from the time he was a little boy, and bring up the whole pack of them. No, no, you can't say anything against Joe. Look out for that in your hand. She stopped, listening, both listened. And sure enough the baby's thin cry could be heard coming fitfully from the back of the house.

Here, said Gurlie, when they reached the kitchen, you can make good cakes. There's all you need — somewhere in there. Make a cake. I don't know what you want, replied Hilda. A cake, said Gurlie, any kind. There's flour, butter. What do you need? Here are three oranges. Make an orange cake. All right, said the thin auntie, but it's only four o'clock.

Take this, said Gurlie, handing her an apron. Roll up your sleeves. And before she knew much more about it Hilda was hard at it mixing up a cake batter while Gurlie was prodding the range with broad skillfull hands until she had a roaring fire there. Her hands were grimy and her blonde hair was in wisps flying about her forehead and temples.

Vinie! she called and the lanky colored girl came in with the baby on her arm and Lottie traipsing after her. Come here, put down that baby. Yas'm. Take the things off those tubs. Yas'm. And the baby having been propped up in a high, rolling chair with a pillow, was given a wooden spoon to play with. Lottie wanted it and deliberately pulled it out of the baby's grip, tho' the mite, who had been trying to suck it, held on with might and main — yet it was taken from her.

Waaaa! she yelled.

Then the door bell rang. Vinie went. And with a great clatter in came Oscar, a case of beer on his left shoulder and a bushel basket heaped with small packages, unwrapped vegetables and a bottle, in the crook of his right arm. Here we are, he called out. I rang the bell with my elbow. Couldn't push the door open.

Oh! shouted the ladies in amazement. Oscar! what have you done? But with that case of beer on your shoulder that way, you shouldn't . . .

Who? laughed the man.

But you've bought too much. What is this?

Everything. Then he saw the baby and stopped. The baby! said he. And he dropped everything to the

floor and went over at once to the chair where little
Flossie was still sobbing, broken-hearted, over the loss
of her spoon. Then he turned seriously to Gurlie: Is
she all right? Of course, she's all right. Who's taking
care of her? He turned to Vinie who backed off with
a scared expression to her face. She's too thin. Why
don't you feed her?

Leave the child alone and mind your own business,
said Gurlie. We have work to do if we're going to cook
all that stuff you've brought in. I think you're crazy —
for four people.

And there was Lottie crowding in — or trying to —
between him and the baby, looking up at him with
big, reproachful eyes. Let's see what they gave us,
he said.

Gurlie started to laugh in spite of herself. And
who's going to fix that chicken? Me, I suppose.

Watch someone as *can* fix a chicken, he replied.
And to Vinie's intense amusement, he threw off his
coat, rolled up his sleeves, tucked a kitchen towel
around his waist — he wore no vest — and the game
was on.

But not until he had opened up three bottles of beer,
filled three glasses, and: What about the gal? he said
turning to Vinie. But Gurlie shook her head. No! at
Vinie behind his back. No, not for her, said Gurlie,
she doesn't like it. So Vinie looked down and sucking
in her lips tried not to laugh.

Here's to success! said Oscar, come on Lottie, take
a sip. Success! and the ladies said the same. And some
meat on your bones, Babes! He leaned down to the
baby. Pros't! And he drank the glass down as if in one
swallow to the baby's health and filled up another.

The time flew, as did their fingers. Soon the kitchen

was filled with delicious smells. Whee! said Gurlie,
open those windows at the top.

And how old were you when you were in the German army? asked the thin auntie.

Eighteen, said the man, in the Kaiser's Dragoon
Guards, not a man among us under six feet in his
stockings . . .

I want to know all about it. It is very romantic, said
Hilda. Was she very beautiful?

Oscar gave Gurlie a broad wink. *Wunderschön!*
It was love at first sight.

And then? said Hilda eagerly.

And then, when it was too late, I found she was my
captain's wife.

Nonsense, said Gurlie. You must have known who
she was.

No, no, said Hilda, such things do happen. But you
do not understand, you are not romantic, she concluded addressing her sister.

On my soul I didn't, said Oscar melodramatically.
I thought she was free. What could I do when I found
otherwise?

But what were you doing when they found you?

There we were, continued Oscar. It was a dark
moonlight night. I had climbed from the back window
of the *kaserne,* dropped twenty feet to the
ground . . .

I don't believe a word of it, said Gurlie.

Why yes, said the thin auntie. That is how these
things happen. I believe in love . . .

Whoops, said Gurlie. I'll bet you do. Wait till you
try it. I'll bet she saw he was a nice boy and took him
by the ear . . .

But did you . . . did you? Did they catch you? continued Hilda ignoring her sister.

No, not exactly, said Oscar, a little sobered in spite of himself. Not exactly. Or else I wouldn't be here. Well, here's to the living. And he downed another glass of beer. Anyhow, she was a fine woman.

The baby was crying again. Lottie had pushed her sister's chair far over, little by little, while they were talking, against the wall with her face the other way.

Look, said Gurlie, laughing. Look what she's done. Vinie, come here.

But Vinie who had been setting the table in the other room frowned heavily at the older child as she brought the baby, still crying, around to face the room again.

Take her out, said Gurlie, she cries too much.

No, said Oscar, let her stay. They like to cry. That's their profession. The first thing they take up is crying. And with that the baby stopped at once and a broad, sunny grin spread over her features all running wet with tears — the toothless grin of a five months old baby — while she snuggled her face down shyly into her pillow having attracted attention to herself at last.

Why don't you get married, you like babies so much, said Hilda.

It's bad luck, said the ex-cavalryman. I once heard of a man who did it — and his wife lived to be a hundred.

Well look out, you smart guys, began Gurlie. But she suddenly changed her mind. What time is it? Look and see, Vinie.

Ten minutes past six, Ma'm.

Then a wild scramble ensued. Why, the baby should be fed and asleep by this time. But she was jabbering loudly and gaily along with the others and banging her chair with the spoon. Let her stay up, said Oscar. I'll have to clean myself up, said Hilda. Chairs were rushed about. Then, as it approached six-thirty — all traces of excitement were ironed out, not an unusual sound or sight prevailed, just the smell of the roast chicken, and — the sound of a key could be heard in the front door. It was Joe.

Hellooo! he called out. No answer. Hey! he said then. Where is everybody?

Oh, is it you, said Gurlie coming forward. Then she lost control a little, took him by both cheeks, pinching him hard with her strong hands and kissed him vigorously all over the face. It's me darlint, she said, my little Dutchie.

Leave me alone, he protested harshly. What's the matter with you? You've been drinking. Get out of here.

And with that Oscar and Hilda rushed forward into the hall.

Hello Joe!

What's this! What's this! said Joe.

It's a party, said Gurlie, hilarious now. For what? said Joe. A party? For us! said Gurlie. It's Oscar's treat. That's good, said Joe. I suppose he has lots of money. Well, how are you? Glad you came. Let's go into the other room.

The dinner was tremendous. Skol! said Gurlie holding a glass up to her husband's nose. Skol! come on, you. Drink.

Joe, though, somehow couldn't get himself up to the mood of the others and gradually, as the effect of the beer wore off and they had eaten more and more, they grew soberer and soberer. Hilda had let her head fall on Oscar's shoulder and he had placed his arm around her gallantly. Vinie was a little bored. The baby had been put to sleep earlier and Lottie who had been kneeling on a leather pillow behind Oscar's chair ended by going to sleep there also.

Why did you say you came east? said Joe to his brother finally. Have one of these nickel cigars, he added, they're good. No thanks, replied Oscar. I'm going to fill up the old pipe in a minute. I just felt like it, so I came.

Good, said Joe, that's the way to do things. Just quit, eh?

Oh, it must be wonderful to be a man, commented Hilda drowsily.

Yes, just stepped out, said Oscar, for a little vacation.

Are the meat packers pretty well organized these days? asked the older brother.

Stop it, said Gurlie. What's the matter with you? Skol! Oscar. He's too serious.

Well, somebody has to be.

What's happened to you, Joe? said his brother. You were always a hard worker but . . .

Shame on you, said his wife, this is no time for such talk. Oh, she said rising, I know where there's something in the pantry. And you're going to drink it, she threatened her husband.

Yes, I wondered where you were hiding it, replied he.

All right, she came back at him, Why don't you let yourself go then?

Go on, said Joe, get out of here. Can't a man talk

to his own brother? Are you a member of their union? he continued, addressing Oscar.

Sure I am. Please, said Hilda, don't quarrel. Joe gave her a look and laughed in spite of himself. Here we are, said Gurlie, coming in with a half bottle of brandy. She poured out a small glassful and held it to her husband's lips. Drink! she said, drink! I'll drink it, he replied drawing back. Give it to me. He took it and smelled it. What's this? Let me see the bottle. Oh, you make me tired, she answered him. It's poison! Can't you see it written here? It's poison, I tell you. That's why I gave it to you. Forget it.

All right, he said. I want to see it just the same. *Was der Bauer nicht kennt, das frisst er nicht.*

What's the matter, Joe, something on your mind? asked Oscar.

Why should there be? Ain't I married?

What do you mean by that, came back his wife swiftly.

Plenty, he grinned at her, frowning to keep himself from breaking into a laugh.

Look here, young man, she went on. If it wasn't for me you'd be in the soup. I'm the one that stands behind you. I'm the one. Isn't it so? Don't you know it down in your heart? Don't you know it? Tell me. Don't you know that I'm the one that makes you get anywhere?

Well, where are we getting to? That's what I'd like to know. The poor house, as far as I can see.

Bah, bah, bah, bah! She got up and tousled his head in her rough, caressing manner. I'll bet my little Dutchie against the world — raising her glass in a powerful gesture.

Hoch, hoch!

You have, and how I know it, said Joe.

What do you mean by that?

What can I mean?

Look here, young man. If you don't think you're lucky to have me pushing you where you don't want to go yourself . . .

You'll see! she continued, ignoring his answer. You'll see. You have everything — but the courage. And I have that. You wait and see.

Gedul' bring' Rosen! I hope so, was Joe's rejoinder before Oscar broke in with: You take too much on your own shoulders, Joe.

Well, it's lucky someone does.

That's right, put in Gurlie. Listen to your brother, he knows how to live.

No, it isn't that, Oscar answered quickly, but Joe's too good. Gott! What difference does it make whether you're dead or alive — in the end, I mean — as far as the world is concerned! You've got to think of yourself more. This idea of thinking you've got to take the whole business on your own shoulders — I've noticed it's usually you little fellahs who get the weight of the world on your necks. While you're studying your latins and getting your scholarships . . .

Yes, exactly, said Gurlie defensively.

. . . why, continued Oscar, we're out . . .

Yes, said Hilda.

. . . living, concluded the ex-dragoon.

Ha, ha, said Joe, you're right. But what exactly he meant by his laughter it would be hard to say.

This is the end. We're living in the last times. Read the Bible, broke in Gurlie.

It's the women coming into business that's doing

it, said Joe ignoring her. They're too damned lazy to stay home and take care of their own work. They want to put men out to show how smart they can be, to make money to fix their hair and paint their faces with . . .

Nonsense, answered Gurlie quietly. Give us enough money and we are satisfied. Whoop la! she shouted, then *la de da dee da dee da dee!*

Na na, na na! Can't you keep quiet for a minute? Can't you let us talk? No, you are too serious, said his wife. You're drunk, he replied. Who's drunk? Not I. But you ought to be, that's what's the matter with you. You need it. Who's going to give us a toast?

I will, said her husband suddenly, and paused. Down with the unions, he cried out, standing. Come on, drink it.

There was absolute silence for a minute. Nobody drank but Joe who finished his glass. Let's have another, he added, holding his glass out toward the wife. What's the matter? Are you having trouble down at the shop? said she shrewdly, not filling his glass as he had asked her to. Not a trouble in the world. Come on, give me something to drink. Down with the unions! And he laughed his chuckling, half mocking adult laughter. Come on, all of you. Drink up.

All right, said Oscar. Down with the unions. And down went his dram.

Now then, tear up your card, said Joe, with a malicious twinkle in his eye.

Right you are, replied Oscar, reaching into his pocket. He had his eye fixed on his older brother.

No, said Gurlie, stopping him. Papa, what's the matter with you? Are you crazy?

Well, are you going to let me talk then?

Not when you talk that way.

All right then, forget it. To hell with the politicians. Vote for Cleveland. *Hoch soll er leben, hoch soll er leben! Drei mal hoch.* Is this all you've got to drink?

My God, Joe! said his brother, I've been hoping to see you lit all my young life. Gurlie! The champagne!

Whee pee! I forgot it. And she jumped up and went running out of the room.

Champagne? said Joe.

I love champagne, said Hilda. It makes you feel so — I don't know what.

No, I guess you don't, said Joe.

You're right, said Oscar. That's right. Listen to old Joe, said he to Gurlie returning. He was just saying . . .

I think you're terrible, said Hilda.

What are you men after, embarrassing my poor sister.

Oscar was working at the neck of the bottle by this time. He didn't try to hold back the cork. Pop went the cork, bouncing sharply from the ceiling directly into Hilda's lap. Good luck, good luck shouted Oscar.

Say Oscar, this is fine, said Joe after a minute. You shouldn't have done it. That must have cost a lot of money. That's fine of you, though. We haven't had champagne — how long is it since we had any champagne, Mama?

Oh, this is delicious, said Hilda. It reminds me of when I was in Paris.

And here's to your health, all of you, said Oscar. To us all — God help us!

And down with the unions, said Joe laughing. The unions and the politicians.

Say, is Sis still playing in the Black Crook? That's

one of the main reasons I came down this time. Sure, she's still in the chorus, said Joe in his usual cryptic manner. Want to go and see her? Yes, said Oscar, I was thinking we might all go down there now . . .

Yes, yes, broke in Gurlie.

Not tonight, said Joe. Not me anyhow. I'm sorry. Take the ladies if you like but I've got to go to bed. I've got a big day ahead of me tomorrow.

CHAPTER VIII

Men

STECHER! He took a step out onto the floor where every press was going full blast. Stecher! he yelled at the top of his voice. Then he turned back into his office again. Where the hell is Stecher? Boy! Go find Mr. Stecher and tell him I want him in here at once. Yes sir. And the boy came around from the window and went out through the office door closing it behind him.

Joe was back of the No. 3 press at the far end of the second row, in his shirt sleeves, crouching down, almost to the floor looking in, over the upturned Brodies, the overalls and body of the head mechanic who was lying on his back looking up under the rollers. This press was still. This one only.

What is it? said Joe at the top of his voice.

One of the roller gears is snapped, came back the voice.

God damn it to hell, said Joe under his breath. Then, Where is it? Put your light up.

At that moment the office boy came up from behind. Wanted in the office, sir. Joe paid no attention to him. Didn't even hear him in fact. Hold your light up higher. Higher, I said. Put your hand on the break. He got down on his knees, then drew back and spoke to the pressman who was standing by.

Is the power off, Carmody? She's jammed, said the one addressed. Won't move one way or the other. I didn't ask you that. I asked you if the power is off.

Yea, said the man, drawling out the word slowly. With that Joe went around to the controls and looked for himself then came back behind the press again.

You're wanted in the office, sir, said the boy. Joe looked at him as if he'd never seen him before. Then he started crawling in under the press near the mechanic. When he was in there their faces were only a few inches apart, both were looking up at the under surfaces of the rollers, the mechanic's face was smudged diagonally across the forehead. Look out for your head, Stecher, he said. It's a dirty place in here.

Joe was looking carefully at the place that had been pointed out to him. Suddenly he started, almost microscopically, didn't say anything at once, but reached up and tried to take hold — but couldn't quite reach it. What's that? What? said the mechanic. That, said Joe, sticking out there. That's not a part of the machine.

If you'll let me get where you are I'll see what it is, said the mechanic. All right, said Joe and he crawled out backward. The mechanic moved over, lifted himself up and took hold of the object Joe had pointed out. What is it? I can't move it, said the mechanic. It looks like part of the gear. Get it out, said Joe.

The mechanic seemed awkward and slow.

Mr. Stecher. Wanted in the office.

All right, said Joe. Can you move it? he spoke again to the mechanic.

There was a hammering, a metallic grating and muttered curses under the press then the voice, saying, I can't make it. It'll have to wait until we take the press down.

No, said Joe. Get it out now.

I'm likely to damage the roller if I go hammering.

Get that gear clear and bring out any loose pieces, said Joe. There was more pounding, then a clatter of falling metal and something dropped out from under the press and bounced on the floor. The pressman reached for it, picked it up. But Joe went up to him and took it out of his hand roughly with a quick wrench of the wrist. He looked at it. It was the shaft of a small screw driver. This yours, Carmody? he asked. Let me see it, said the man sulkily. No, said Joe. Show me your kit. The man slowly got his tool kit out and loosened the strap. Joe looked in. Then he looked at the man, square in his eyes. The man returned the look without a quiver.

Well, what about it? said the latter.

Nothing, said Joe quietly. Report tomorrow morning at the usual time. We don't need you today. Better leave now. And take better care of your tools next time. Then he burst into a rage. Haven't I told you . . . the man took it like a lamb. Yes sir, said the man.

Now get out, said Joe. Every press was going at full tilt and every man in the place sensed, and saw, almost one could have said, they heard every word that was uttered in that irregular clatter and clash. Carmody hesitated a moment, looking right and left, then walked over to the lockers.

The mechanic was out from under the press and on his feet by the time Joe got around to him again. How long will it take? said Joe — leaving the rest of the sentence to be understood. It all depends on whether I can get a part in the city. Well, get on your clothes and go out and get it, said Joe. But don't you think I'd better start? Can you fix it without the part? No, but couldn't you send one of the boys while I

. . . Then do what I tell you. Get what you need, wherever it is made. Get on the train. Go where they make them. But get it. Work all night if you have to but this press has got to be running by tomorrow morning. Do you understand me? Sure, Stecher, I understand you.

Then Joe went to the basin, holding his delicate soiled hands out before him, washed them, dried them, put on his coat and went to the inner office.

For Christ's sake, Stecher, where the hell've you been? Didn't the boy tell you I wanted you right away? Joe made no answer. But the old man went on as if he had. Drop what you're doing and come on the run when I call you next time. What's the matter anyway back there?

One of the presses, said Joe. Broke down? said the old man. Yes, cracked gear.

For God's sake, Stecher, you knew what we had ahead of us this month, why can't you keep those presses in order? I told you time after time to see that everything was up to the minute. That's your job. I told you to have the presses put in trim for a heavy load. Which press is it? No. 3, said Joe. That's a brand new machine. We haven't had it in the shop a year. What's the matter? Can't you take care of the equipment?

This made no impression on Joe. He knew and knew that the old man knew he knew there was no one that could take his place. He knew too, that the old man had to work off his steam some way. Let him blow. But Joe didn't enjoy it. He just kept his mouth shut and looked his boss in the eye as Carmody had looked at him only a few moments earlier.

And what have you done about it?

We'll be rolling again by tomorrow morning, said Joe.

The old man said nothing for a minute then turned to his desk and picked up a letter. Look at this, he said handing it to Joe, God damn 'em. It had the U. S. Government Seal at the top — an order from the Post Office Department that they were to double their deliveries of money orders beginning the next week. Joe read it and handed it back to his chief. We can do it, he said, if you'll let me run a night shift.

Christ, what can I do? Let you run it? How in hell are we to do it if I don't? Costing how much? Joe again didn't answer.

That's all, said the old man. Fix it up and go ahead. And what do I get out of it? Nothing. Nothing but a kick in the ass. And next time I call you, Stecher, don't keep me waiting a half hour, come at once.

All right, said Joe and went out.

Carmody was still hanging around the shop at the lunch hour.

I guess the little Dutchie called you that time, huh, Irish? said one of them.

Balls, said Carmody under his breath.

Yes sir! that's the way to talk to him boy. Like a — Yes sir! he says, as sweet as you please.

Didja hear him? Yes sir, he says.

What j' drop your screw driver in the press for, Car?

Shut up, you bastard.

Sure you did, didn't you? Did it on purpose.

That's what I did.

Like hell you did. You haven't the nerve, said one of the older men. Do you know what that might cost?

What the hell do I care what it costs?

Well you're lucky. If I was him, I would have fired you ass over teakettle out of the place on the spot for carelessness.

I got that bastard's number. He didn't have the guts to fire me. I know they need the press. They're up against it and don't want to start a night shift. Afraid we might earn some money! Let him fire me. I'll close the whole God damn shop down on them. This is Government work. Let him try it.

Aw go soak your head! said one of the others.

I told you . . .

What j'a throw it in for?

I didn't tell you . . .

You said you did.

It fell in.

Come on out for a smoke. Coming, Jim?

Joe was sitting at his desk a couple of days later, when he saw, out of the corner of his eye, a man in a derby open the shop door, come inside, close the door and stand there a moment looking around. He was smoking a cigar. Without further ado he came down the press aisle toward the floor manager. Joe continued at his figures.

'Lo, Stecher, said the man. Like to have a little talk with you. 'S all right if I sit down? Busy? Go ahead if y'are. I'm in no hurry. And he took the idle chair and leaned back in it looking over the shop. Several of the men, one after the other, cast quick glances in the direction of the newcomer but without hesitating in what they were doing.

You don't smoke in here, said Joe.

All right, said Mr. Burke, taking the cigar out of his mouth.

Drop it in there, said Joe, indicating an empty

metal waste basket. The man looked at the cigar which was only a third consumed and placed it on the edge of Joe's desk. Joe picked it up and dropped it into the waste basket. The men looked at each other but said nothing further for a moment

What do you want? said Joe.

I wanted to see the old man, but I understand he's out.

It's funny you didn't meet him on the stairs, said Joe.

Look here, Stecher, said Burke. No use shinanigin around with you. I can see that. I'd like to talk a little business with you. What do you say? You're the real boss here, everybody knows that. If you and me can agree on th' proposition I'm gonna spring on you in a minute, I know it will be all jake with that crowd in there. He jerked his head toward the office. Now I don't want no trouble. I come in here as a friend of the workin' man. I always want to see things arranged amicable. What do you say?

Well, what is it? said Joe.

Well, I wanna know how you feel about it first, said the man.

About what? said Joe.

Say, listen, Stecher. I got a rotten cold today. I feel like hell. Tell you the truth I ought to be home in bed. When I got the call to come up and see you people this morning, I says to my wife . . .

What do you want? said Joe again.

Well now, why can't you talk reasonable with me, Stecher? Listen, you and me can do business if you'll give me the high sign you're on the level . . .

That's why you waited until you saw the boss go out? Joe came back at him.

What! said Burke jerking himself up straight. What's that?

Joe had turned his back on him for the moment and was drumming his fingers rapidly on the desk, thinking.

Now listen to me, Stecher, said the man, assuming a threatening tone, none of your damned back-yip. Or I'll pull every pressman from in front of them presses so fast it'll take the breath out of you.

Joe didn't bat an eyelash. Show me your card, he said.

Burke took a leather card case with a celluloid front to it out of his pocket and held it in his hands. Let me see it, said Joe. There it is, said Burke. Let me see it, said Joe. And he took it in his own hand.

And you can look at this too, said Burke pulling back his coat and showing a bright nickel badge pinned to his vest — Pressmen's Union at the top. And across the middle — Delegate.

I see you're a master printer yourself, said Joe.

Yes, said Burke, a little proudly, I am.

We need good printers these days, it's a pity you gave it up. What do you get now?

Oh, it ain't the money so much, said Burke. But that's got nothin' to do with it. You can't work these men the way you're doin' it in this shop unless you give them more money.

What do they want? said Joe quietly.

Well, it ain't what they want so much, but it's the principle. You're paying them time and a half for the night shift. We want double time.

Well, that's business, said Joe. I'll talk to Mr. W about it and you can come in at the end of the week.

No you don't, said Burke. Got to know today. Hey,

listen, Stecher, it's worth something to youse here to get this government contract off your hands on the tick. Right? Well, why not give me a break, then?

Because I'll be God damned if I'll pay you a nickel, said Joe suddenly flaring up, for your crookedness. And if you don't like that, get the hell out of here and tell Sam Gompers I sent you. Do you understand that? Tell him Joe Stecher kicked you out of the door and tell him why I did it. Now get out.

Whoa baby! laughed the man without stirring. Yes, I know all about you and Sam Gompers. You and Hillyard and him started the Typographer's Union, didn't you? They said you was a tough customer. How come you didn't stick by it, Stecher? Huh?

I've got no more time to spend with you, said Joe. If you want to call a strike go ahead and call it now, we're ready.

What'll you do then?

Try it and see, said Joe.

Scabs, eh? said the man. But I don't wanna call no strike. This is a good shop. The men need the money. What do you think about it yourself? Don't you think they ought to be paid more?

Do you want to know what I think? said Joe.

Yes, said Burke, I'm interested.

Well I'll tell you then, and Joe looked at him quizzically a moment, as much as to say: I wonder if you have the brains to understand anything. I think the men should get more money. I'd like to see them get it and I've tried to get it for them. But I couldn't do it — not yet. I know the men are better off in this shop than in hundreds of others all over the city. We keep the place clean. They get fresh air. They have individual lockers. They have a decent washroom and toilet — not one of those stinking — Joe made a disgusted gesture with his hands. But this is not my shop any more than it is theirs. You can't come in here right when we're in the middle of a government job, just when we need to work, and to work hard, and every day at our maximum capacity — you can't come in here at such a time and ruin the work. That's why I quit their union. They want too much. They want to own everything. They want to tell me how to run a shop and what I must do. That's too much. And what are they thinking of to call a strike now? There's work to do. So that's just the time they choose to make trouble. When there is work that must be finished. That's wrong. That's not manly, it's not honest, it's not upright. The unions have got into such hands and that's why I got out. They want too much. Wait till we have finished this contract. Come back then and I'll work with you to get as much for the men as I am able. I'll work with you. I'll do the best I can. But not now.

Yes, that's all right, said Burke. But I don't know nothin' about all that. I was sent up here to get more overtime money for the men . . .

And you couldn't do it, sneered Joe, so you had to call a strike. And you've got to sneak back and tell the gang that sent you, that you couldn't make Joe Stecher come across. You got to say he licked you, you couldn't do it. You didn't know how. You weren't good enough. Go on home, like a whipped cur, and tell 'em. You can't call a strike today. I know the game better than you ever could or will. Try it. Go on walk out there on the floor and try it. And I'll fire every man on the spot that so much as turns his head to listen to you. I'll give you free leave, go on walk out there and talk to 'em.

Burke did not stir. Now he began to tap the desk with his hands.

But, I'll tell you this, Burke, went on Joe. They can call a strike if they want to after they hear your report this afternoon. We don't want one now. Tell them they're right. The men should have double time. Tell them Joe Stecher said he will *try* to get it for them. And come back tomorrow — about two o'clock — and I'll give you your answer.

That's fair enough, said Burke. Put it there. And he held out his hand. They shook hands, Joe quickly drawing back his. Burke left the shop. As he did so, Joe followed him with: And take my advice, Burke, as soon as you can, get a decent job for yourself. We need good printers.

Will you give it to me? came back Burke.

Ask for it and you'll find out, said Joe.

In hell I will, said Burke, and went out.

The old man wouldn't hear of it. No, he roared out. No. God damn it, are the Unions going to own us entirely? Or is this my business? I won't pay them another fokin' nickel for their time. They get too much now, the swine. What do they think I run this place for anyway? For them? Where would they find a place to earn their lousy dollars if I didn't give them a chance to work for it? It's my shop. What are we coming to anyway? I put up the cash for the rent, don't I? I buy the presses. I go out and get the business. Where would they be?

Yes, and you also get most of the profits, said Joe almost to himself. The old man wheeled on him like a flash. Joe turned white. He had not meant to speak that way, but he did not flinch from the stare which met his. The expected explosion did not occur, however. Instead the old man contented himself with saying: So you're going back to them, are you, Stecher?

No, said Joe, I'm not. But in this particular case I think they are right. Men working at night that way should have double time. I think, besides, that we are in a difficult situation. I'd pay it now just to have peace . . .

Never! said the old man. What? Buy peace from a lot of dirty thieves, a lot of highway men who . . . He stamped about in a mounting fury.

. . . if you don't, went on Joe coolly, we are likely to have the place shut down tomorrow.

There was a long silence between the two men.

Well, my answer to you, Stecher, said the old man finally, is that I won't pay it. Tell that to the bastards and let them take a fit for themselves. What do you think will happen? said he in an altered voice.

Joe thought a minute. Are you quite sure you want to fight them?

Yes, said the old man.

I don't ask you for much, Mr. Wynnewood, went on Joe. But I'd like to see the men get this increase today. I think we can carry it in several ways. I've been thinking it over for a long time. And as a matter of fact, said Joe, I've been convinced for the past four months that it's a general strike.

For what?

Shorter hours and a probable 10% increase in wages.

Why they'll ruin the business.

The smart move in my opinion is to beat them to it. Give it to them, if we are the first shop in town.

What! My God, man, you're crazy. Are you . . .?

I think it's policy.

Never.

Well, this is what will happen. This man here today was just a lot of bluff. But it's coming soon and when it does happen they're going out all over the city at once. We might buy immunity long enough to finish our present contracts. I think . . .

A general strike.

That's my opinion. And it will be hard under such conditions to get non-union men. We'll have to import them.

All right. Let it come, said the boss.

Am I free to act if it does? said Joe.

Go to it, beat them if it costs the works.

It may be an expensive fight, said Joe.

Can you win it?

I can, said Joe.

Then fight 'em, said the old man. Go the limit.

I'll need a liberal account to draw on.

No questions asked. Go to it. Win, that's all.

All right, said Joe.

CHAPTER IX

Strike!

It was six o'clock, perhaps a few minutes earlier. Joe was in his stocking feet, his suspenders hanging down.

Why in hell don't you keep some toilet paper in this house? he shouted sticking his head in at the bedroom door.

Gurlie was hardly awake. Lottie sat up in her crib. What's that you're yelling about? said Gurlie.

What kind of a house is this?

Oh, forget it, said his wife, what's the matter now?

No toilet paper in the bathroom. No order anywhere. Where are my clean shirts?

Have you looked in the drawer of your chiffonier?

Yes.

Well, look again, said Gurlie and you'll find them. And you'll find the toilet paper on top of the medicine cabinet if you have any eyes.

I can't for the life of me see what you do with yourself all day long, continued Joe, you never do any work that I can see. Nothing is taken care of.

Look here, young man, said Gurlie sitting up suddenly. Mind what you're saying. I work. I hate this being cooped up in a box like this all day long. I'm not used to it. I can't keep every button on your shirts and every hole in your socks stitched up just when you think I ought to. But you're no wonder yourself — at a lot of things.

Well, all right, all right.

Yes, it's all right when you want to yell but I must keep quiet.

I never heard it yet, said Joe.

Well, I'll tell you one thing. Get me out of here, went on his wife, I want to get into the country. I need air. I want to feel the dirt. I'll show you what work is. I can work. But I can't do this housework all day long. I'll go crazy.

Go ahead, said Joe, it won't be any different than it is now.

Gurlie checked herself at the instant of a blind fury as it flashed into her mind what day it was and the dangers that lay ahead. Stepping down a peg from an instinctive retort in kind to her husband's irritable attack, she contented herself with: You! You know as well as me that you'd wear the same pants, and shirt too, from one year's end to the other if I didn't take them away from you, before you disgrace yourself . . .

This ended it. Joe had to smile to himself — but wouldn't show it. Well, get some toilet paper in the place.

There's plenty of it in the kitchen closet.

Why don't you put it in the book case where it will be convenient when we need it, said Joe. But she didn't answer him this time. She kicked her feet out sidewise from under the sheets and in her nightgown walked barefoot to the kitchen, dashing some cold water into her face at the sink and then opening the draughts of the range, put the kettle on.

The baby was crying. The new maid wouldn't come for another hour. Gurlie took up the baby, put it on its chair, pulled down the hinged tray and let it stay there while she went back to put some clothes on.

Joe came in and looked at it. The baby was in a wonderful mood.

Joe sat there, contemplating it with affectionate pleasure. Gurlie came back, having put on a new face with her dress, gay in her rough manner — carelessly sticking up her hair any old way — fastening her dress. There, sit down, she said to Joe as if he himself were a baby, sit down and let mama feed you. Poor man, you must have lots on your mind. Shall I make some toast?

No, said Joe, I don't want anything but a cup of coffee.

Oh, but you must eat something. I'll fry you an egg — with some bacon.

All right, said Joe, only do it, and do it quick. He turned to the baby again which was grunting in a succession of grunts and doubling its face down on the tray of its chair, afterward, laying its cheek on the cool wood and then turning and looking at the wood with curiosity, then laying its cheek down again and grinning, then banging the wood with its open fists. Squealing with pleasure. Joe snoozled his face up to the baby's which the mite tried to avoid hilariously. But suddenly it reached out and grabbed Joe by the moustache, wildly with a spasmodic jerk. Joe's head went along involuntarily, he could not pull away. So he took the baby's tight little fist in his own, tried to loosen it.

With a terrifying shriek the baby let go of the man's hair. Joe sat up. But the baby shrieked and shrieked in terrific earnest. Gurlie dropped her cooking. The child was in agony.

Suddenly Gurlie lifted up the tray and, as she did so, both saw that the little finger of its other hand was dripping with blood. The nail was almost off. In Joe's struggle to free himself, he had slightly lifted the tray and the infant placing its hand in the open hinge to steady itself in its struggles had been caught viciously in the trap. Joe went white, sat down to keep from falling. Helpless, speechless.

Oh, said Gurlie, oh!

Joe took out his handkerchief.

No, no, said Gurlie.

Send for a doctor, said Joe.

The doctor? Go on now, she added roughly — gently, get out of here. Drink your coffee first. I'll take care of this. It's nothing.

But . . . the baby was still shrilly screaming but Gurlie just shook her head deprecatingly and with one hand on her husband's back, had him soon at the door. Go on — and don't get hurt. Come back to me tonight.

It may not be till late, said Joe.

The day was a hard one for Gurlie. The morning paper mentioned it but the evening paper seemed made of nothing else to her uneasy sight. They've had a hot time down town today, Mrs. Stecher, said the old fellow who sold papers under the elevated stairs at the corner. They'll be bloodshed tomorrow if it keeps on this way.

Gurlie's code forbade any sign of fear in public. I suppose you'd be scared of your life to go down there, she replied to the man, who looked up at her sharply. But her heart felt weak. She turned and left him, it seeming a mile she had to walk nonchalantly to her front steps, slowly, as if it didn't matter, and into the house. She stood inside the door without going up and scanned the headlines — Strike! Scenes of disorder!

Violence! Typographers being imported from Paterson and as far west as Buffalo. Both sides girding their loins. A general strike among the printers unless the pressmen's demands are acceded to by noon tomorrow. Winthrop, Hallowell & Co the center . . . She read no more. Folded the paper. Went upstairs to make supper.

The enforced inaction all day, violence within herself, had Gurlie nutty. As she moved about the house, she brushed the children aside or stuck things into their hands in a thoughtless way to which they responded very nicely — it must be admitted.

After a while they seemed to act just as if she wasn't there, amused themselves with all sorts of little ordinarily forbidden tricks. Lottie dragged an old coffee pot, which she loved, onto the kitchen floor and the baby — the bandage off her finger, — smeared herself gloriously with her oatmeal, finally succeding in getting the empty bowl right on top of her head.

Gurlie sat by the window but couldn't stand it. The strike — the word " strike " made her strike out with her two fists, into the air. Images of men taking hold of each other. Joe standing up and trying to get through a crowd of hostile pressmen lined up by the door to the place. Joe, of small size, but determined, walking right past them. One of them knocked off his hat. Joe leaned to pick it up. They kicked him. He stumbled. He tried to see who it was when they closed in . . . Gurlie leaped to her feet from before the window — her hand flew to her throat. Then she — walked to the kitchen. So it had gone all day long. Now it was dark.

She washed the children, did up the baby's finger again — somehow or other the little thing had never paid any attention to the sore finger after the first shock of pain. The children in bed asleep, supper at the back of the range, she couldn't stand it any longer but went out into the street and walked up and down. About ten o'clock she saw Joe come out of the elevated exit.

What are you doing here in the street, he said and kissed her. He looked dirty and tired. Are you all right? Sure, why not? Humph! she replied — and they walked back slowly to the entrance to their building.

It had been a tough day, but not so bad — not yet, Joe told her chuckling. She was relieved and thrilled seeing him in such a capital mood. Sure, he replied to her, the streets are full of them. What did you expect me to do, run?

But . . . you're not hurt?

The whole police force was out. Anyhow, we kept the place open. And we'll keep it open. We won't miss a day. I'll beat 'em so bad they'll never get over it. A pack of dirty, lowdown thieves and blackguards — yelling and throwing stones — breaking windows — they can't even throw straight. Have 'em arrested! Arrest them all if it comes to that.

Gurlie was relieved, delighted, sat close to her husband with one hand on his shoulder while he was eating, eagerly, hungrily, talking between mouthfuls. Suddenly he stopped. How's the baby's finger? She's all right. I couldn't get it out of my head all day long. Pingh! said Gurlie puffing her lips out, it's nothing. Every once in a while I could see that broken nail and the blood. Sure she's all right? A little piece of rag around it. She's forgotten it already.

I'm tired, said Joe, I want to go to bed.

And is that all you're going to tell me?

Well, what is there to tell? We kept the shop open. They can't do anything. Let 'em try it, that's all.

And you're going down there again tomorrow?

What do you think I'm going to do? Joe looked at her surprised. Expect me to run away?

But if they hurt you. I'm going down there with you. If you think it's any fun to stay shut up in this prison all day long while you're down there likely to get hurt . . .

Agh, they're afraid, said Joe laughing. A lot of cowards.

Next day Gurlie was beside herself. Joe left before six, pulling his hat on, bending his shoulders a little forward it seemed as if conscious of the approaching attack. The newspapers were again full of it. Carrying on her feud with the old newsdealer at the corner, she went out for the morning paper and a noon edition. But sensing his scorn, not a word spoken, in the afternoon she walked three blocks to another news stand for the latest.

It was Thursday, the girl's afternoon off. The babies were alone for the moment. Both children were asleep. She didn't realize how long it would take her.

Lottie woke on her mother's bed where she had thrown herself and looked around. The baby in its own little wooden crib was lying on its back both arms flung wide, completely relaxed. Lottie got up and walked all through the house looking for her mother, then came back to the bedroom. Mama's gone, she said.

So she returned to the kitchen and got herself a glass of water at the faucet standing on a chair to draw it and drank some. Holding the half full glass in both hands, she went into the baby again and drank some more. Then with the glass in one hand, she pinched the baby's outflung arm through the bars of the crib, pinched it hard. The baby waked, pulled back its arm, sat up with a struggle — and blinking its eyes grinned at her sister.

Lottie tried to feed it water from the glass through the wooden bars. It spilled as the baby tried to grip the glass. Then the baby choked and some of the water went into Lottie's face. Lottie took some water into her own mouth and, imitating the baby, blew it out into the infant's face in retaliation.

Flossie was delighted. Lottie did it again. Great success, spitting out magnificently.

Lottie now handed a rattle in to the baby which she promptly threw out again with great gusto. Now the older girl put a rubber ball into the crib between the bars. The baby crawled to it. Managed to push it to the floor again. And laughed excitedly. Lottie put it back. The baby threw it out. Each time she did so she slapped her hands together in wild excitement. So the older sister began to fetch and throw everything loose she could find into the crib to beat the baby to it. Books, an old pipe, a pillow, a paper-cutter — anything — shoes, and the baby took each thing as it was able and threw it out again looking delightedly into her sister's face for approval and crawling all over the crib, falling, rising again, the best it was able.

Till finally Lottie could find nothing else to throw in, she had finally done it so fast the baby couldn't keep up with her and had just sat back and watched — thrilled at so much attention. So Lottie got a chair and climbed into the crib herself, over the top, to get

them and threw some of them out again, the baby
leaning over to watch each object as it fell and perhaps rolled away. Then Lottie had an idea. She tried
to loosen the movable side of the crib. Failing to do
that, she got behind the baby and tried to lift it up
over the top. Impossible. But she chided her little
sister. Climb up, she said. And again she grasped the
infant around the waist from behind and pushing
with all her might lifted her up a little to the edge of
the cribside.

With tremendous effort, pushing hard, finally she
succeeded and the infant hung face down over the
edge of the crib. It wasn't frightened but seemed completely serious and submissive before its sister's efforts,
passively waiting. As it teetered there, Lottie a little
afraid now, holding it back by the skirts its head went
lower, then with a sudden slip it went all the way down
with a rush over the edge — on its back into the chair.
As it went, its marvelous little hands flew out and
finding them clung desperately to the crib bars. And
remarkable to say, still there wasn't a sound more than
a little grunt and sucking of the breath on Flossie's
part as she labored.

There on its back in blank astonishment balanced
on the chair hanging on to the crib for dear life lay
the infant until Lottie could slide over the edge of the
crib to the ground again. She looked critically at the
child a moment then, leaving it, ran off instinctively
to find her mother. Coming back and seeing the baby
in the same position, she stood and looked at it again
from both sides at a loss. Then she tried to loosen
its hands. Nothing doing. The infant wasn't convinced though it smiled a little appreciatively. So
Lottie changed tactics, took hold of the chair, pulled

it from under until one of the baby's hands slipping, it suddenly slid sidewise and down square on the top of its head to the carpeted floor. Lottie watched it with fascinated interest. The baby lay still for a moment, you couldn't tell which end was which. Then, still without a sound, it found itself, got up on its hands and knees and looked around.

In a moment it was creeping. In another it had found something small, a button, which it picked up. Sitting down abruptly, it examined the strange object, then put it into its mouth, turned on its hands again and headed for the back of the house.

What a mess when Gurlie came in. Lottie and the baby were in the middle of the kitchen floor, Lottie with an apron around her neck wielding a broom. The baby black with coal from the scuttle, her mouth as black as the scuttle itself. Just as Gurlie came in the baby was clinging uncertainly to the scuttle's edge, trying to turn her head around without falling and . . .

Lottie! shrieked the mother, what have you done?

Joe didn't come in till nearly midnight, dog-weary and serious, uncommunicative this time. He wouldn't open his mouth more than to say, We'll beat 'em. He'd had his supper. Took off his things and was asleep almost before his head hit the pillow.

But next morning, the sun up and Gurlie ahead of him this time, he was ready — eager even — to talk. She was a fascinated listener.

Saw the old man. I mean all the partners were there. I mean Seymour. He's a fine old fellow. I always liked him. Kindly — no good in business. They're scared this time. Means a lot to them to win this strike.

What'll they do for you, if you do win it?

Fire me, I suppose, said Joe in his old time cyni-
cal good humor.

But what happened? What kept you so late?

Moving mattresses, said Joe.

Mattresses?

Yes, mattresses — fifty of them. The damned scabs.
We got to lock 'em in. As soon as one of them went up
to the hospital, they all wanted to quit.

The disgust Joe put into that word " quit " con-
torted his whole body.

So I had to lock 'em in. Now let 'em think. Let
their strike *leaders* — and again he emphasized the
word with savage purpose — tell 'em what to do next.
And he laughed his half bitter, Ho, ho, ho, ho!

What! said Gurlie. Is it as bad at that?

Well, we've got to get the work done, don't we?

But isn't it dangerous?

What? To sleep on a mattress? Sure. You might
catch cold.

But what good is that? insisted Gurlie. They have to
go out to eat.

Oh we don't feed 'em so bad, said Joe. Gurlie was
looking at him in admiration. We got plenty of water.
Bread. A little butter, not much because there's no
place to keep ice. But canned beans. Tomato soup.
Oh, they're having a regular picnic.

Gurlie shook her head silently. You're the only one
that's going in and out then. Sure, said Joe. The bosses
decided they'd spend the weekend in Newport.

Breakfast done, Joe left his wife at the downstairs
door where she had gone with him in her uneasiness.
She watched him go along the nearly empty street to
the elevated entrance. His narrow, straight shoulders,
the black coat, his determined even-footed walk —

he didn't look very strong to her, smoking his cigar
— his cheap cigar. I wonder how long it will last.
I don't think he can beat them.

The third night Joe came in jubilant. The regular
money order shipment had gone off on time. The
fourth night he confided to his wife that in a week he
wouldn't care what in hell the pressmen or anybody
else wanted. We'll finish the government contract
then close the place down till they come begging on
their knees for us to open it again. I got 'em where
I want 'em this time. The lazy suckers.

But Monday night the following week he was again
later than usual. Gurlie had begun to relax, the strike,
after all, was only a strike, everything had been going
along smoothly in spite of the hard feeling. The men
were afraid of the police. Joe had been jostled once
or twice. A boy even hit him in the back with a small
stone one morning — but that was all.

But when he did finally appear this time his tie
was crooked, his shirt collar mashed and blackened,
his hat out of shape.

They held me up, he said. He was extremely serious
and low-voiced. Are you hurt? No. Where were the
police? Oh, they laid for me, at the entrance to the
Chambers St. elevated station.

What did they do?

Stopped me. Put a pistol in my face.

Joe! What did you do?

Well, I'm here, ain't I?

Did you fight, then?

No. I didn't have a chance. Two of them. I recognized one anyhow. Who was it? No, I'm not telling
anybody that just yet. I suppose it's that gas house
gang.

What did they want?

Want me to call off the strike.

What did you say?

I told them I couldn't call it off. They told me I'd have to. What did you say then? I didn't say anything. One of them grabbed me by the collar while the other stuck the pistol against my side.

Oh! said Gurlie, I refuse to let you go down there tomorrow unless you are protected. What is the city thinking of?

The city can't think, said Joe.

I refuse to let you. I've got something to say about that. I don't want you killed. What about me and my children? Sure, the Company don't care if you're killed. They can get someone else. If you go, I go with you.

Calm down, said Joe, seriously, however, I'll get a cop to take me to the station at night after this. And meet you in the morning, added Gurlie. All right, said Joe, but they haven't the nerve to do anything in the daytime.

But what about up here, coming home late? They'll follow you —

I'll take out a license to carry a pistol — tomorrow morning. But — but — but! Can you shoot? said Gurlie. As well as they can.

But you didn't finish telling me what happened.

Nothing happened, they heard someone coming and beat it. I got on the elevated and came home.

But what about tomorrow? What will they do next? What will happen?

Nothing, said Joe. What do you expect?

CHAPTER X

The Giveaway

HE WAS a nice old gentleman with pince-nez glasses and·spats, sitting in the middle stall of the only available bench in that part of the park. The other benches, though cleared of snow, were either in the shadow and icy or in the sun, where it was warm — delightfully warm for December — and so wet from the thaw. He had several sheets of newspaper under him.

He looked up and smiled at the girl with the baby carriage. He could see she wanted to rest.

Better join me, he said. I don't think there's another dry bench in the neighborhood. She stopped a moment, looked at him — and she was tired of pushing the baby carriage on the uneven walks.

It must be rather hard work, he commented, seeing her hesitate. Won't you take a piece of this newspaper?

But instead of waiting for him to get up and give it to her she sat down quickly toward the end of the bench so she wouldn't have to accept his offer.

That's all right, he went on, seating himself again, it's not wet there.

She turned deliberately away from him frowning and leaned into the carriage to arrange the baby's covers. The thing was sleeping blissfully, just a little face showing between the wooly cap and the blanket edge.

How old are you? said the man, speaking very gently and quietly.

Fifteen, said the girl — and then bit her lip for having answered him.

Do you often come out here with the baby?

Sure. Everyday sometimes. That's dumb, she added to herself.

About this time in the morning?

Sure. Why not?

Not many people do it, these days. The finest of the year I often think, gloomy, quiet — but very restful. But a person of my age is often lonesome. Do you know anything about that? No, of course not. Young people have the better of us but they understand very little. A good thing too. Don't you think so?

She looked at him as if she thought he was dippy. Do you come of a large family, he continued.

What do you take me for, a dictionary? she decided to be rude.

He laughed. Well, maybe you'd tell me the baby's name then.

Spider.

What?

Spider.

Your sister?

No, I'm just the maid. And she started to get up to be on her way.

Please don't go, he said. I'm sorry if I've bothered you. Please. Please, I'd rather go myself. I won't bother you any more. So she sat down again while he leaned on a cane he had between his knees and looked the other way. She gave him a good look while his back was turned and felt sorry for the old geezer. She had nothing to do but sit there.

Gee, it's terribly cold today, she said after a while as if speaking to the trees. The old fellow turned toward her quickly with a smile on his face. Anyhow, it's cold for a baby, I think, she said.

It's good for them, said the man, so long as they're properly protected, especially from the wind. The wind is a baby's enemy. It's especially important to keep cold draughts from coming up under the carriage and blowing through the mattress. Did you know that? All carriages should be lined with some impervious material, like oil cloth or paper, for instance. It keeps out the wind. Is the child warm enough?

Sure, said the girl. She'd let you know if she wasn't. She says " mammy " and " baby." She won't stay in your lap any more. You know there's about fourteen kids in the block where we live has whooping cough.

You don't say? said the man. Does she creep? And with that he ventured to get up and look at the little sleeping thing. But it wasn't sleeping. I let her go everywhere, said the girl. She's very friendly, except to people with glasses.

Yes, the man took her up, to an infant I suppose glasses seem like big terrible eyes. The girl looked at him as though she thought there might be something in what he said. Yes, it's the glasses scares her.

But the baby wasn't scared. So she continued, But she isn't afraid of anything at all. See! she spoke to the baby, who's that?

The baby looked wide eyed at the stranger, lost in wrapt attention, moving her eyes the least bit from time to time from point to point over the features of the face leaning above her. The man patted the blanket where she lay very gently and then sat down again near the girl. A smart little thing she seems, he said.

She can say so many words. I think she can say fifteen words.

What! So many?

Well you know, they sound like words. Yea. She has four teeth, two up and two down. She fell out of bed this morning. But she always looks up smiling.

She's rather small, said the man. Does she eat?

She eats everything now — except cow's milk. I've given her cow's milk and she vomits it. I give her a whole tomato yesterday.

A tomato at nine months!

Sure. She wanted it. She sucked the middle out of it and threw the skin away. Bread. An egg sometimes. That's the only thing she eats greedy — that's an egg. She's never hungry in the morning. Say are you a doctor or something? said the girl finally, checking herself.

No, no, said the stranger, but I have two little nieces of my own and I'm very much interested in children.

Well, I hope she doesn't get whooping cough, that's all I say, went on the girl. If she does, I quit. I've seen enough of that.

You wouldn't do that, would you?

Sure I would. I've got myself to think of.

But they'd need you more than ever at such a time.

Oh, I ain't been working there long.

Are they nice people?

Germans.

The man smiled to himself quietly and cleared his throat quickly. Oh, whooping cough isn't so bad if you keep them out of doors, I guess.

Yea, I heard that. But the reason I keep her out most times is that she eats better. Days that she's out she'll eat a pretty good dish of spinach. She needs it, believe me. You never seen such a skinny kid. But you ought to see the little red-head down stairs from us over by the river. He's so dumb. Yah, yah, yah! that's all he says but you can't help loving him.

You must like children.

Them and talking. God give me the gift of gab — once I get started. That's about all he did give me, Ma says. I make use of it though. Guess I better get moving, she added thinking maybe she had been getting a little bit too confidential toward the end. So long.

Good bye, said the old man getting up politely. It's good of you to have let me talk to you in this way. Take good care of the baby. I hope it doesn't get whooping cough.

She just stared at him, once again, and left. The baby who was sitting up by this time, took hold of the edge of the carriage with its little mittened hands and kept straining out to keep sight of the figure sitting on the bench now fading off across the snow behind them.

Say Jim, said Maggie to the cop on the corner, you ought to have seen the old bird tried to pick me up in the park.

You don't say. You mean the old gentleman with the side whiskers?

Yea.

The cop laughed. He wasn't trying to pick you up. That's the governor's brother. He lives around here.

Yea? Well, he can be the pope's uncle for all I care, said the girl to show what she thought about men like that. The cop laughed at her some more. You better be gettin' home, he said. It's past noon.

It was whooping cough. Lottie came down with it first and then the baby, struggling to hold back each racking paroxysm. And Christmas coming on. Gurlie was angry. Whooping cough should come in the spring time, not now. But she didn't pay much attention to it.

The main thing was to keep the baby out of the house as much as possible. Only it started to vomit everything. So she told Maggie not to feed it too much. What! said the girl. At night they burnt a lamp in its room with a smell of creosote to it.

It's fine today, said Gurlie once about the twentieth of the month, out wid yez! Take her to the Park. And remember what I've told you: don't feed her any junk. And keep away from other children, she added as an afterthought.

Maggie started toward the west. But at the corner she took a good look back and went round the block heading east then toward the river. *I'll* take you to the park, she said. And away she went, lickety split, tearing along with the carriage joggling in front of her as if it were a race. *I'll* take you to the park, she said again to the back of the baby carriage.

So the baby began to cough and vomited. Whew! said Maggie all in a sweat when she had to stop and take care of the brat. If you hold me up this way, we'll never get there.

Then she lit out once more and pretty soon she arrived at the Carl Schultz Park overlooking the East River at 89th St. She went in one entrance of this, round one of the paths and out again — just so I can say I was in the park. At the exit she met another girl with a carriage.

It's got the whooping cough, she said. Keep away.

Wait a minute, said the other, what's your sweat? They stood away from the carriage talking a few minutes.

Don't give her this, don't give her that, she says, said Maggie in a mocking affected tone of voice. Aw, they make me tired. The kid's lost a couple of pounds already. Ma says feed her anything she'll take. Milk's the worst. She vomits that easiest. You ought to see her sometimes when I pick her up, she's covered with it. In her hair, in her eyes. And smilin'. You gotta laugh, I wanna give her a break. I'm takin' her up to the gas tanks. Ma says if you walk around the gas tank, it'll cure her.

Well, so long, said the other girl. See you Saturday night.

Maggie started out again toward two red painted gas tanks that could be seen now a few blocks north on the river. As she went she walked slower and slower. She was a little scared. Suppose they should blow up! She looked around too, to see if anyone was watching her, thinking maybe someone had been spoofing sending her up there — she felt kind of foolish. There might be men or boys in a place like that that would get fresh. Then the baby had another fit. That decided her, she'd do it. Once around anyhow. To go around one of the tanks seemed to be the idea in her mind. You got to go all the way round, she said to herself.

It was a relief when she got there to see several other women with carriages and small children sitting behind a wire fence close to the tank on boxes in the sun. They didn't pay any attention to her at all. Now she could smell the gas. Gee, that can't be good for a baby, she thought. It was quite strong near the enormous tank. The middle part was half way up in its frame and gave out a creaking sound from time to time as it filled. She was wondering what would happen if someone should light a match when she saw an old man in a cap sitting in a broken chair near the gate to the enclosure. He was smoking a pipe. She thought maybe you had to have a ticket or something to get in. Good afternoon, he said to her with a strong burr to his voice and with that she headed the carriage in and started around the tank. It was quite strong in there.

First she headed away from the other women who were on the sunny side of the tank intending to go around it.

Hey, you can't go around there, said the old man.

Why not? said Maggie.

There's a barbed wire fence twenty feet ahead of you, said the man. That's why. If it's the first time you're here, I'll tell you you can sit there where the others are sitting or no place at all. And don't throw any fruit peelings or waste paper around the place either, he added.

The baby has whooping cough, Maggie said.

Well, what else would you be here for if it didn't? said the man. You'll find an old box beyond, he added jerking his thumb over his shoulder and paid no more attention to her. The other women and children had been out of sight during this talk. Now one came with a baby in her arms and went out of the gate and away. Maggie, with her heart in her mouth, started the carriage along the rough gravel.

Now she could hear them . . . I'm not so fussy any more. You ought to see Winnie's baby. She eats everything and honestly she's beautiful.

Then they came into view, one wiping the nose of

her own child and saying, she's getting an awfully gubby chin, sticking it out that way — honestly, it's terrible.

But as some of them turned to look the baby in the next carriage sort of choked and began it. My god, there she goes! said one of the women. It was the worst Maggie had seen. While the woman was tending the child in its paroxysm she kept talking, describing the events as they happened — as if to relieve herself of her concern. Maggie watched fascinated. First she gets red, then purple — even her legs get blue and then her face is green. Look at her put her hands back of her head. You'd think she was going to choke to death.

Indeed Maggie thought she was.

Then the baby stopped her cough and began to vomit. She vomits twenty times a day, concluded the woman. And so that emergency ended. Maggie wanted to run. But someone laughed and the women started to talk again and so Maggie pushed her carriage past them, while they looked at her in talking, and found the old box the man had told her about.

Mine sits half the time with his mouth open. I can't fill him up.

The wall of the tank was close behind her. Though she felt a little creepy about being so near the gas — still the others didn't mind it and so she began to realize — thinking of the stinking lamp they burned at night — that it was the gas maybe that cured the cough — not just walking around the tank that did it.

There were four or five women who had their boxes gathered around in a small group in the middle of which was a rosy cheeked woman with greying hair who was always talking and laughing and keeping the others with their eyes pretty much upon her all the time. By her talk and her looks Maggie put her down at once, like herself, for a mick. There were only two other carriages but at least three babies in arms and a few older children who kept sneaking off behind the tank whence they had to be fetched out yelling.

Get out of there, shouted the old man going around the fence with a stick in his hand to some older boys who had climbed on the fence after a ball. One of the women got up and threw it out to them.

Do you know what he says to me? I don't care how the hell sick you are so long as the kid's all right.

I had her down to Coney Island Tuesday. I think it was Tuesday. Wasn't it, Rose?

Hallo, Mrs. Falori! called out the rosy cheeked woman in the group to a big Italian woman going by.

Agh! and the one addressed, raising her hand, let out a sudden high pitched hawk's cry in answer to her, smiling the while.

Yeah, they're gettin' in averywhere now, said one of the women. And the funny names they have. Mrs. Magazine, I heard someone say in a store yesterday. Mrs. What? I says. Keroseno? I sez. And she laughed along with the rest.

Then little Flossie choked and went herself into a paroxysm. Maggie felt the other women looking at her and her own face go crimson. One of the women came over to help her. Aw, that's not so bad, said this one. My uncle told me with mine that when she goes into a kink to throw her up in the air and catch her.

Aren't you afraid you might miss her, said Maggie.

No, I don't mean so high. I tried it and honestly it brought her out of it.

Spinach poisons her, one of the other women was saying, everywhere it touches her. She likes it well

enough but it doesn't agree with her. The first time
I gave it to her she broke out all around her mouth.
I didn't know what it was but I found out later.

He's got a good pair of eyes, said another of the
women, speaking of one of the older children whom
she had just captured and whose nose she was vigorously wiping of a chocolate smear. Yes, he don't miss
much, so long as it's for his stomach.

I'll get money out of youse, said another to a small
boy, if you don't keep off that carriage.

Know her? Maggie heard then, why Effie and I
used to stand in line to sit on the same pot when we
was kids. And all the women laughed uproariously.

Yes, kids is funny, said the rosy faced woman. I saw
him walking round the kitchen yesterday with the col-
lander held up against his back side. Me's giving me
a ride, he said. And they all laughed again.

Mine fell, boom! on his bottom the other day, said
another. What did I do? he asks me looking up kind
of stunned. Then he gets up holding his breath and
walks into the next room, where I couldn't see him,
before he'd cry.

They hate to be put down. If they have any spirit
it's an insult to them.

You don't have to tell me. I got one too. Always up
to something, a regular rip. But he hasn't slept so
good for the last couple of nights.

They're down like a stone, up like a cork.

No, I sez. There was no money born with ye and
there'll be none buried with ye.

Now he's this way — he's good in some ways. If I
brought him here and you told him to take the nasti-
est medicine, he'd take it. But if his father or I tried
to make him take it, nothing doing.

You got nothing to kick at, said the rosy faced woman to the one who had last spoken, with that angel out of heaven you're holdin' there to keep you company.

Oh she's all right, the woman replied. But that other blister . . . ! Oh my! It's a wonder he's still alive. I could kill him sometimes.

He wants to sit up and he's fresh — he's a sassy boy — but he hasn't slept so good for the last couple of nights.

Oh Jesus, Mrs. H! Don't let her get started crying.

Well, they're here and you got to do the best for them. But I'll tell you the truth, it's a thankless job sometimes.

You're right it's a thankless job, said a heavy-browed woman who had not spoken until then. My youngest was that kind. He was a wicked one. She paused. I'm ashamed to tell it. And a faint smile crossed her thin lips.

No one opened her mouth knowing she'd go on if they waited. Maggie sat straining not to miss a word. The woman seemed to be talking direct to her.

I've got an awful temper, she said. When it gets the best of me I'm like crazy. I'm afraid of it myself sometimes. Well, one Sunday morning he disgraced me. I had him all dressed for Church and he didn't want to go. So I let him downstairs while I was getting myself ready. And when I went to look for him you should have seen him. He was black from head to foot. So I took him home and beat him and even then he wouldn't stop his yelling. He'd get purple in the face with it. His father had been up all night and lay asleep. I couldn't make the kid stop. So I took him downstairs and threw him in the ash barrel and cut all his head. I thought I'd killed him. My sisters heard the racket and came running. They had to take him to the hospital to be sewed up.

Oh my God, said one of the women.

I got an awful temper . . .

For a while Maggie turned away. When she listened again they were talking about doctors. You're a wonderful patient, he says. Yes, I says. And I was for the shape I was in.

There's a bride in our block is expecting sometime next month. And is she scared! So I says to her, you got nothin' to worry about. She's always thinking maybe she won't get to the hospital in time. So I says to her, my first was born in a cab and my second in the toilet basin. And look at 'em now, I says.

Did you ever hear of giving them bay leaves for gas, said another. They cook them down with water, some woman told my husband.

I want to pippy.

Lord, if I had a thousand I'd think I was in Heaven sittin' down.

His bowels were terrible, something awful. Phaugh.

Sure, he climbs out of his carriage already. I have to keep him strapped in. He's up to such mischief when he's small, what'll he do later?

So it went. Maggie listened, watched them — all older than herself and she didn't think much of them. No kids for her. They'd have to chloroform her first. She looked in at her own little Flossie and decided she wasn't so bad though. Guessed she'd go home.

Everyone of mine come to supper, another of the women was saying. And they are the hungriest kids! I never saw anything like it.

Good bye, dearie, said the rosy cheeked lady, as Maggie finally walked off.

Good bye, said Maggie without looking at her. And as she stopped a minute to loosen the brake of the carriage which stuck she heard finally:

I had it easy.

You must have had a left-handed doctor, someone else answered her.

Say, he was left-handed. How did you guess it?

Didn't you say it come easy? And once again Maggie heard the women laugh as she went out of the gate. Good luck to you, said the old man there. Maggie gave him a smile but he wasn't even looking at her. She hurried off.

On the way she decided to try the baby on some crackers like she'd seen the women feeding their children back by the tank. Maybe they'd stay down better than the milk did. She went into a store she was passing and got a few for a nickel — chocolate covered. She gave one of them to the baby and put the rest in her pocket. The infant was delighted.

Maggie was late. She hurried. At the corner of their block she took out her handkerchief and went carefully over the baby's face to remove all signs of the cracker.

Where in the world have you been? said Gurlie.

Over in the park, said Maggie. Where did you think I was?

No impudence from you, Gurlie came back at her. I've been waiting almost an hour for you. I want those potatoes peeled. It's long past the baby's eating time. It must be starved. Has it coughed much?

Not much, said Maggie.

Then the baby began. And before it was through the chocolate cracker was all over the blanket, all over the floor — it seemed five times as much as had ever gone into it.

Then Maggie grabbed her hat and fled.

CHAPTER XI

Ständchen

How DID the strike finally come out, Joe? said Mr. Lindquist looking at his cigar as he pushed his chair back from the table and took a deep breath.

Put her down, said Gurlie to her sister before Joe could answer.

No, said Astrid snuggling the infant closer, let her stay here. The child was leaning forward with both hands on the littered table and reaching for the handle of a fruit knife. No, no, mustn't touch! Aunt Astrid took it away from her. Little Spider, she concluded kissing the child. Put her down, said Gurlie. No, said her sister, I want to hold her. The others looked and laughed as the infant glanced triumphantly at her mother and lifted the knife again tentatively. Put her down, said Gurlie. But the fat auntie paid no attention. Yes, tell us how you came out, Joe, she said.

Well, tell them then! said his wife to him.

All right, what do you want to hear?

How did it come out? Who won?

That's it, said Gurlie. Who won? And she laughed sharply slapping the table with her two hands.

Humph, said Joe carefully tilting the ash off the end of his cigar onto the metal ashtray. He paused.

Go on, said Gurlie. You've been sitting there for an hour without a word to anybody . . .

You mustn't say that, spoke up Mathilda.

I've been enjoying the conversation, said Joe. Tell them how much they raised your salary after what you did for them, said Gurlie. I want to hear you say it.

Joe looked down. Well, didn't I tell everybody long ago how much I'd get? They gave me the business, it's all mine now. All the partners resigned in my favor. All I have to do now is find money to pay the bills with. And he chuckled to himself and put his cigar slowly to his lips. *You* better tell them, he turned to his wife, you know more about it than I do. And he blew a cloud of smoke gently into the air and looked at it as it rose against the ornamented Christmas tree beyond the curtains in the next room. They were all waiting. He kept them that way for a moment. Then he continued, everybody won. We finished our contracts then closed down. When we reopened last month the typographers got what they asked for and so everybody is happy.

And how did you make out? asked Mr. Lindquist at his side.

Well, I still have my job, said Joe.

They didn't even say thank you, broke in Gurlie. And that man there, after risking his life . . . Nonsense, said Joe. Nonsense, eh? replied his wife raising her voice. Do you think it's nonsense when I sit here night after night . . . ? Would you have been better off if they fired me? said Joe. Oh you're crazy, said Gurlie. He's crazy.

Joe you're a case, said Lindquist. That was delicious wine you had today, he changed the subject, good stuff, do you know it? Where did you get it?

Somebody gave it to us, Joe told them, for nothing.

Yes, said the big fellow with the pleasant face and the scar through his upper lip, very good. I'll bet it cost you a penny, Stecher. Well, one more year will soon be over, he continued. New Year's Day in a little less than a week, think of that. Another year gone.

Ow! What's that under my feet? suddenly cried out Astrid. Oh, the cat. The cat came out and put his feet up on her chair then, and Mrs. Lindquist, whom everybody called Mathilda, stroked his head. Pretty pussy. Then the conversation broke in half. Gurlie and Mrs. L, with Astrid listening and shaking her head, were still at the treatment Joe had received from his employers after the strike. While Mr. L and the other couple with Joe between them started to speak of a friend who had recently lost his wife from pneumonia. Grandma, who didn't sit as high as the other ladies, sat alone trying to get the meat out of a nut.

Come on with us, said Mathilda. You shouldn't sit alone like that on Christmas. Move over here. We young people forget that you are here, sometimes. We are so selfish, we think only of ourselves.

That's right, Grandma agreed. I was young once too. I know. But I have had my time. It's you who have to do the work now, so you must have the first place.

Things were different then, weren't they?

Yes, different. I should say so.

They used to begin to cook for Christmas two months ahead.

What is that?

She's a little deaf, said Gurlie.

I say, they used to begin to cook two months before Christmas.

Yes, I've been cooking a little.

She made the cookies, *sandbackles*, a month ago.

They're delicious — these little cakes. How do you make them?

You have to have cream and eggs, began Grandma. And they all laughed. Yes, but eggs and cream cost too much now. I can imagine, said Mathilda. In the old country they would use cream by the quart and two dozen eggs in one cake.

Oh well, that's past now, said Grandma. Perhaps it's better so. We used to eat too much and too rich food too.

I thought it was Americans who did that, said Mathilda. You know what they say about Americans: They dig their graves with their teeth. Oh! Mathilda went on, seeing a mark on the back of the old lady's wrist, you've burnt your hand, that's too bad.

That's nothing. I can't see so well now. I forget the pan is hot.

You know what they say: It's only good cooks that get burned.

Anyone can cook, just give them something to cook with, answered the old lady in her gruff voice.

Sweet little Spider, said Astrid at this point to the baby, I'm going to take her in to see the tree again.

There she met Joe who had preceded her and was standing near the tree looking out of the front window as if judging the weather.

What are you doing, Lottie, so quiet here all alone? said the fat auntie with the baby in her arms to the older girl who all this time had been in the front room without a sound out of her.

Reading, said she without looking up. Oh no, said Astrid patronizingly, you're not old enough for that. Yes, said the child with great determination as she looked up from the picture-book before her. Her

eyes were resentful and determined so Astrid turned
away from her and walked toward the tree with the
baby eager to touch everything.

Come look, she called to the other ladies. Come
here a minute. And she turned and nodded with her
head toward Lottie. Isn't she beautiful! And the ladies
all looked at Lottie reading on the sofa, who smiled appreciatively and went on with her book. But look.
Lottie, look up. Look at those eyes. And Lottie oblig-
ingly simpered and made big sentimental eyes. She
was pretty with her long black curls.

The baby by a sudden swing of its arm managed
to bat an ornament at one of the branch-tips. No, no,
mustn't touch. But the infant leaped up and down
humping itself and relaxing while ecstatic grins lit
its little face — so the Auntie glanced covertly toward
the dining room where the other ladies had returned
and gave it just a taste of a candy cane.

Joe, came Gurlie's voice from the other room.
Astrid jumped. What kind of a host is that?

Come on, said the pretty Mrs. Lindquist entering
and taking him by the arm with a laugh, we missed
you. Come in with the ladies, you can't run off like
that.

What! Are we going to eat again? said Joe.

Coffee and cake. You must come. And then we
want you to play the violin for us. Isn't that right,
Captain?

Yes, yes, said the big fellow.

You think so, said Joe. Look at this place. I better
pick up a few things.

No. You must come with me. You're not going to
clean it up now I hope, are you?

But we've just finished eating.

Astrid, shouted Gurlie from the other room. Coffee. Come. We want to talk to you. Give me that baby, she said then, appearing suddenly. Give her to me. And she gathered some toys at random and heaped them on the floor — a small doll, an animal on wheels, a small music box to which she gave a few turns to attract the baby. Leave her here now. And down she sat the baby in the middle of that litter. Lottie, watch the baby.

Lottie looked over the top of her book, looked, came over, took the small music box away from the baby and went back to her reading.

I should think she'd put things in her mouth, leaving her that way, said Astrid, with all those broken ornaments on the floor, they're glass you know. No, she won't, said Gurlie. Let her learn. Someday you may be sorry, said Grandma.

Yes, said Mathilda. And I noticed a lot of pins on the floor from the packages and all that.

No, said Gurlie, she won't swallow them. She knows. But Gurlie ... Oh there are pins here on the floor all the time. I showed her one and stuck her finger. Pin! I said to her. Pin! Pin! So she must learn.

Pin! said the baby suddenly with exaggerated exactitude. Pin! And everybody jumped. She had her back to the room and was holding up her right hand with the index finger and the thumb together and trying to look over her shoulder.

Look at that! said Astrid, as she and Mathilda almost fell over each other as they ran in to her.

But it turned out to be nothing at all when they got there. Oh you little faker, said Astrid. She must have heard what we were saying. But isn't that cute! said

Mathilda. Isn't that cute. Think of it. Let me sit here and play with her.

No, said Gurlie, from the other room whence she had not stirred. This is Christmas, we can't be watching babies every minute. Come. You must come. I want to see your ring. Take it off. I want to try it.

Mathilda was obliging. With the ring on her firm finger Gurlie got up and went over to her husband. Look here Mr., she said, shaking the ring on her finger under his nose. See what smart men give their wives. Oh but look what you have, chided Mathilda. She can't see that, she only wants more, said Joe. You ought to be glad, answered his wife. You need someone to make you go ahead. Oh you're terrible, Gurlie, said Mathilda. It's a fine ring, said Joe.

No sooner had the ladies left the front room than the cat walked quietly in, flopped down on the floor and began to roll over with its four paws in the air for all the world like a dog.

Look at that cat, said Astrid, won't it hurt the baby? Gurlie didn't even answer her.

The baby sat where its mother had placed it for a long time without moving. But now it seemed to come to life. She struck right and left with her hands at the jumble of toys before her and looked up delightedly at the havoc she had wrought. But seeing no face above her she grew serious. Then she looked, saw and began reaching. It turned out to be an abacus. Leaning far forward from the hips until she was almost on her belly she managed to just get hold of it.

Having possessed herself of the object she looked at it intently, critically, then, touching the colored beads with her left hand she saw them move. Cautiously she withdrew her hands, then half advanced them to the beads again, stopping and looking around into the dining room for support. When a violent . . . She stopped, swallowed hard and then held her breath as hard and as long as she could. The cough began but she would not give in till it burst from her against her mightiest efforts to control it. She bowed her head struggling and clasped her little hands tightly together before her. She made so little noise, her back to the talkers, that she was not noticed till with a stifled gasp she ended — and sneezed violently.

Once more, everybody but Gurlie came about and the Auntie and Mathilda ran. It's only the whooping cough, said the Mother. Bring her here. The infant was sobbing a little but brightened after a moment in Astrid's arms. Put her back where she was, said the mother, I can watch her from here. So back she went to the toy-heap. The abacus was still before her. She looked at it as if recalling what had happened then with one pointing finger began to move the beads one at a time, carefully. But in the end, emboldened, she struck the beads with both hands, bang, bang! and pushed the thing away.

What is Christmas in this country? the old Captain was saying. It's not the same as at home.

You're right. It's to see who can show off the most with presents, and expensive presents. There ought to be a *law* against it, said Joe in his imitation coarse voice, frowning darkly.

Yes, there is nowhere the real feeling of Christmas and all the color and so quiet. Music and bells and real happiness. Not here.

But I notice, said Joe, you don't refuse the presents.

Oh you, said Mathilda, you always say something like that.

Why should we, said Gurlie, it's coming to us.

Then what do you expect? said Joe.

It's because there is no tradition here, no peasants that love the land. There is no feeling of . . . of reality. I can't express it.

You express it well, said Joe.

No, I'm sorry but I don't, replied Mathilda sadly smiling.

It's because everybody wants to beat the next one, said Joe. That's the American way. Unless you have more than anybody else you have to feel ashamed of yourself.

Oh you shouldn't talk like that, Joe, said Mathilda.

No. He's right, said Gurlie. So give it to us.

Sure, said Joe. Give us another bottle of that Rhine wine. The Captain's glass here has been empty for the last half hour. Come on. Think of somebody else for a change.

Look at that cat, said Lindquist suddenly. Is he crazy?

Vicious, his look wild, suddenly the beast had galloped up over the back of an upholstered chair in the front room, clawing it wildly. Then diving under it he lay on his back, clawed at the bottom, propelled himself upside down sliding on the floor under it with vigorous strokes all the way under the chair and out again on the other side.

Look at that beast!

He's drunk, said Joe.

Won't he hurt the baby?

No, said Gurlie, he just wants to play.

I know but . . .

It's the booze, said Joe.

The booze? What do you mean?

Everybody has to have booze, the cats too.

It's catnip, corrected Gurlie.

Oh, said Mathilda, that explains it. I see now. Booze.

Yes, that's good, said the big fellow. Everybody has to have booze. That's right too. Very good.

It had been five cents worth of catnip which Gurlie had tied in a little cotton bag with a red ribbon at the top and hung on a low branch of the tree. The cat had chewed a hole in it and scattered the stuff on the carpet the first thing in the morning. They all watched.

The cat was now walking slowly over the carpet, his head down, his nose just touching the floor delicately, regularly as he walked, snuffing the aromatic dust. Now he found the bag again. He batted it with his paw and it disappeared under the tree. The cat stopped suddenly not having seen where the bag had gone and looked right and left a little bewildered. Then lifting his head high and cocking it to one side he saw the bag and crouched down at once, his neck stretched out, and began to tread quickly with his back feet, wiggling his haunches eagerly from side to side. Then with a dash he pounced on the object, tossed the thing into the air, rolled over holding it in his arms and biting it while he brought his back feet into play, jabbing with spasmodic tearing motions.

There's the wild beast for you, said Lindquist. Look at that.

And again the cat batted the collapsed bag, then with a long run and a slide, the forepaws held rigidly before him, he drove it under the cloth around the tree and as suddenly turned his back on it and sat down, turned up his rear parts and began to lick them carefully. After which he flopped once more to the ground, completely at rest, as though nothing had happened and in another moment was fast asleep — his forepaws folded in under his furry breast, his eyes closed and his head sunk forward until his nose rested drunkenly on the carpet.

Look at him, said Mathilda, that's the way we all feel after we eat too much.

A silly beast, said Lindquist. Is he a tom?

Yes, I prefer a female cat every time, said Gurlie, they're much smarter.

Give him time, give him time, said Joe. He isn't a year old yet.

He doesn't even catch the mouse we have. If it was a female she would have caught it weeks ago. He's stupid, he has no sense at all, said Gurlie, but the children like him.

Yes, he has a big head like a tomcat. The female has a much smaller, prettier face. But I think the male is a nicer pet, they are not so suspicious.

He's too stupid.

He hasn't such a bad temper, said Joe.

And what have you been doing with yourself, Astrid, asked the big fellow with the scar across his upper lip. You know it's five years since I've had a good talk with you. What are you doing? Still with the same people. They must be treating you well, you look fine.

Yes, said Astrid, let me pass the cookies. How was it in Norway this summer?

Oh, we had a good time. I did a little fishing, a little shooting.

But you came back, broke in Joe.

Sure, said the big fellow, there's no money there. But the country is beautiful. Wish you could go there some day, Stecher, you'd like it.

All the pictures I've ever seen of it are nothing but rocks, said Joe. You don't know what you're talking about, Gurlie interrupted. Wha! said Mathilda trying to save the situation, can't you see he's only teasing you? You shouldn't let him tease you. Such a sweet man. Skol, Joe! she smiled, you ought to see the pretty girls in Norway.

My glass is empty again, replied the latter. What kind of a house is this?

Get it yourself, said his wife. Norway was civilized before Rome even. Everywhere in Europe you will find it, everywhere. I'll bet that is where the race began.

Which race? said Joe.

We have Nansen, we have Grieg and Ibsen, we have . . .

Well, said Mrs. Lindquist, I can't say that I enjoyed him much. We saw a play when we were there last — about typhoid fever I think. I can't see much in that. I think it's the Germans and the French that have given him such a name.

Huh, huh! said Joe, you see . . .

You shouldn't back him up . . .

Astrid, spoke up Mr. Lindquist, we've been waiting to hear you tell us something about the people you work for. Are they as rich as we hear?

I suppose so, yes.

How many servants have they?

Oh what do you care about that? I'm curious, tell me. Oh I suppose with the butler and the cook and the upstairs maid. Of course there's the coachman and the stable boy. Oh I suppose they keep ten or twelve most of the time. Phew! said Mr. Lindquist, that must cost something.

Now tell us, Astrid, he went on, we're all friends here — what do you do?

Well, what do I do? I am I suppose what you call a housekeeper. Astrid is a trained housekeeper from the other side, you know *that* Alfred, said Mathilda to her husband. I do everything, Astrid went on. When they need help I get it for them. I pack up when they go away. I open and close the house. I pay the servants and discharge and hire them. Don't make me talk about that.

No, tell us Astrid, I'd like to know how those people live. The eyes of the stout lady, the Captain's wife, were closing drowsily. Her husband gently smiled. Look, she's falling asleep, he laughed good humoredly. Louisa, wake up!

Well, said Grandma, I think I'll leave you now. The men stood up. Sit down, sit down, she said. No use to be so polite. I can go alone. And slowly she left while they waited, standing, for her to go.

Now go on with your story, said Lindquist to Astrid. I'm curious.

Yes you are curious, said Astrid. That's what's the matter. Well, they . . . Well, what is there to say? There's nothing different from ourselves.

Are they good to you?

Mrs. Haggerty is a dear old lady. What do you want to know? They have a house on Fifth Avenue. They have another house on Long Island. They go to Europe and Florida like the rest of the rich people . . .

What are they doing today?

Today? said Astrid. Mr. Haggerty had his break-

fast at six o'clock as usual and then went down to
the office.

What! on Christmas Day?

No, no, no. Not downtown. But he has an office on
the first floor of the house and he goes down there
every morning and every evening working at his
business, whatever it is, and usually Mr. Tim is with
him.

Arbeit macht das Leben süss! interjected Joe, when
you have a couple of million dollars to shake around
together.

What, every day does he get up at six? asked
Lindquist.

Yes, about six o'clock — and works until he leaves
the house to go downtown.

What do you suppose he's doing every day like that?
asked Lindquist in the direction of Joe who sat at
his side.

He's probably getting ready to skin more suckers,
said Joe getting up and pushing back his chair. You
shouldn't talk like that, said Astrid, you've never even
seen him. He's a nice man. She's so loyal she
wouldn't say a mean thing about anybody, chimed
in Mathilda.

It's stocks and bonds he has to figure out I suppose,
said Astrid, he always looks at the newspaper first.

Tammany graft, said Joe. He made his pile selling
lumber to the people who put up the elevated
railways.

He's a smart man just the same, said Astrid.

Sure. If you get half the lumber in Maine from a
lot of farmers and don't pay anything for it and then
sell it here for five times what it's worth of course
you'll make money.

No, he was smart. He floated it down here in rafts and saved the carfare. Everybody laughed.

That's the way they make money in America, Gurlie spoke up sharply. Why don't you listen and learn?

Because you have to be a crook to make money that way, said Joe. They're all dishonest, every one of them. That's why they're what they are — Great men! Master minds! — while everybody else starves. Nobody can make as much money as that honestly.

If you're too honest you don't get anywhere either, said Lindquist.

Agh! What's dishonest? That's nothing. Everybody is dishonest, said Gurlie. It's the way to make money, that's all that counts. Afterward there is time to be honest — if you want to make a name for that.

Now children, children! Mathilda admonished them. But Gurlie couldn't be stopped that way. She continued her tirade. You should listen to what Astrid is saying, you can learn. But he's Dutch, she went on, turning to the company in general. No, no! he knows everything. But this is America, Dutchie! She made a snoot at her husband, that's how they make money here.

Only here? said Joe — and turned to go into the front room, smoking.

I'll bet he could give you some good tips on the market, persisted Lindquist. Does he ever do that, Astrid?

Yes, said Gurlie eagerly, that's it.

No, said Astrid, of course not.

Why not? Why don't you ask him? You must have money to invest sometimes. One good stock can make a lot for you if you know how to watch the market.

Nonsense, said Astrid.

No. Alfred is right, Gurlie insisted. You should ask him.

No.

Oh well, then that settles it, said Lindquist. Never mind, Astrid. But maybe you'll tell us what they eat. They all laughed.

You're funny, said Astrid. What is there to interest anyone in that?

I just want to know what makes them so smart, said Lindquist. No, I'd really like to know. What about his breakfast?

Astrid looked at him for a moment as if the whole thing were below her notice but finally she thought she might as well tell them. Well, for breakfast he has sometimes ham, bacon, three or four eggs. Meat and potato sometimes. And always a big bowl of Irish oatmeal which he gets especially for himself from Ireland. Two cups of coffee, sometimes three. Bread. Butter. Plenty of butter. Now leave me alone.

Phew! said Lindquist. What a man. But wait a minute. You mean to say he worked all day today?

No.

Well?

Then Mathilda stopped her husband. Don't you see that Astrid doesn't want to talk about that any more? Stop it.

No. Just a minute. Didn't he go to mass this morning?

Yes, said Astrid, finally. His wife took him away from his work and made him go with her and the children.

What is the baby doing, Joe? his wife called out to him.

I hear Hilda has bought a farm up in Vermont,

said the big fellow at this point. And his wife who had hardly opened her mouth all afternoon said, yes, is it true?

The answer came from the next room. Joe laughed and said, Yes, it reminded her of Norway — solid rock. But anyhow she had the money to pay for it.

What did she pay?

A hundred dollars down, said Joe coming into the room.

You make me tired, said Gurlie. It's a lovely, romantic place. And the cat raised up and stretched, arching its back and yawning as it clawed the carpet lazily. Stop that! said Gurlie. Then it lightly batted a hazel nut, which it encountered, lightly over the floor, licked itself behind then walked slowly through the room where the people were assembled and went off down the corridor to the kitchen.

Look at that baby, said Mathilda. It's incredible that a little thing like that can be so good.

Yes, she *has* been quiet. She's been too quiet, said Gurlie, getting up and going into the next room.

Oh leave her alone, said Astrid, she's so cute. But the baby, seeing her mother moving toward her immediately started to cry, and lustily too. Look at that, said Astrid. She knows.

Yes, she has a good memory, said Gurlie picking her up. That's what I thought. Now the baby kicked and screamed until it went into a spasm of coughing again as Gurlie started off toward the back of the house with her — but had to stop a moment to allow the infant to catch its breath. What's the matter now? said the big fellow.

It's the lying down, said Gurlie. She hates to be put down on her back to be cleaned. She always fights it.

She likes to be dirty. I think it's time for her to go to
bed anyway.

My heavens yes, said Mathilda. Look! it's almost
dark outside. And we sit here . . .

That's all right, said Joe, don't be in a hurry. For
sure enough the light was rapidly failing and Lottie
had fallen fast asleep on the lounge in the next room.

Light the lights.

Well, this has been a fine afternoon, Stecher, said
the big fellow in his slow positive way. A fine old-
fashioned afternoon. This is what I call good company.
That's what it means to have friends.

Yes, I tell you that's true, Lindquist added. Joe, you
said you would play for us.

No, no, no, no, said Joe.

Yes you did. Get out your violin, Mathilda kept
after him, and we can play something. We need music
to finish it up just right. Come on now, don't be a
backslider.

So Joe very reluctantly got out his fiddle, tuned it
and with Mrs. Lindquist accompanying him played his
favorite *Ständchen* very slowly and carefully while
the others listened and applauded well afterward.

By God, I didn't know that Joe could do that, said
Lindquist.

His brother is a violin teacher at the conservatory
in Prague, said Gurlie proudly.

Yes, that's one of the reasons I'm in America, volun-
teered Joe.

So? said the old Captain.

CHAPTER XII

A Visit

I DON'T WANT another creeping baby, said Gurlie. When they creep they never seem to walk until they're about two years old. Can't we get one of those things on wheels for her?

Sure, said Joe. Why not? Do you want me to bring it home today? he added ironically.

The last Saturday in January, it was snowing hard outside, the driven flakes striking with an almost imperceptible seething sound against the back windows of the flat as the husband and wife sat in the kitchen for Joe to drink his hot coffee before starting downtown. The baby was at his knee holding on precariously and grinning up at him as usual. It's little hands, none too clean, rested on his pants' knees but he didn't disturb them. When the baby put her mouth down on the cloth however and began to bite and slobber he objected.

Take her away, he said. Here, he added, and placed the baby back in her chair. I think she's getting more teeth.

It's snowing hard, said Gurlie who had not heard him. It must be beautiful in the country.

Yes, I suppose it is. And plenty of shovelling on their hands before they can move, too. Work for the city's unemployed.

They should go out where there is freedom and fresh air. Why do they want to huddle all together here in their filthy homes the way they do? They make me sick. I have no sympathy for them.

Well, so long, said Joe. I'll see if I can find one of those roller things for the baby.

Oh, she'll be all right, said Gurlie. It's you I worry about.

What! chuckled Joe. What did you say?

Take care of yourself, said his wife. Here put on these goloshes. Yes, you must put them on. It looks like a blizzard I tell you. Perhaps you'd better stop at the Market and bring home a chicken tonight, I don't think I'll go out. And tomorrow is Sunday.

Where's the money? said Joe.

What money?

For the chicken.

Well, if you don't want to buy it you'll have to do without it, said his wife.

That's the way to close a deal for a profit, said Joe. Look at that baby. He was out in the hall looking back. The baby had somehow slid from its high-chair and was coming, hinching itself down the hall in grand style, putting its two hands forward on the floor and hauling its body, in a sitting position with one leg bent under, swiftly after them. So long. I've got to go.

He was the first down the ten steps to the street, the snow was already deep on them so that the footing was deceptive. There was a cold wind at his back as he headed, wading in the heavy white fall, toward the elevated station. The street otherwise was empty.

In the car Joe watched from a west window, the sky full of dark-winged gnats. They drove aslant past the windows of the moving train and fell white on the roofs of the houses.

Everything was muffled, giving the illusion of peace,

as if the city were changed rather than merely weighted down and smothered. Yet it *was* peaceful to the ear and to the eye from the obliteration of meaningless detail. And it was strange — an unreality — a softness which yielded to some wish — which triumphed and gave an exhilaration to the mind — the body? — relieving unrest. The illusion of an imposed order, the cleanliness — touched Joe and gave him contentment watching the storm.

Downtown earlier passersby had trod a narrow footpath from street to street — further illusion, he was walking through woods and fields — though at windy corners the bare pavement brought the city back quickly enough.

As Joe approached his own building he had his head bowed and did not look up until he was right at the door and had started to kick his toes against the sill before opening and going inside.

Are you Mr. Stecher?

Joe came up with a start. There was a woman standing to the left in the shelter of the doorway, grey eyes fastened steadily on his own.

Yes. What is it? Joe had his hand on the door-handle ready to go inside.

Can I talk with you a minute?

Come inside. He opened the door and they went into the chilly corridor. Her shoes were soaking wet.

I'm Mrs. Carmody.

Look here, said Joe losing his temper a little. I have no time to stand here listening to such stories. Do you need money. Here.

I'm not asking for money only, the woman began.

But Joe broke her off. You tell Carmody if he has

anything to say to me to come here like a man and say it.

It's a cruel thing, the woman began again. She stopped suddenly and drew the shawl about her face as someone came into the building and glancing quickly at them talking, went by. Good morning, Mr. Stecher. Good morning, Tom.

It's a cruel thing, the woman began again.

Wait a minute, said Joe. Where do you live?

Second Avenue, sir.

Where on Second Avenue? said Joe.

She looked at him suspiciously a moment. We live at number two hundred and thirteen, sir. The third floor in the rear.

Joe took a small pad from his vest pocket and made a note of it while the woman waited patiently.

Have you any family?

Five small children, sir.

All right. I'll see what I can do. But the woman did not move. We're in great need, sir.

Have you had any breakfast?

No sir, said the woman. Joe reached for his wallet. He took out a dollar bill and folding it once handed it to the woman. She took it. God bless you, sir . . . turned, opened the door, hesitated a moment and went out.

God damn it to hell, said Joe mounting the stairs. What in Christ's name are you gonna do about a thing like that?

During the morning he tried to reconstruct the picture Mrs. Carmody had made standing speaking to him — a woman almost fifty he thought, with a white, pinched face, a sagging mouth but fine eyes — truthful eyes. Says you. What would Gurlie say though. And what if Carmody should try to start something? Well, the only way to find out if people are lying is to go and find out. But later on in the morning he shook his head more than once at what he had determined upon — for those kind of people — on a day like this — or any old day for that matter.

But he had been careful not to give himself away to anyone in the shop — nor even to Mrs. Carmody. It was just that he wanted to see for himself — during the noon hour — just how bad things are in the houses of these people. He could easily take the hour off and no one be the wiser for it. He never ate much at noon anyhow, but he noticed that his cheeks were burning as it grew closer to the time and he, unusually at that hour, felt the need of a cigar.

It was dark, almost, as twilight under the elevated road as he faced north up Second Avenue a little after twelve and began to watch the numbers on the glass over the narrow doorways as he walked. The pulsing roar of a train overhead caused him to look up apprehensively. One hundred and fifteen. Almost a hundred numbers more. All the houses were about the same, two or three steps and the door, with two small-paned windows to the right.

The snow in the center of the street was by this time trampled and scarred by the traffic, blackened and dung-stained. But it was still falling and covering again that which had been swept off earlier.

A few cheap restaurants. A Chinese laundry, the two Chinks hard at it behind the frosty pane. But aside from that not much life anywhere. No children to speak of and only one other man going in the same direction twenty feet before him. Slow-moving steaming horses passed occasionally, dragging trucks with difficulty through the street.

Joe passed the swinging doors of a saloon, whiffed the sour smell, thought he might stop. But the seriousness of the errand wouldn't allow it. He was hungry too, now. What is it in America makes the drinking of a glass of beer just a little shameful? He could still remember an entirely different mood about such things, places where families sat about tables, neighborhood cafes, no better than these in some ways — but different. Not that the beer isn't pretty good either. Of course not like *real* beer — but you have to be in Germany for that.

Another saloon and a girl coming out of the side door with a can in her hand which she carried away from herself carefully, looking right and left at the street crossing before hurrying over. It's the Irish of it. He could never understand them.

Somebody had spit squarely onto the middle of the first step at 213 in the freshly fallen snow. A child's face was in the window at the right of the door its hands close up to it on either side shielding away grey lace curtains. It stuck out its tongue at Joe as he stood on the small platform before the door looking for the bell. The child laughed, looked back into the room, said something. Then another child and finally a grey haired woman came and looked out also. They eyed him up and down as he stood there and the woman gestured vaguely.

Finally he realized there was no bell, only a hole where one had been, all hacked about with pen-knife whittlings and a cork shoved in to keep the wind out. As he stood undecided an enormous woman came struggling up the three steps behind him, raised her face, looked at him squarely and went heavily by. A terrific smell of urine stood out in her wake and other gynecologic odors which it would have been impossible for Joe to identify. Are you comin' in? she said as she held back the door without any effort at all, by the sheer presence of her body in the doorway. Then laboriously turning to him she said, who are you lookin' for?

Where does Carmody live? said Joe carefully avoiding to say, Mrs. Carmody.

The woman looked him over. You'll find Mrs. Carmody and the children on the third floor in the rear. Go on up ahead of me young man, I'm slow on the stairs.

Joe could hardly pass her in the narrow hallway poorly lit as it was and a smell about it, the further he got from the woman herself, of generations of filth and decay. It must be in the wood itself and in the cracks of the floor, thought Joe.

At each landing there was a toilet with the door open and a sink and faucet for drawing water beside it, bare, wet, unappointed in any way, the seat raised on a little platform above the floor. For a good reason. Good God! — the doors of each hacked and maltreated each in a new way. All seemed to have had the original lock avulsed from them by — Time, it must be. While about the torn opening were remains of nails, bolts fastened in fresh places — wherever the wood would hold them.

He could hear the slow tread of the old woman ascending heavily behind him in the semi-dark. The smell of the dreadful toilets was even worse than she. He went ahead.

On the third floor Joe stopped a moment undetermined after all whether to go in or not. There were three doors as a matter of fact and no mark of identification upon any one of them. He stopped and listened. A door opened on the floor below him, it crashed shut and he could no longer hear the tread of the old woman. It would be easy enough to turn and go back the way he'd come. He could put a couple of dollars in an envelop and send it back by mail. He smiled to himself and rapped sharply at the rear door.

It was opened almost instantly by Mrs. Carmody herself, and wide. She stood with her face thrust forward as if startled and for a moment neither made a move. Then Joe felt a blast of heat coming out of the room for which the woman immediately apologized: Come in. I keep it warm here for the children. The rest of the place is like an icebox. He had walked directly into a kitchen in which a range stood with a washboiler on the top of it. I'll take your coat. Won't you please sit down. Tommy bring that chair over here for the gentleman.

But as Joe made a slight forward move, suddenly, from under the range half darted, half scuttled one of those always begrimed white dogs of which you can't see the eyes for hair and yelping, barking furiously, launched herself at his feet.

Don't mind her, said Mrs. Carmody, she has pups back of the stove. Shut up, Jenny! And she reached for the coal shovel. The bitch instantly retreated still yipping and shivering.

In the first place Joe hadn't realized she was so young. Her hair, glossy black, was parted in the middle and drawn into a knot behind. Her bodice, folded in at the neck and her sleeves, rolled high, showed a milk-white skin. Hm! thought Joe. That's different.

The room was pretty clean too, as clean as could be expected with five children packed into it in various corners. There were several unironed patched shirts over the back of a chair.

The oldest of the children appeared to be a boy of about ten, dark and thin, with grey eyes like his mother, who had been busy looking at part of an old newspaper when Joe entered. After fetching the chair he went back to his reading and seemed to pay no more attention to the visitor though Joe saw by the way he raised his eyes from time to time how closely he was listening to what was being said. There were two girls of about five or six with thick disheveled lighter hair, another boy, perhaps about three, whose face was scarcely recognizable from something he had smeared on it and a small child which because it had nothing on but a shirt reaching to its belly-button and a bedraggled pair of shoes Joe saw to be a girl.

This chubby and delightful thing came at once staggering with a spoon in its hand toward the visitor. It rocked and hesitated as it progressed, unseen by its mother, but kept on upon its sturdy legs until it landed full upon Joe's knees and looked up gurgling.

Instantly the mother had it, put it into a sawed off packing box over by the window and with a moistened towel went to wiping Joe's pant knee.

Oh, don't bother, said Joe as he looked squarely down between her breasts — impossible to avoid doing so — and was again struck by the incredible whiteness of her skin. Something to admire. Something unusual. He had heard that the Irish sometimes have skin like that though it's often, too often, badly freckled. He took out his watch.

I tell you what I've come for, Mrs. Carmody, he began . . . where's your husband?

The woman looked at the children, then at Joe. He went out last night, she said, and I'm expecting him any minute now. Joe had himself well in hand ready for anything the woman might be up to. But when she raised her face it was quiet and her eyes were not pleading. Her forehead was straight up and the hair came out of it in a clear line going off to either side smoothly and giving to the woman an almost intellectual look in spite of her obvious condition. Joe even felt a kind of protection which she had assumed over him. He relaxed accordingly.

You mean, he said, you don't know where he is.

The woman nodded her head.

Drink? asked Joe bluntly.

Yes, said Mrs. Carmody, but I think if you'll give him another chance I can get him to go straight.

I can't do it, said Joe. But I'll tell you what I came here for, Mrs. Carmody. I'm sorry for you. We've got enough troublemakers to deal with in business every day but these are hard times and when you came to me this morning . . . well, something's got to be done to take care of these children. How old is that little one?

She'll be a year in April.

Joe smiled to himself. What's her name?

Kathleen, said the mother. Have you children of your own, sir? Seeing you look at them that way makes me think it.

Yes, said Joe, I have a little girl the same age as your daughter.

God love her, said the woman. Isn't that fine now. This one's a wonder, she went on. She has a great habit of tip-toeing, she likes to tip-toe and creep. But when I call her she always answers. If she's under the bed she sticks her head out and says, Ah! We have a lot of fun with her now. She says mom and dad. And when she hears a train she goes, Ffth! and she points outside and listens.

That's a nice little fellow you have there too, said Joe, meaning the one with the dirty face.

The redhead? He's a scallywag. The greatest boy with a hat I've ever seen. He'll play all day with it.

But Joe took himself in hand again quickly and returned to business. Now listen to me, Mrs. Carmody. No use mincing words. I see you haven't much to do with. I want to know plainly just how much you do have. If I may ask that question.

We haven't a red cent to our names, sir, and that's the truth or I wouldn't have been out in that storm this morning to see you. He took the last quarter I had hid in the cup on the shelf there and went off last night with it just as the snow was beginning. When I went out of here this morning I had nowhere to go but the mission — until I thought maybe you could help me. I've often heard him speak your name.

Yes, I can imagine that, said Joe.

He's a foul-mouthed man, my husband, the woman replied, you mustn't mind that. But you can see for yourself I'm not lying. You can come into the other rooms . . .

Never mind, said Joe.

There's nothing in them but the beds and an old rag of carpet. Will you make a place for him, anything at all? I'll promise you he'll work steady and cause no more trouble to you.

I'm afraid that's beyond you, Mrs. Carmody. There's

nothing he can do there anyway and the union wouldn't let him take less than he was getting, said Joe his lips curling. She saw it. Neither spoke for a moment. The children seemed mesmerized by this strange visitor with an unusual accent. But the big boy continued to or pretended to go on reading the old paper.

Joe looked again at the little gurgling girl in her improvised play pen and thought, as many have before him, what wonderful children sometimes come out of such places as this. She seems twice the size of our baby and as round and rosy and generally good looking as the finest in the land. Mrs. Carmody turned to look too following his gaze, nodding to the child and clapping her hands to make it crow and chortle. The two little girls went over to it then, seeing it had the spot light, and they too began to give it some attention. But Joe wanted to get the job over with.

I'll tell you what. If you'll sober up your husband and send him over to me next Monday . . . now I'm speaking plain, Mrs. Carmody. There's no use keeping anything back in a case like this. If you'll have Carmody come to me Monday morning, I'll find work for him. I can't say it'll be anything much, and I can't say it'll be with me. But it will be something. And, he added getting up, I'll advance you a week's salary for him right now. That'll be twelve dollars.

No. I can't do that, said the woman.

Joe waited, the money in his hand.

Maybe tho', she added, you could loan me another dollar till over the end of the week.

Make it five, said Joe.

Give it to me in ones then, she answered. Joe counted them out to her one at a time while the big boy looked up for once attentively. She folded the bills together and put them into the bodice of her dress.

Until Monday morning then, said Joe.

God bless you, said the woman, and a thousand thanks for your kindness. Watch the stairs.

Joe was back in the pressroom at the usual time.

About six o'clock that night Carmody came stumbling home to his family — hard to tell just how drunk he was. He wore a cap pulled well down and under it his eyes were malicious — one of those red prince-of-the-barroom-types, with a strong jaw, a rough face, lean, built for courage and looking anything from twenty to fifty years.

The first thing he shot at his wife was: Who was in here today? Don't lie to me now you crooked white bitch or I'll . . . He made a pass at her but she was too quick for him and he fell across the table, rolled into a chair from it and sat upright.

Gimme something to eat, he roared and as he swept his arm around he struck one of the little girls. Uncertainly he picked her up off the floor then and raised her to his lap kissing her with exaggerated solicitude. Your dad's drunk. Your dad's drunk as hell, he told the child. But do you see that dirty white bitch standing over there by the stove? Do you see her? Well, I'm going to *kill* her! he yelled out. And up he leaped spilling the child on the floor again and went for his wife.

Leave me alone, Mike, she said. You're drunk. Leave me alone or I'll tell Father Reilly on you in the morning.

To hell with Father Reilly! the dirty fornicatin' son of a bitch, the man shouted back at her. Come here till I . . .

For the love of God, Mike, sit down and let me get something hot into you.

Something hot into yourself is more like it, you white bitch you. Who was it was here today giving you money to spend down on the block, you lying harlot you.

Sit down there and calm yourself, said his wife to him trying to shove him into a chair. But he was too quick for her this time and got her by the arm. Come here, he dragged her toward him and then suddenly struck her with his fist square in the face so that she went staggering back across the room and fell against the baby's play pen. He was right on top of her when he grabbed her by the throat. Gimme that money. And he ripped out her shirt, money and all with one powerful grasp.

That stopped him for a moment as he fumblingly counted the remainder of the money, three dollars in all. She went to the sink to wash her eye. But putting the money into his pocket he was on her once more and with a tremendous swing knocked her almost senseless with a blow alongside the head.

She fell to her knees and grabbed him about the ankles in self defense. As he struggled to free himself he lost his balance and fell backward striking his head on the edge of a chair. But he was up in a moment.

He cursed and swore, burning himself on the stove, as he pursued his wife about the room, blocking the door though she made no attempt to go off by it. She fought doggedly trying to protect herself and the children, saying once, You fool, you won't know a thing about this tomorrow.

But when he grabbed her again she screamed at the top of her voice he hurt her so. Shut up, he said putting his big paw over her mouth. But she sunk her teeth into it this time and struck him in the face, scratching and tearing.

You will, will you? he bellowed and lifted his knee up suddenly into her stomach so that she folded up with a groan under the table. You will, will you? he kept on saying. You will, will you? rubbing his hands together as if to dust them off, panting. Let that teach you a lesson. And seemingly sobered but panting with exertion he looked at his bleeding finger and went out and down the stairs again.

As his father had begun to shout when he first came into the room the ten year old boy with a white, drawn face, moved over along the table edge until he was close against the wall and kept his eyes glued to the eternal reading which he had been at again as if to shut out the world. As each scuttle reached the point of a cry or a crash he would look up with terror in his eyes then quickly bend to the reading again in mortal terror.

Once during the fight an elevated train had gone by outside shaking the building.

The two little girls had clung together, crouched in a corner sobbing but not daring any longer to come forth. While the two year old, seeing his opportunity and profiting by it, crawled in to where the pups were concealed, oblivious to the racket, as if he had been waiting for this chance for a year. The bitch, strangely, didn't molest him but lay aside raising her head now and then yipping, yapping and barking, or shivering all over as a dog will when cut off from escape.

Without knowing anything — save the shattering of an afternoon — the infant alone let go its full voice. It shrieked. Tho' it had grinned Da, Da, Da, Da! when the man came into the room earlier. Now it stood with both hands on the edge of the enclosure, its feet apart and screamed. It stamped its feet, held on and with rigid neck shut its eyes in a futile rage and yelled.

When the mother fell against the pen she knocked the baby over. It landed in a sitting position but with great alacrity rolled over, got to its feet and was back at once in the old place hanging on and screaming louder than ever.

Once it stopped to let go its bladder and for a moment seemed interested in that. But then, pulling itself back and forth, knocking its head against the cage-edge it started screaming once more. Still nothing happened. It held on, closed its eyes and rasping out its yells seemed bent by the very fury of its efforts upon gaining attention.

Then a change came over it. Achieving nothing, it began to look around even while crying. Then it forced its screams but without any heart behind them as if it were listening to itself. It was losing interest in the proceedings. Then its mother went down heavily.

In the sudden silence after Carmody had left the room when for a moment the whimpering of the pups was the sole disturbance the baby stood without moving. Then it gave a few snuffling sobs, squared its jaw, sat down and began to look around as if for something to play with.

CHAPTER XIII

The Flirtation

THE CHURCH BELLS were ringing in the March wind, the sound rising and falling as the gale whistled and shook the windows of the flat — calling the Easter crowds to eleven o'clock service. For heaven's sake, said Joe, aren't you ready yet? Well, what do you expect? his wife answered him. You make me nervous walking up and down that way. Take Lottie and go on ahead, I'll get there. Here, put on her hat and coat and get out of here.

How did she get this cold? Joe replied.

She goes to the parlor window, she just about reaches the frame. And I suppose the little wind that comes in there . . . Joe went to see. He put his hand down and sure enough there was a cold current of air coming steadily in under the frame. We ought to put in some weather-stripping, said he.

Spend money? Not on this place, said his wife. They do nothing for us here.

Well, if the child gets cold that way . . .

Here, said Gurlie to her elder daughter, bring me your hat and coat. You're going with your father. We're not staying here after this winter, Gurlie went on while she was clothing the child. I won't do it. This isn't a life.

When we can afford to buy a house of our own — in about ten years, Joe answered her, then you can begin to talk. Meanwhile we better get that window fixed.

Huh, Gurlie answered, ten years? You wait and see.

There, now go with your father. She had dressed Lottie in a heavy brown coat and a cap, or hood rather, which closed snugly under the chin and left the little face with the dark hair caught at the two sides a perfect oval.

As Joe, leading the child by the hand, walked along — with that feel of spring in the air which even the darkest March days possess — he was answering the child's small questions while his mind reverted to something his barber had been telling him the day before. Three boys, the barber had. Better than girls. You don't have to worry so much later. That's what I tell my wife. A boy you can put a pair of pants on and send *them* out. But a girl, that's different. If something happens she blackens up the whole map. You can't do a thing about it. She's the daughter of this one and the sister of that one and the granddaughter of the other one. And so it goes. There's always some sweet tongued bitch to spread it a little further . . .

Look! said the little girl.

Gurlie came along later in a cab with the baby. They arrived long before Joe could manage it. The Captain let them in himself. Look who's here, he said. Well! Where's Joe? And Lottie?

They started to walk, Gurlie told him, blowing a little after the climb upstairs. Whew! You've got it warm here.

Well, we're glad to see you. You're sure Joe's coming?

Yes, he was so *dumb*, he couldn't wait. That's the Dutch of it, he makes me tired. So I took a cab and beat him.

Gurlie! said Mrs. Neilsen bursting in from the kitchen, what a trouble, eh? to come out for dinner to two old people like us. You poor thing. So much trouble to do with small children. We're so glad to have you. That's right, make yourself at home. And the baby! What a little doll. Now Elsa! This she spoke to a beautifully groomed Irish setter which had come waving its plumy tail toward them from another room. She's a good dog. But so big for a little place like this. She won't hurt you.

I know that, said Gurlie. I love dogs. When I am in the country I want to have dozens of them. The Captain enjoys to go shooting sometimes, said his wife, but I'm afraid she's getting too fat now to help him much. No, she's still a good hunter after the first day, said the big fellow defending his pet.

Gurlie had put the baby down on the sofa all wrapped up in its coat and with a shawl pinned over all under the chin. It couldn't move anything but its eyes as it looked up in wonder at being in a new place and seeing strange faces above it.

That's a sweet baby, said the Captain. A sweet baby! That's something I always wanted to have. But I think it's better so. For a young man a sailor makes a poor father. He is never at home. Well, that sounds funny but you know what I mean. And he laughed his quiet laugh while he kept his keen eyes steadily on the face of his listener — he did not close them for amusement. Let's see, how old is she now? Eleven months. I wonder what she's thinking? It's funny, they will not remember one thing of it afterward. But they look so knowing. A girl, eh?

I'll see you later, said Mrs. Neilsen, I must go back to the kitchen.

It smells good, said Gurlie, can't I help you?

No, no, no, no. I wish we could have had the Lind-
quists here too but our place is so small. You understand. It's so nice of you to come here.

Not at all, said Gurlie. It's a lovely place, plenty
big enough for two people. You mustn't make excuses.

I can't get over such a fine baby, the Captain went
on as Gurlie was still unwrapping it. They are like
little flowers, a flower that is just opening. When you
take off those clothes it makes it look really as if it
were so. The baby yawned widely, then swallowed
and began to move its head around a bit — it had had
its eyes fastened almost without moving on the Captain
until then, studying him intently, as it lay still on the
sofa being mauled about by its mother undressing it.

I wanted six boys, said Gurlie.

Well, why don't you have them then? said the Captain. You're still young. Whoops! laughed Gurlie.
Will you pay for them? Well, said the Captain, I wish
I had them too. Six boys! Yes, that's the old idea. And
a stand in the country. But we Norwegians are wan-
derers still, so we think we want to buy a farm. But
we are for the sea in the end. So a big man like me
wants to have a baby. It's funny. I was reading the
papers just now, he went on. We have had quite a
gale along the coast I understand.

Yes, I read it.

Come in. Come in here. We call this the dining
room. But we spend most of the time here. You can
see the river . . .

Oh but what beautiful plants, said Gurlie. She's
lucky with flowers, I can see that. Why you have a
regular hot-house here. Look at that lily. What do
you call that?

I don't know, said the Captain, you'll have to ask Louisa. Yes, they are pretty fine. She likes that kind of thing.

But what is this? said Gurlie.

I think she calls it a waxplant, or something like that. Ha, there's Joe. The frontdoor bell had just rung, the Captain hurried off to welcome his friend.

Hello Stecher. Well, I'm glad to see you. And Lottie. How's my little sweetheart? Elsa! he added to the setter. Charge! But Lottie wasn't a bit afraid and put her hand out to the dog who looked askance at it and turned to Joe instead. He patted the beast on the head.

Come in here and look at these plants, shouted Gurlie from the next room.

That's a nice dog, said Joe. She's no good, the Captain answered as if to his pet. Just a nuisance. We pet her too much. Come in, your wife has been here a long time.

You see, smarty, said the lady in question appearing through the curtains, you thought you'd beat me. Who got fooled?

We had a nice walk, said Joe.

Mr. Stecher! burst in Mrs. Neilsen once more, How nice it is to see you here. I hope we haven't put you to too much trouble. I know what it must be to come out with children on the only day in the week you have to rest. And Easter Sunday too. But it's so nice to have you. Come in. Don't stay here. We haven't many rooms. Come into the dining room you don't care if the table is all set, do you? We like it here, we have such a nice view.

Yes, the Captain added, every room in the apartment has a window looking at the river — unless we

are unlucky and somebody builds a house next to
us.

Well I should say, said Joe approvingly. This is
what I call a lovely room.

Huh! burst out Gurlie. So you don't like what I
give you . . .

But Gurlie . . .

Everything he sees in somebody else's house he
likes . . .

But Gurlie . . .

I call this a fine, homelike room, said Joe. It looks
comfortable. You could sit down here and take it
easy.

Well, it's shipshape, said the Captain. We don't
need much. With my leg and my job on the dock,
what else do I need? We haven't two fine children like
you have. What wouldn't I give for a little girl like
that, he continued looking at Lottie. And a baby . . .

He's just a baby himself, said his wife. They all
laughed. Look at these marvellous plants over here,
said Gurlie dragging her husband to the window.
What do you think of that?

The baby was drowsy after the morning outing
so Gurlie decided to give her her bottle and see if she
would go to sleep. That's right, said the Captain,
we've fixed up a place for her in the bedroom.

So they put the baby to sleep. Gurlie fed it first
and it went off like a lamb. She came back to the
others relieved. Lottie was wild about the dog who lay
on its side under the table with Lottie right by it putting her arms around its neck and kissing it on the
head passionately.

How did you break your leg, Captain, said Joe
when they had been left alone a moment by the

women. Oh, I fell down a hatchway like all sailors do
finally, said the one addressed. That was the last
time. But that finished me. I'm just a landlubber now.

And here's dinner!

Mrs. Neilsen hooked back the kitchen door and began to bring in the food. I have to do all the work
myself, she told them, so you must excuse me.

That's all right, said Joe. We'll excuse you by what
I can smell coming. Just like a man, said Mrs. Neilsen
beaming, you like to flatter us women.

Vegetable soup first. Then they had a roast leg of
lamb with cresses around the plate and caper sauce.
The potatoes were browned whole and smothered in
butter. They had red cabbage with cardamom seed.
Fresh peas.

Fresh peas! said Gurlie, look at that — at this time
of year. Why, if I had such things on the table my husband would think I was making him broke. Do you see
that? she slapped her spouse on the arm. See what
people eat.

Oh you mustn't say things like that, Gurlie, said
Mrs. Neilsen. This is a big occasion to have our friends
here to see us. We don't eat like this every day. If we
don't treat you well you'll never come back again.

And celery and olives, white bread and brown. I
bake it myself, said Mrs. Neilsen. The Captain won't
eat store bread.

You like beer, Stecher. All good Germans like beer.
We have plenty of it in the house. I can't serve you
Champagne like you did us . . .

That was Christmas, said Joe.

Well, we can each finish a couple of bottles and if
you want more we have it outside. Come on Stecher,
you ought to be able to give us a good toast in Ger-

man, you must remember some from when you were a young man there.

Oh, he's not a sport, said Gurlie. He don't know anything like that.

Skol! said Joe. That's good Scandinavian.

That's right. Skol! said Mrs. Neilsen and they all held up their glasses.

Lottie, as usual, was no prattler but ate her meal quietly — leaning over the side of her chair every once in a while to touch the dog's head where the beast sat close beside her.

So they all ate and talked and drank their beer.

Then they heard the baby!

Goodness gracious, said Joe who had taken out his watch at the first sound from the other room, three o'clock! Think of that. And here we are still at table.

That's fine, said Mrs. Neilsen.

When Gurlie reached her the baby was out from under the covers trying to push away the chairs they had put with their backs against the bed to keep her from falling out. She was picked up and taken into the dining room.

Each time they wake from sleep it is as if they were just born, said the Captain. Look at her! She doesn't know what to make of us. Here! And he jumped up to help Gurlie.

He got a rocker, propped two books under it so that it stood solid, filled it with pillows. His wife let him do it. And there they sat the baby who with wide eyes still watched the big man while he took a long kitchen towel and whirled it between his two hands into a sort of rope. Running it from one arm of the big chair to the other across the baby's chest he soon had her securely lashed in place.

He think's it's a ship, said his wife.

Flushed from sleep the baby continued to look un-winkingly at the Captain in obvious wonder. The others sat watching.

But now the baby dropped its look, then bent its head forward and remained that way staring down into its lap.

Look at that! the little flirt, said Mrs. Neilsen. Would you believe that, at her age.

The Captain was delighted and laughed aloud. At this the baby bowed her head still lower but tried to look up with her eyes, sideways.

Oh you big elephant, said Mrs. Neilsen to her hus-band, you'll frighten her.

She's getting shy, said Joe.

He's frightened her, said Mrs. Neilsen.

Nonsense, said Gurlie. Here, she added to the in-fant, don't act so silly. Hold your head up.

Of course he's frightened her, said Mrs. Neilsen. A big thing like that, he ought to know better, putting his face up suddenly to her that way. You should be ashamed of yourself.

Hold up your head, said Gurlie again to the infant.

Oh don't bother her, said the Captain.

At this the baby began slowly to wave her upraised hands round and round at the wrists, faster and faster until they were going like small propellers. She raised her face and with an offended look fastened her eyes straight on the Captain.

You see, said his wife.

The poor man was crushed.

Helplessly the little hands waved round and round. Then the child's lower lip protruded. She jerked her

breath once or twice. Tears filled her eyes. Then she
gave in and sobbed convulsively.

You see, said Mrs. Neilsen to her husband. You see?

Joe laughed.

I wish she was grown up, said Gurlie soothing the
baby as she placed it on her lap. I don't like them at
this age.

But that's when they are best, said the Captain re-
covering himself.

I wish you could take care of her then, said Gurlie.

Mrs. Neilsen burst out laughing. Imagine it! she
said.

But she's pretty smart, said Gurlie. If I do say it
myself.

I can see that, said the Captain, like her mother —
and her father.

Ho! ho! laughed Joe. If she's smart like her mother
she'll grow up and marry a rich man like her mother
did.

Well, you'd better be rich pretty soon, said Gurlie,
that's all I can say. Why don't you make enough
money so you can retire young? If I were a man that's
what I'd do.

Good for you, Gurlie, said Mrs. Neilsen. That's the
way to talk. I'm sure your husband is luckier than
many men.

Yes, I'm lucky to be alive, said Joe.

With that Gurlie, tired of holding the baby, placed
her on the floor where she was struggling to go anyway. Is it all right? she asked her hostess.

Why certainly, said Mrs. Neilsen. There's nothing
she can harm.

Lottie was still in adoration of the dog — but now

more quietly, the affair having progressed to that stage. The baby was put down in a sunny spot and sat with a thumb in her mouth watching her sister.

Well, here we are, said the Captain. Come on Stecher, another bottle of beer.

I don't mind if I do, said Joe. How old were you when you first went to sea, Captain?

Well, the first time, I don't know. I must have been a baby. But one of the first times I can remember I was about six years old . . .

The baby gave two parrot-like squawks and went down on her hands, eagerly watching the dog lying there by her sister.

Let's see. I was sixteen years old, went on the Captain, when I broke my leg the first time.

What happened? said Joe. Oh you don't want to hear that story. Yes, said Gurlie, tell us. That was when I got this cut on my lip too. Have one of these cigars, Stecher, they're clear Havana filler, I get them from a friend. No thanks, said Joe, they look too strong for me. I like my cheap smokes better.

The baby crawled to within reach of the dog and sat down by her tail.

Look at that baby, said Mrs. Neilsen.

That's all right, said Gurlie. Go on with your story.

Oh it isn't much, said the Captain. We had a small schooner that time, somewhere in the Bahamas. You know there are lots of little islands down there. We had just unloaded a cargo and were on our way to pick up another I don't know where — some other place. We never got there anyway. The captain I suppose wanted to save money so he thought we'd get there without bothering to take on ballast. That's a nuisance to a sailor, you know that. Well, we were sailing

along with all hands taking it easy and feeling pretty
fine. It was a nice day but pretty hot. Just about noon
it was, I think, and I was down below in my bunk.

The next I knew everything was going upsidedown.
I don't know what happened after that, how I got
out or anything about it. But after a while I
came to and I was on top of a piece of wood, it
turned out to be a hatchway cover. The ship must
have turned right over. The wind caught her in a
hurry I guess and over she went. I couldn't see her
anywhere. Or any of the crew. There had been six of
us on board, I was the youngest. Everything had
disappeared.

The worst of it was it got so hot. That was a bad
time for me I tell you. I got pretty thirsty. I don't
know how I kept on that piece of board but I did,
for three days. I got sunburnt, I tell you, pretty badly.
The last day I don't remember anything.

I was lucky though. The wind must have blown
me on a shore sometime that night. I don't know how
long I lay there, the waves must have washed me up
and down quite a bit. It broke my leg and cut me up
pretty badly. It would have drowned me but I guess
I was pretty tough in those days.

Lottie didn't want the baby to have a share in the
dog and kept pushing her away, or trying to, but the
baby wouldn't move.

The next thing I knew, said the Captain, I woke
up in bed all bandaged so I couldn't move. I didn't
know where I was. At first I thought I was in
heaven . . .

Under the table the children continued at odds
over the patient animal. But Lottie was really in love
with it, stroking it and patting it understandingly as

the beast lay relaxed under her soothing gestures. But the baby had a different idea of what to do. She sat straddle-legged by the dog's rump and with beaming face whanged it with her two small hands in an unrestrained delirium of joy.

This both Lottie and the dog resented, the dog not so much as Lottie. The beast every now and then would throw her head back toward the baby in a more or less casual way as she might were a fly bothering her and that was all. But Lottie went into more serious action. No, she said softly under her breath so that the grownups might not hear, and frowned severely. No. Stop that. The infant looked at her astonished for a moment but soon went back to her amusement. Joe alone was watching them.

With that Lottie moved over closer to the infant, covertly, without attracting attention, and wearing a perfectly expressionless face dug her fingernails deeply into the child's bare knee.

A sudden tumult occurred. The child screamed. The dog jumped up. The women pushed back their chairs.

Lottie pinched her, said Joe. Lottie come here to me . . .

Nonsense, said Gurlie. What is the matter with you? she said to the baby. Can't you be quiet.

Did the dog harm her? asked the Captain. She couldn't bite her.

Joe made no further move. So after a moment the infant was put back into her chair where she kept looking down at her sister and the dog once more happily playing.

We never heard the end of the story, said Joe.

Oh well, there's nothing much to tell, the Captain

went on. An Englishwoman was walking down on the beach in the morning and she saw me lying there with the waves knocking me around. She thought I was dead. But she had them take me up to the hospital anyway and that's where I was when I woke up.

That was a lucky thing for you, said Gurlie.

Yes, I was in that place three months. They were good to me all right.

CHAPTER XIV

Gurlie and the Jewess

THE DAY the baby was a year old there was a pretty card from the fat Auntie in the morning mail and a short note saying she had been extremely busy opening up the Long Island house but that she would stop around that evening for a little while. Joe had not mentioned the event when he left that morning. And Gurlie, as a matter of fact, had not thought of it until an hour later.

The card was just a colored picture of a bunch of daisies, cornflowers and wild roses with sanded gilt letters under it — Happy Birthday! Lottie took it and rubbed her fingers over the colors as if to feel them but the roughness of the lettering made her stop and look again.

It was a superb April day. All morning Gurlie kept the windows open, going restlessly back and forth among the rooms as if she might be working. Lunch was a joke. But by one she could stand it no longer and went down to the street. Take care of the children, she told the maid, I'm going out.

But Lottie was behind her. All right. Only take the baby in by three. Yes, ma'm. And off they went toward the Park, Gurlie with her short quick steps and Lottie running after.

What a relief!

In the distance, through the veil of trees, rose the walls of the reservoir. Gurlie took a narrow path which ran curving south. But after a few moments, feeling warm from the walk and the heavy clothes she wore she sat down on a bench and looked around.

I'm hot, said the child and started to unbutton her coat.

There was a willow off to the right beside a small lake. Green threads of branches hung almost to the ground. In fact they touched the ground. While at the top the faint green was quite lost in the sky's brightness. As Gurlie had sat down she had first brushed the bench off with her bare hand. Now she saw that it was small brown flowers which she had struck away. Some had in the meantime dropped upon her lap and the air was very sweet. It was an elm. As she looked up the twigs of it were knotted with those flowers.

You could see quite a distance through the trees which were no longer a monotonous and uniform tangle of bare branches. Individual trees could be distinctly made out on the general background by their green or red outlines. Small points of green which near at hand you had to look close to discern in the distance took on a shape.

Lottie had spied the water and some white birds floating on it so Gurlie got up and ambled after her, thinking.

Here the grass was brilliant and the water caught the sun. A dozen ducks and two swans — more aloof — came thrashing to the edge of the lake as Gurlie and the child approached. Lottie was frightened and fled behind her mother. But Gurlie laughed and spoke to the birds.

I haven't a thing to give you. Shoo! Go along with you. But the birds thinking something had fallen among them as Gurlie raised her hand rushed into a struggle and then, turning about, swam off turning their eyes quickly right and left to see that they were not being cheated.

Behind them a white feather floated on the water. The wind took it and it skated toward the center of the lake till one of the ducks bore down on it, seized it in its bill, champed it a moment rapidly and dropped it — to sail no more.

There was nothing to do but look and walk, the place was quiet at that hour and Lottie was very good. Presently they came to some higher trees on a knoll with rocks and rhododendrons to the north of them. Gurlie had grown warm again and was glad to stop once more. It was dark and cool behind the rocks. Underneath one of the rhododendrons in a hollow of wet leaves was actually a small patch of fast melting snow but almost black with dirt. As Gurlie put her foot to it it fell apart, rotten.

From there the two took a turn down toward a tunnel under the carriage driveway. No one was in it but themselves so Gurlie yipped and yodeled to amuse the child. Yip! Yip! Yip! It sounded loud and hollow. Lottie didn't like it and wanted to go back. They went on and came out into the sun again on the farther side where three laborers were spading up a flower bed.

The two stopped to watch them. The men glanced up sidewise but kept to their work. Gurlie moved closer. Is it good soil here? she said. I shouldn't think so in the city.

The men, evidently foreigners, said something to each other in an undertone, glanced toward the woman's legs and one of them spat into the new dirt. Dirty pigs, said Gurlie half aloud and went on.

It was a lovely day. Lottie had some peanuts after
an hour or so and Gurlie bought a glass of lemonade
from which both drank a little. And so the time passed.
As the afternoon wore on more and more children
came out to play. Lottie watched them with her wondering eyes but she was bashful. Once a woman
stopped her when she had got twenty feet or so in
front of her mother and asked her who she was. The
woman was smiling and old but Lottie would not
answer her. I think she's lost her tongue, the woman
said to Gurlie as she came up. Oh no, said Gurlie.

Then in that part of the park where they arrived
children were everywhere running and rolling on the
grass. It was permitted. Close to the two walkers were
a dark girl and a blond of perhaps four or five years
of age. The blond one, with her two arms held out
like wings and wearing fuzzy blue gaiter-pants, was
turning round and round and round. Both were laughing as the spinner went more slowly and more slowly
wavering and laughing drunkenly until she fell to
the ground.

An older boy almost knocked Lottie down dodging
back and forth behind her while another larger tried
to catch him. They were out of breath and laughing.
Finally the smaller one gave up and bending down
the other leaped from the front upon his back and
taking the first one's head between his knees began
to slap his rump with both hands.

Stop that! said Lottie.

Children were lying and rolling all about them,
the boys especially, wrestling and chasing each other
up and down.

I want to go home, said Lottie, I'm tired.

Come on, it's too nice to go home yet. We'll sit

down again, said her mother who was tired too. Whew!
it *is* hot. And we'll take another little rest.

Home on the block Maggie wheeled the baby up
and down but it wouldn't go to sleep. So she put the
carriage top back and let the thing sit up and look
around. It was very warm on the sunny side of the
street so Maggie turned the carriage around to keep
the sun out of the baby's eyes and sat down on the
steps, blocking the carriage wheels with her feet so
that it wouldn't roll as she leaned her arms over the
side of it and made funny faces at the baby.

She'd push her face forward to within an inch of the
baby's face and say, Ah there! then draw it back again.
Then she'd put her face slowly forward once more
until she was close up to the baby, then draw it back
and lean it forward again — tilting the carriage a little
toward her each time — and saying, Ah there! until
the baby got to expect it and would lean her own face
forward openmouthed so that her nose actually
touched Maggie's each time the game was repeated.

At first the infant blinked a little to see Maggie's
face coming at her, even tho' she liked it, but after a
few tries she gave a little laugh and then with each
new approach she laughed louder until she went
into fits of laughter followed by an exciting period of
waiting as the girl drew back once more. It ended in
an embrace and the girl snuggling her nose down into
the baby's tummy. You're a little darling.

Whew! it was getting hot. Maggie took her hat
off and threw open her coat. The baby also looked hot
so Maggie loosed the ribbon of her cap which was tied
under the chin. At this the child reached up and
wanted to drag the encumbrance off. No, no! Mustn't

do that. The baby looked at her and the minute Maggie had lowered her warning finger she did it again. And so this too became a game until Maggie grew a little impatient and slapped the baby's hands. She whimpered and threw herself back on her pillow.

Hello Maggie! came the voice of another girl who had approached from up the block, she also with a carriage. So the two maids got together and talked. The second baby was a very small one and sleeping. But little Flossie was up again all smiles and started to chatter and cry out. Shut up! said the other girl harshly under her breath. You'll wake my kid.

But Flossie thought this a game also. She looked at the newcomer a moment seriously and then said, Huh! and waited for a reaction. Shut up! I told you, said the new maid. Huh! continued the baby. Shut up! said the girl. Huh! said the baby with curiosity written all over her face. But the girl didn't answer her this time so she shut up.

The girl was too interested in what she was saying to Maggie to bother with the baby further.

You're making a fool of yourself over that nut. Maybe I am, said Maggie, lowering her face. Why, he's playing you for a sucker, can't you see that? You don't think you're the only one he's filling full of his crap, do you?

Maggie didn't have a word to say.

Come on with me and Jim. I want you to meet his kid brother.

No, said Maggie.

O.K., said the older girl, but don't say I didn't give you the lowdown on that cheap sport. Why, Mag, he isn't worth wasting your time on. What'd you ever get out of him anyway? Did you ever get anything?

Everything Maggie could think of at that moment seemed more than a little insignificant.

I could tell it. Why he wouldn't give up a nickel without you'd hold him up and rob it off him. He's the worst I *ever* seen . . .

He's good looking, said Maggie.

Sure he's good looking, that's how he gets away with it. Aw come on. Give him a stand-up for once. It'll put him in his place. He needs it bad. Come on with us. It'll be a grand dance and the kid's a wonderful stepper, take it from me. You'll have the time of your life.

No.

What are you gonna do then? He'll probably take you out in the park and give you a free seat on a bench for your trouble. Honestly I didn't think you was that weak.

Now the new brat set up a squawk and Maggie's friend had to get up and tend to him. She joggled the carriage violently a while but the baby still continuing to yell in a high maddening voice, Come on, she said to Maggie. Walk down the block with me. So the two went off wheeling the carriages side by side down to the corner.

There they stood talking, rocking the infants back and forth pendulumwise as they themselves stepped back and forth from one foot to the other.

How are they treatin' you? said the friend.

Pretty good, said Maggie.

I wish I could say the same for the pain in the neck that's got me hired. What a washout she is. Katie! she says, as if she was gonna break down and cry on your shoulder. But don't fool yourself, can she find things for you to do. She's got the feet run off me.

And that piece of cheese — pointing to the baby — you can't hit him with a brick and put him to sleep. I'd like to push him into the river.

A boy whistled to them from a delivery wagon which went crashing down the street on the rough cobbles. They turned their backs on him.

Remember now, the new girl was saying, Saturday night. Tie a can to that piece of boloney and come on with us. I'll remind you of it tomorrow. Good bye darling.

Maggie got fed up with the kids playing ball on the block a while later and took the infant into the house. It looked as if it might rain, also. Where in hell is your mother? she asked the infant when they had got upstairs. She's got big ideas, that woman, about what she expects me to do around here. Why don't you go to sleep? she said to the baby. But she loved the baby and kissed her on the head when she spoke to it. It's little head was all sweaty from the heavy hat it had been wearing.

Maggie got a brush and sitting in the open front window where the warm sun was still shining she brushed the child's yellow hair out into a halo about its head. It was really very pretty with the sun streaming in on it.

At the sight of the child's hair Maggie became interested and having nothing else to do she just went on fiddling with it tying a small piece of blue ribbon around it at the back in a very abbreviated pigtail. But that was no good, there wasn't enough of it, so she parted it in the middle and tried to gather it at the two sides. That was better. The effect, in fact, was striking, making the child look very much older than her one year.

So it went on — from one thing to another. The hair threw the rest of the get-up out of scale so Maggie fished out an old summer dress of Lottie's with which she further dolled up her little charge. Then seeing the child so pale she rouged her cheeks. Finally as a last touch, she took off the yellow glass-bead necklace which she herself wore and putting it over the baby's head she tied it into a knot at the back. It made a perfect baby-faced prima donna.

Now grin, she said to the baby. Look. Like this. Show your teeth. The baby wasn't long in imitating her perfectly — till Maggie almost fell over laughing — and again and again.

But where the hell is that mother of yours? A fine birthday she's giving you. Listen. She leaned down to the baby. Damn. Say it. Damn. Damn, said Maggie. Say it.

Da! said the baby trying very hard.

No. Listen. Damn.

Da! said the baby.

Anyhow you're my little sweetheart. And Maggie grabbed and kissed the baby impulsively. Then she took her into the kitchen with her and began to look around for supper . . . or I'll be slaughtered.

Beside the bench where Gurlie and her daughter were sitting ran a hedge and by it were three children cutting up high jinks. One was a mannish little fellow, four years old perhaps, in a big cap who was marvelously showing off before two girls. Shuffling up and down and making grotesque faces with his tongue stuck out. The girls were seriously attentive. Finally in the excess of his gyrations the little sport crashed into the matted hedge which, bending solidly, elastically bounced him back again. That was a great discovery. At first he was surprised, a bit taken aback. Then finding he was not hurt — much, he crashed, backward, into it again. The little girls were delighted and as he did it again and again all three began wildly laughing.

Finally one of the little girls herself essayed it and the stiff hedge branches went up her coat sleeve and scratched her. She pulled back and began to rub her wrist while she looked at the offending hedge reproachfully and tears came to her eyes. Then growing angry she stood off and struck the hedge with her uninjured hand, repeatedly, blow after blow — so that all laughed again and she too amid her tears.

The boy then attacked the hedge in earnest, pummeling it and finally, since nothing happened, he took hold of several individual branches of it and bent them downward trying to break them off. This was too much for Gurlie.

Stop that! she said, naughty children. What are you trying to do? No wonder we have no parks. Can't you see these things are planted to be taken care of? Look you're breaking all these branches. And look here on the ground all the green shoots you've knocked off . . .

The children came to with a start and backed away while she was talking. Then they turned and ran, laughing and skipping sidewise when they were a few yards off, then whispering.

So Gurlie sat down on the bench again with her own quiet child beside her. Baby carriages went by and then a little boy in a heavy overcoat with breast pockets and wearing a sailor hat came directly up to Lottie and stood there leering. Hm! said Gurlie.

Lottie shrank against her mother. The little boy reached out and deliberately laid his hand on Lottie's breast. Lottie lowered her head but kept looking at the little boy under her hat brim. He crouched down and looked up into her face. A tall smiling woman came along the path and said, Ah ha! so there you are. I told you not to run away. She looked at Gurlie, smiling.

Do you like the little girl? she asked her son. Gurlie understood at once that they were Jewish. She did not smile.

Come on Sidney, you mustn't bother the little girl. Come *mein Kind*.

Nothing doing.

The woman who was gentle faced and well into the thirties took the small boy by the arm — or tried to do so. He shook her off. Come, said the woman. It's going to rain and thunder. And sure enough dark clouds had come up. But the small boy fought his mother the more.

Gurlie burst into her harsh, uncaring laughter and said, You should spank him if he does that.

No, the woman shook her head, he's a good boy.

It ended in a scene. The boy struck at his mother, repeatedly, even tried to kick her. So, so, *mein Kind*, she said. What will the lady think about you? But Sidney didn't give a damn, apparently. He lost himself in a blind fury, threw himself on the ground in his blue coat and lying there kicked his heels up and down and yelled. The mother tried to pick him up.

Leave him alone, said Gurlie.

With that the woman sat down on the bench exhausted. The child rolled over on his stomach all covered with dirt.

But Sidney, look at yourself, said the woman. Ach! that child. He's killing me.

That's because you don't know how to bring him up, said Gurlie.

The woman looked at her as her son, finally getting first to his knees and then his feet, and with dark looks at Lottie, went to his mother and put his head in her lap.

Don't cry, *mein Kind,* don't cry. But now the little boy was saying, By, by! to his mother, By, by! wanting to go.

By, by! All right, she answered him, we're going right away. Sit up. So. Let me wash your face. Stick out your tongue. So she took her handkerchief, moistened it on the child's tongue and washed his face with it.

Why is it all you people always insist on staying in the cities? Gurlie spoke again. Why don't some of you go out in the country where there's light and air. That's what you need. You've got plenty of brainy people. I should think you'd see that.

My husband has a store, the woman answered her conciliatingly. But Gurlie went on. You're always blaming us for doing things to you but it's your own fault. You crowd into the cities. You have no love for the land. That's what makes all the trouble.

I'm sorry we bothered you, said the woman not a littled frightened, excuse it please.

A little sprinkling of rain had begun.

With the rain newspapers came out over hats, the nursemaids rushed off with their carriages, the children shouted their delight, holding their faces up to feel the rain — but scampered. It's not going to rain hard, Gurlie said aloud, though a low rumble of thunder sounded in the distance. She did not move but gathered Lottie close to her and watched the rain. The child watched the splotches of dark color come upon the asphalt, one at a time. But in a few moments it was over and the warm smell of it filled the air. Gurlie breathed it deeply in. April!

So presently the two got up leaving a dry mark on the bench and started home.

On the way they came to a place where sheep were going through a gate in a fence which an old man was holding open for them. There was a dog beside him as the grey bodies shuffled through, knocking together and backing up then flowing again past him. Gurlie was surprised.

Sheep? she said. In Central Park? I didn't know that.

Yes ma'm. He was a longfaced individual with scanty sideboards and a worn hat. The last sheep went in and he closed the gate.

It makes me think of home, said Gurlie.

Yes, sheep make one think of home, said the man. Gurlie noted a new accent. Are you Irish? she said. No, said the man. Scotch? No, ma'm. I'm from the North of England, ma'm. You look like the men from home, she went on. I mean Norway. I've never been there, said the man. That explains it, went on Gurlie, we're all the same people. We're all mixed up together — Norwegian, English, Danish . . .

I want to go home, Lottie tugged at her.

I love the country, Gurlie added. It's the only place to be.

If you were brought up there then that's where you want to go.

Yes, said Gurlie, I lived on a farm till I was nine years old.

You'll never get over it then. There's been little rain this season, he went on. It's not a good thing for the country. I was hoping we'd get a good shower to-day.

Oh we'll have a wet spring yet, said Gurlie.

It'll be no good if it comes all in one day the way it does here and the next day drier than ever. The trees in this place can't live. Nor the grass either.

Why do they keep sheep in the park? asked Gurlie.

It was to keep the grass down on the lawns. But I think in a few years they'll have to plant more grass to feed the sheep. There's no rains here the way they are in England and you can't have grass without it.

Maybe it's the city keeps it off.

Perhaps you're right, ma'm, but I don't think so. Good day, ma'm.

Gurlie shook her head gloomily and marched on.

It was five o'clock when she reached home. The maid had nothing much for supper and the fat auntie had been waiting for an hour doing what she could meanwhile to get things ready. Where have you been?

When Joe came he brought a package. You darling, said his wife bussing him on both cheeks and acting the infant as she could at times. Have you brought something nice for me?

It's a birthday present for the baby, said Joe. Be careful now you'll break it.

CHAPTER XV

One Year Old

Stand up, he said as she sat naked looking at him from the table. He gave her his two index fingers. She struggled to her feet and stood there, legs apart, uncertainly. Just a year old, eh? He tried to loose her but she clung to him tenaciously.

Shall I hold her?

No, no. She should stand alone.

Of course she can, said Gurlie.

Come, said the doctor to the baby. Walk. And he drew it by his fingers carefully along the table.

How can she walk there? It's too soft. Put her on the floor, said Gurlie. But the baby put out her feet one at a time, stuck her tongue in her cheek, turned up her toes and did very well. So. Now sit down.

I don't believe at all in you doctors, Gurlie started.

That's right, no more do I. But you better listen to what I tell you — if you want to keep your baby.

Why what's the matter with her?

How do I know? I'm no genius. And he turned toward a cabinet on the far side of the room. She had not expected him to be a hunchback.

Gurlie stood there, looking. Shall I dress her now?

God knows what you women bring your babies here for. I don't, was what he answered.

Well, she isn't very strong and so I thought you'd tell me what to do to build her up.

You thought so. Who told you to come here?

Some of my friends told me that you know all about children . . .

So? They told you that. A pack of fools.

But doctor . . .

I'll tell you what you came here for. You came here to have your child examined. That's what you came here for. Sit down. Gurlie sat. A gnome, a troll, a funny man.

He put his stethoscope to his ears and examined the baby's chest all over, grunting to himself now and then, stopping, tapping with his fingers here and there, then listening again.

Who in your family has had tuberculosis?

No one, Gurlie answered him. We are all healthy. Why? Has she . . . ?

He turned and smiled at her. When you consult a doctor tell the truth. Gurlie flushed, wanted to speak but didn't. His eye held her fixed. This is your second child, he said. Yes, said Gurlie. And the first's a girl? Yes, said Gurlie. You wanted a boy? Yes, said Gurlie. Miscarriages? No. You're sure of that? What do you mean? said Gurlie. Did you have a hard labor with this one? Very easy, she was a little premature. Did she breathe right away? She did. And yelled too, said Gurlie. Did you nurse her?

No.

The doctor shook his head. Did you try? Yes, I tried, said Gurlie. Then you gave her the bottle. Did you have trouble then? Yes, said Gurlie, till an old German woman told me what to give her. I had no help from you doctors.

Did you consult a doctor?

Yes.

How many times?

Gurlie did not answer him.

Carefully the old man picked the baby up and carrying it to a scale weighed it. Then he measured it, the length and round the chest and round the head. He took the temperature and grunted. What have you been doing to her? he turned again to Gurlie. When was the last time you saw a doctor?

She was doing very well until she got the whooping cough.

So? The whooping cough. That's how you took care of her.

I didn't come here to be insulted, Gurlie flared up.

Insulted? That's what you mothers need, to be insulted, said the old man looking at her stonily. Here we have a female infant, he went on as if before a class. At one year she weighs seventeen pounds six ounces. She can't walk alone . . .

He ran his fingers up and down her spine.

But she is straight. No rachitis. No deformity of joints or bones. On the other hand the muscular development is weak and flabby. She is undernourished — he pulled the infant's lower eyelids down — and anemic. A very good child, he added. Indeed she was a good child, not making a sound of protest all the while. But now she got down on her knees and started to crawl off.

Come back here, said the doctor. He felt her head. The anterior fontanelle was still open. That's right, he said.

Oh, don't press there, said Gurlie. Won't that hurt her?

And a clean scalp. The integument of the limbs and body is clear. No rash. The finger nails a little pale but aside from that normal in shape and color.

He looked into the baby's mouth. The infant gagged and cried. Gurlie rushed to rescue her. Stop that! said the doctor. You do it once. You do it twice. And that's the end. She's ruined. I'm not killing her. Let her get used to it. Eight teeth. Good. The throat is clear. She hears. She sees. She is properly aware of things — for her age. You say she says a few words?

Oh yes, she's a regular chatter-box. She sits and talks to herself by the hour.

You take her out into the air sometimes?

She's out every day.

She doesn't look it, said the doctor. You mothers think that just because you put a child outside the door all wrapped up to the eyes that's out of doors. You're mistaken. Unless the sun gets on her body — it must touch the skin — it does no good. Someday, when you have learned sense, you mothers, the sense of animals, you'll take babies to the sun, in winter too, every baby, like they do now the sick in sanatoriums. Outside.

Isn't that the Kneipe cure? said Gurlie.

What's that — the Kneipe cure? We wear too many clothes. We dress our children up in wool like Esquimos. It breeds all kinds of sickness. We lock them up in caves with just the head stuck out. The skin must breathe . . .

Then you think the baby's all right, doctor?

Put on her clothes.

Gurlie began to dress the baby. But doctor, what can I do to make her eat? I've tried to force her but she spits it out.

Never do that! he roared. Never. What is she, a goose you're fattening for Christmas? If she won't eat, take the food away. And find the reason.

But I see so many bigger children.

How big is your husband?

He's not so big.

What do you expect then for a child, a mastiff?

But what shall I feed her?

Feed her anything she'll eat.

Anything?

Yes. Anything she'll eat.

She don't like milk.

The worst thing in the second year of life is too much milk. A pint a day's enough. Feed her eggs, pot cheese, fruits, meat, vegetables, raw and cooked. I had a baby that ate raw string beans and thrived on them. My friends call me a crank. That's right, I am. But I am peasant stock. There's not much to eat where I was born — and the children eat it and grow strong. With some exceptions.

But isn't it the air that does it? Gurlie questioned.

Here it's ice cream, sugar, candy, the doctor sneered. The little darling won't eat his dinner, mother has to give him a cookie afterward so he won't starve. And another because mother doesn't like to hear her baby cry. And still another after that — because he wants it. And a piece of chocolate. And some ice cream for dear mother — and the baby gets his share. The poor thing didn't eat his dinner! Sugar. That's what they live on. Naturally they won't eat.

Isn't sugar food?

No. Sugar's fuel. It takes the place of food.

But they like it, doctor.

Of course they like it. All they want to do is go. They don't care if the engine falls apart.

But you said give them anything they want.

Yes, anything they want.

I don't understand you, doctor. You said give them anything they want and then you say, don't give them sugar.

Sugar's not food I told you. Fuel. Do you understand?

Oh, yes.

Put the food before them, on time, regularly and well cooked. Without a word. They'll eat it. Unless they're ill. If they eat it — and want more, give them a little sugar. Sugar is the alcohol of children, to be used the same. And chocolate is their tea and coffee. Naturally they want it — it contains a drug. And drugs — are useful.

Yes, but you haven't told me what's the matter with my child. Gurlie had the baby near her on the couch.

But the doctor had got started by this time and would go on while Gurlie sat and listened.

I'm afraid there must be other patients waiting.

Let them wait. Yes, what's the matter with the child? That's what they ask me.

Isn't that what we come here for?

What's the matter with the child? It makes me laugh. The child's alive, that's what's the matter with the child. But now that I've examined her I have to tell you in three words just what's the matter. Then I should give you a big bottle of red medicine and presto! not only is she cured but it has made her beautiful, intelligent and strong as a bear. He laughed. That's what they come to doctors for. And if he doesn't do it he's a thief, a blackguard and in fact killed the child. Is it any wonder the profession's rotten through and through with cheats? What people want to buy there will be those to sell it to them always. I can't do that.

But doctor, you must give me some advice.

We'll come to that. What is the matter with the children? They are unhappy.

She's not unhappy.

Almost, one should say, they're born to be unhappy. Every generation kills the next's chances of being happy in its children — out of envy. Malice I tell you. And that grows up into wars. Hatreds, hatreds against the parents — that is the rulers — of the world. And what do we do about it? We build schools. Schools, mind you, those factories of despair. Fools, that's what it rhymes with. Fools who build them to the destruction of the natural ingenuity of childhood which should be learning the world, the world, mind you, and not the disappointments of elderly females who are in the menopause and cannot know the subtleties — of history — of mathematics. Bah. What can they know? To venture. To penetrate. To strike home.

The unfortunate little man was beside himself with just fury looking at Gurlie, as he walked up and down before her, where she sat, her strong legs crossed at the ankles, her hands in her lap, nodding her head vigorously in approval. You're right, she said. You're right. Yes, I know I'm right, he answered her. But what can I do about it?

Schools! he went on scornfully. That's our excuse for doing nothing. What is a school? It is a place where knowledge is forbidden. The first law is that a teacher and a pupil must not be intimate. It is a prison. It is a place to kill a child — with stupidities they drip into their heads one drop at a time until it stupefies them. Makes mules of them. And we can do nothing to prevent it. There is no knowledge to be got in schools, only make-believes of knowledge. An imitation of what knowledge is. A bad picture, painted by sick people. What kind of man is your husband? The doctor scowled. As big as you?

Oh yes, a little bigger than I am.

That's not so small then. A German?

Yes.

Well, I tell you. Whooping cough is not a good thing in the first year. I don't like your baby's chest, her lungs, you understand. But I can't put my finger on anything specific. And I can't say she won't be worse tomorrow. She seems to have a good heart. That's good, she'll need it. Fresh air. Sunlight. Take her away, I can do nothing for her.

No medicine? Nothing?

Nothing. Take her to the country, to the mountains. Give her good food.

But when? When must I go?

Now. At once. A summer in New York will kill her.

Gurlie came to with a start. I don't believe it.

That's your privilege my dear lady. The attendant will take care of you outside.

THE SECOND YEAR

CHAPTER XVI

Flight

W<small>ELL, WE'VE</small> been talking
here for the last half hour and we haven't decided
anything yet. Are we going to stand all summer and
look at her suffering?

Oh, you make me crazy, said his wife. Take her to
the country, then. Have you the money? You're always saying you're so poor.

Next day the fat auntie who had run over to hear
the doctor's verdict settled it by saying she knew just
the place, at least she was pretty sure it could be
arranged.

How much? said Joe.

I don't know, as long as you keep yourself, maybe
nothing. I don't know. Wait a couple of days. I have
a friend.

It must be around the north pole if it's for nothing,
said Joe after she had gone. I think we'd better look
for the address of some good boarding house in the
papers.

A boarding house! said Gurlie. Not on your life.
What do you think I am? I'd rather stay here. You sure
want to kill the lot of us. In the paper? That's about as
much sense as you have.

Well, that's what papers are for, aren't they? To
advertise what's for sale.

The fat auntie's hunch proved good. She was back
the next day with the whole thing written down on a

sheet of lined writing paper. The night boat to Troy, New York. The train from there to a place called Shelborn Falls, I think — somewhere, I don't know exactly where, but that's the name. Then a stage or a little train, she wasn't sure which, to another town about twenty miles up into the mountains. No, she had never been there but Hilda had and it was all right. Beautiful! No need to be afraid. An easy trip.

Beautiful! Yes, I can imagine, was Joe's comment.

But what kind of a place is this you're shipping me off to to get rid of me, said Gurlie. I don't want to go away somewhere where I can't get everything I need.

Agh! said Joe and stood up, taking out a cigar and turning his back to them.

What do you think I am? bridled Gurlie raising her voice. To go off alone somewhere with two children, no running water, no conveniences, no place where I can get help.

Gurlie, you ought to be ashamed of yourself. Nobody's trying to do anything to you. You ought to be ashamed.

Send her to Newport, remarked Joe over his shoulder from the window.

But just then the baby could be heard whimpering in the bedroom. With a great contortion of its body, jackknifing itself up into a sharp angle, it had rid itself once more of the foul excrement which had been tormenting it periodically for the past two weeks.

Phew! said the fat auntie when she got to it, that's awful. Poor little Spider.

Gurlie laughed at her but said, Well, what shall I do then?

Get your things packed, tonight. I'll help you. And

so it was agreed. Joe set his seal of approval to it on the spot. It would do Lottie good besides.

But you haven't told me the name of the place yet. Where is it?

Westminster, Vermont. It was a compatriot, in a sense, a fellow Scandinavian in any case, a Swede, who had the place. Or rather it was an old couple living alone there on a small farm, kept by their only daughter, Astrid's acquaintance, who managed a commercial laundry in the city. *Wunderschön!* High up on a hill, the finest spring water. Their own cows. Now, she can have fresh milk. The air is different. They are good, kind people.

How much will it cost? said Joe.

They are lonesome. I don't think it will cost anything except you will have to pay for what you eat. But you can give them something, a few dollars, if you want to. In the country they don't need much money.

Don't they have to pay taxes? said Joe.

Oh well, the fat auntie looked at him reprovingly.

All right, said Joe. What's the name?

Payson.

The address?

Just Westminster, Vermont, I think. E. Payson.

All right, said Joe writing it all down carefully in his vest pocket notebook with the gilt edged pages. And how do you get there?

By the Hudson River boat. I'll come in the morning to help you, said the fat auntie. Oh you darling, poor little Spider, she added going to say goodnight to the baby. Now, you're going to be fine. And in another few moments she went out the door where Joe was waiting in his shirtsleeves to lock it after her. Good night. And much obliged.

He went over to the baby's crib and wondered if it would last long enough to get there. Be sure to take everything you need, he said to Gurlie as he was taking off his collar in the stifling bedroom.

Get me the tickets and give me some money, that's all you have to think of. Where are you putting that shirt? He had thrown it behind the chiffonier. What an idea! What in the world do you do that for, you, a man that's supposed to have some sense? *Schweinerei!* his wife continued.

But this wasn't one of the lucky times for saying things like that. A flame of anger shot into Joe's eyes. Why don't you put a dirty-clothes basket where I can see it then? I can't put dirty things back in the drawer. I'm not going to throw them on the floor. And I won't have them lying around on the furniture where I can see them.

Here, give it to me. And she threw it into the closet.

That's right. Fill up the closet till it stinks.

No answer this time.

And don't get up there and begin writing me to send you this and send you that. Think *now* what you'll need and take it with you.

Oh, go to bed, said his wife in a milder voice. I wish they'd send you up into the mountains. You're the one that needs it.

Yes, said Joe. You stay home and run my business for me.

The next day was scorching as it so often is toward the end of June in New York City. But by the middle of the afternoon Gurlie and Astrid and the two children with all their miscellaneous small packages were on the L bound downtown. The house had been left as it was and the larger baggage had gone on ahead by express.

At 23rd St. they scrambled out, descended the stairs still swaying uncertainly from the departure of the train. Be careful you don't drop the baby. Be careful now. Be careful, said Gurlie to her sister.

There at the corner they took the horse-car. Then they had to transfer at West St. to get to the dock. The time was slipping by. This is awful, said Gurlie. Can't he make that man ahead of us get out of the way? I'd get out and tell him. This is too much.

Don't excite yourself, said her sister. We have time. What is the matter now?

A loaded truck was trying to pull out in front of the horse-car but the front wheels of it stuck in the tracks and it just skidded until the sweating horses stopped and would pull no longer, tossing their heads in a lather as they fidgeted about. Then a hot argument flared up between the truck driver and the old conductor of the horse-car who had gone ahead to investigate.

What are we going to do? said Gurlie.

Finally the front door slid open. The driver poked his head in. Hold on, he said. Then, slamming the door, he geed up his old plugs. They swerved suddenly, jerking the car bodily out of the tracks and had it rattling over the cobbles on its flanged iron wheels. He was pulling out around the stalled truck.

Oh! Oh! said Gurlie. He'll kill us. The windows rattled as if they would shatter into pieces at any moment. Oh! But they arrived at the pier finally to see Joe standing there at the entrance, his watch in his hand.

Whew! said Gurlie laughing. You see, smarty, we got here in time after all.

Yes, said her husband. Thank goodness the trunks came too. They're on board. Come on, hurry up.

Hurry up? said Gurlie. Why we have easily half an hour before the boat sails. Can't you take us to a restaurant or something?

You can eat supper on board, said Joe. Come on.

There were not more than ten or twelve people on the boat as yet. In fact, the purser's window wasn't even open.

Joe had to go and hunt up someone so as to get into the stateroom. They had to unlock the purser's office to get the key.

You make me tired, said Gurlie, bringing us to sit on these plush chairs for another hour on a day like this.

All about them were the noises of shiploading. A hand truck would come clattering up the gangplank, stop, bang! and off it would go again. They tried sitting outside but the heat and the smell and the noise were too much, besides the baby decided to fall asleep — probably as a result of the rigors of the trip downtown. So they took it into the carpeted little cabin and put it on the lower bunk. I'll stay here with it, said the fat auntie. The place was stifling. Lottie was thrilled with the long curving salon of the boat, the stairway, the long rows of cabin doors. Gurlie and Joe went outside. I think I better go now, he said.

Don't go away and leave me, she replied in a pretended, childish voice, pouting and taking hold of his arm. They were at the head of the gangplank up which now, finally, men, women and children were coming steadily. Don't go away and leave me.

For goodness' sake, said Joe, trying to push her off,

don't act like a fool. He looked around to see if she had been overheard. Quit it, he added frowning and ruffled.

I'm not going to see you for two months! she went on in her insistent childish imitation.

Agh! he answered and started down the gangplank.

Aren't you even going to kiss me? she called after him. He merely bowed his head stepping carefully over the laddered planking.

You come back here. That's no way to act. She leaned on the rail talking down to him where he stood three or four feet below her.

Good bye, he shouted over the continued clatter of the hand trucks, the laughing, and scuffling about him. I'll write you. Kiss the children for me.

Don't you go yet, said Gurlie. You've got nothing to do.

Agh! he replied.

Gurlie stopped one of the boat hands who was passing and turned to the rail again. The boat won't be leaving for a quarter of an hour yet.

Joe hated this leavetaking. I'm going, he called out, looking right and left to see if anybody was looking on at this disgusting scene. There was a man in a derby leaning against one of the iron posts of the pier twenty feet behind him who looked away when Joe turned. Good-bye. He raised his hand.

Wait a minute, said Gurlie. What's the matter with you? We're not going yet.

I've got something to do up at the house.

Oh, go on then, she said and made a motion as if she were pushing him away — half waving. Then as suddenly she walked over and came precariously waddling down the gangplank.

What's the matter with you? said Joe. You've left the

children alone with Astrid. The boat may be going any minute. Go back.

Ta, ta, ta, ta, ta! said Gurlie laughing now and kissing him roughly on the cheek to his intense mortification. She almost knocked his hat off. They can't leave me here. Don't be silly. And listen . . .

Go back to the boat.

Listen to me, Gurlie persisted. You're going to be alone in the city all summer. Don't do anything naughty. And take care of yourself. Eat properly — and take a bath once in a while.

Sh! he said. Not so loud.

Listen here, she shook her head as if to brush off his objections, if those people at the office don't give you a vacation so you can come and see us, I'd take one anyway.

Ja, ja! said Joe.

A bell rang. Go on, he said starting to push her ahead of him.

Remember, said Gurlie, and send your dirty things to the laundry. Don't throw them all over the room.

Joe had her on the gangplank now where she turned and kissed him again, then walked up to the ship with a final wave. But once on deck, she went to the rail once more. She wanted to tell him to ask for a raise. A trunk crashed as one of the hands took it up the gangplank on the run.

What? Joe put his hand to his ear.

The boat once out in the river heading upstream, the air was cool, people began moving about in a new world cut off from their former lives — even in this river cockle shell. The baby was asleep, the fat auntie had come up on deck for a moment also. A glorious night and Gurlie, after all, just in her twenty-fifth year. She remained on deck and stood by the rail watching the boats and the piers of upper New York. A tug-boat glided sighing by, a loaded ferry was loafing in the down tide waiting for them to pass. She could see the tide carry it. Then she walked across the deck to see the sun low over the Palisades and the darkness beginning to gather along their lower parts. It was magnificent, it was quieting. She took deep breaths of the river air and remained for a long time watching the sun getting lower and lower. Then sensing that it was time to feed the baby and perhaps eat a bite herself, she went inside.

A few older people were sitting in that rather stuffy interior. How can they with all that glorious air outside! she said to herself, with their packages beside them, people who had not taken cabins, didn't they have the price perhaps or were they too stingy? Five or six small children were running on the carpeted floor, jumping, already half acquainted, running in and out at the open doors. A cat stretched itself and yawned. And shaken by the steady beat of the paddle wheels an old negress in a white apron and with a feather duster clasped in her folded hands was falling asleep in a salon chair.

An officer in a blue uniform passed, looking sidewise at Gurlie as she came from the deck and began on the wrong side, looking for her cabin. But she found it soon, down a little white-enameled companionway — an outside room — and briskly opened the door.

Sh! said the fat auntie lifting her finger. It's asleep. And so it was, in the middle of the lower berth. Lottie's asleep too, in there. She pointed to her own cabin next door.

Why don't we eat then? said Gurlie. I want to go out on deck again. It's marvelous there.

You go, said her sister. I've seen it. No, I don't want to dress again. You go and get yourself some supper. I'll just eat a sandwich and the stewardess can bring me a cup of tea if you'll tell her. No, I'll stay here.

Gurlie was restless to get on deck again. She too took a sandwich from the supper they had brought, feeling that it wasn't necessary to go down to the tables on a boat like this. She did want a cup of coffee, though.

Go on, said her sister. You can get coffee. Go on up on the deck. You go up and get the fresh air, it will do you good. I'll lie here on the lounge. Go on.

So Gurlie went out, had her coffee and returned to the deck once more. It had grown much darker. In the west over the Palisades which they were still passing a cherry red sunset flared into the sky. But lights were already out in the few houses on both sides of the river. She stood in the wind watching the Palisades whose long outline was strong on the illuminated sky. Strong feelings moved in the woman's breast — ships, the floating delights of sailing, the smells of it.

As she stood there watching and breathing deeply of the evening air, people passed behind her talking quietly. A beautiful evening. There's the moon.

Well, we all have our fling, a deep, slow voice began, but the most of us settle down, and make the best of it later.

Yes, said a high woman's voice, me too.

Gurlie raised one foot up on an iron cleat to change her position, lifting her long skirt slightly and stood entranced with the scene, restless, wondering what it was all about. Sailing away. Nature is marvelous, she

said to herself over and over. Mother Nature, that's
what we need.

She was not at first conscious of a man a little way
along the rail from her who too was leaning watching
the Palisades, a man in a straw hat smoking a cigarette.

Gurlie smelt the smoke of the cigarette which, in
fact, passed just under her nose. She turned to look.
The man also was looking. She quickly turned the
other way and walked out along the rail toward the
prow of the boat.

Fifteen minutes later, well up in the prow where she
had found a place with her back to the pilot house
and the lights of Haverstraw beginning to be visible
across the broad Tappan Zee, again she felt that someone was watching her.

She didn't want to go in, she was enjoying the hard,
steady breeze, dreaming, travelling through the air,
through the night . . .

The man came and stood almost beside her. If he
speaks to me, I'll slap his face, she thought. What kind
of people are there in the world, anyway?

The man had done nothing so far but stand there.
But now he turned and looked directly at her smiling.
A lovely night, isn't it? he commented.

Yes, she said, it's a beautiful night. He spoke pleas-
antly in a nice way but moved a little closer to Gurlie
along the rail. Do you often make this trip? he asked.

Sometimes, said Gurlie.

I have heard of the Hudson River all my life, said
the man. It's quite up to expectations. I come from
Milwaukee.

Gurlie did not reply. Then she changed her mind.
Are you with your family? She was going to add that
she was travelling with her sister and two children but

somehow it didn't seem to be the thing to say when it came just to saying it.

No, I'm alone, the man replied turning full face toward her, and you?

My children are asleep, said Gurlie ambiguously. Then wondered why she had put it just that way.

Good, said the man. Have you had supper?

Yes, said Gurlie, determined to be very short this time. What time do we arrive in Troy, do you know?

We are scheduled to arrive at about seven A.M. I believe. Don't you find the wind rather damp up here?

No, said Gurlie, I like it. Yes, but I think you really should have a coat if you intend to stay here very long. Fresh! thought Gurlie to herself. I don't feel cold, she replied.

There was a moment's silence.

You're sure I couldn't help you — in any way, said the man finally, turning his face again toward Gurlie, I feel myself as if I need a nice warm drink, something to warm me up for the evening.

Gurlie didn't want to leave the deck of the ship, she had been perfectly content, ideally happy, in fact, before this intruder had come to annoy her. She didn't want to go in and she couldn't tell him to leave her alone. After all, she felt sorry for the man. Agh, she'd better go. Yes, you're right, it's getting cold here, she said, I think I'll go in.

I wish you wouldn't, said the man, looking squarely into her eyes. Gurlie's eyes shifted, then she raised them and looked straight back at him. Hum! she said shrugging her shoulders and turned and left him.

In the morning they were at Troy.

CHAPTER XVII

The Country

At Troy the fat auntie bid them good-bye, on the train for Shelborn Falls. Wherever that is, said Gurlie. Lottie pressed her nose against the window smiling and waved her hand vaguely to the big woman standing outside. They couldn't open the window. What? She was saying something. Never mind, she signaled with her hands and head, smiling. Good-bye, and she went walking down the platform and disappeared. All gone, said Lottie.

The baby was sitting up on a seat opposite her mother, a seat which had been turned over to give them a little compartment to themselves. A man came by selling candy. Lottie gave him a broad grin but nothing happened. And so they were off.

The baby hadn't done badly on the trip so far, which was quite characteristic of her, she usually did well when it was necessary. For the most part, on the boat, when not asleep she had been content to sit with intensely serious face looking around as if listening. It may have been the noise of the engines. She made little resistance when lifted, shifted. From the boat to the train she had felt tight holds and slipping grasps in complete relaxation. The sun in her eyes, she had blinked, screwed up her face. Going into the tunnel dark she had stretched her eyes wide open.

Smells were new. Voices that were familiar were interrupted by strange sounds. She merely turned and stared, as if questioning. Now she wanted to sit up or stand when she was made to lie down. Now she wanted to remain lying when, ill supported, she was made to stand. She wanted food when none was at hand, was attracted by new sights when food was offered — and looked away from it. Then ate.

In the main, though, she offered no serious objections to anything. And she was dry. That's wonderful, said the fat auntie. She had travelled well.

At Shelborn Falls only about ten people got down. They were in the middle of high green mountains, a swift, shallow stream could be heard occasionally between the shouts, the shufflings and the steady throbbing of the engine at rest. Then the conductor gave his signal, the trainman took it up, the engineer rang his bell and there the woman and the two small children were left in the country.

For a moment Gurlie was at a loss what to do, then seeing her trunk going off with two or three others on a hand wagon up ahead, she followed after, the baby in her arms, Lottie behind her. Is this where we take the train for Westminster? Yes'm, right here — in about two hours. What! said Gurlie. The man didn't give any other answer but continued slowly pushing the heavy hand truck up the platform to another on a curving spur which Gurlie noticed now coming in to meet the main line from the north. The man got the truck where he wanted it, blocked the wheels with a piece of cord-wood, hooked the handle upright and shambled off to the station house in the angle between the two tracks. By the time Gurlie got there, he had gone inside. She went in also.

Most of the other passengers from the Albany train were sitting around in the waiting room with their things. The ticket window was closed. Well, this is the country all right, said Gurlie to herself. Two hours! Whew. It was already almost noon and the baby needed a bottle. No hot water. I wonder if there's a toilet. Nothing, except a small shelter off to the rear with two doors in it: Men — Women.

The baby was fed a cold bottle which Astrid had prepared on the boat that morning. After Gurlie changed her, she wanted to walk. So Gurlie took her outside and they walked up and down. It was beautiful out of doors and as silent as the middle of a field. The shuffle of the baby's small feet on the rough planking of the station walk sounded actually loud to the slow stepping of her mother beside her. The continual rustle of the broad shallow river rushing over its many stones served as an accompaniment. A small breeze picked up the dust. A few sparrows chirped in the roadway. Flies buzzed. Far at the other end of the platform two men walked up and down talking and smoking. The village was close by but Gurlie had no desire to go to it.

Instead, she went on, then continued up the other platform, walking slowly with the baby until she came to the hand truck to see if it was really her trunk they had after all. Two or three of the other passengers were there ahead of her standing around somewhat self-consciously, saying a word now and then and smiling. As she came up, they turned their backs.

There was a curious odor about this part of the platform. Gurlie stopped short. Why, that's whisky. She went closer, then she heard it — drip, drip, drip! It was coming from under the baggage. She laughed. What do you think of that? The others turned where they were and continued smiling. But nobody made another move. So, as soon as she saw that her own baggage was out of the drip, Gurlie turned and went back the way she had come.

Vermont being a dry state, this was a shipment of spirits going disguised in a burlap bag from Massachusetts. One of the bottles must have been cracked when the lot was thrown from the baggage car onto the truck.

The mountains all around them were covered with woolly green and over one of them a large bird, an eagle, slowly wheeled — not a sound once more but the river, the patter of the baby's feet and Gurlie's slow heel strokes, hesitating and beginning again beside them. No, no! The baby wanted to pick up a white button which lay upon the boards. Gurlie held her away from it by the hand.

Then, without warning, the huge engine of a fast moving freight burst with a terrifying crash into the station. The children and Gurlie too were scared almost out of their wits. It wasn't six feet from where they were walking. The ground shook, dust and cinders flew, the light was cut off and then rattling and thumping, clump-clump, clump-clump, it roared by and was gone. Gurlie took the children into the station again. Lottie's eyes were half closed with the dirt. And the baby was crying.

It was cool in there and practically empty now. There was just one woman there, in fact, in a blue mother hubbard, with three children about her, one Lottie's age and two somewhat older. She had several small bundles at her side but one big valise which Gurlie saw her open and from it take four apples which she gave, one to each of the children. They were a poorly dressed, timid looking lot, so Gurlie, bored with waiting and looking around for something to do, went over to talk to them.

Are you waiting for the same train I am?

Yes'm, I suppose so. Whar be you goin', to Westminster?

Yes, said Gurlie, Do you live there?

Well, not exactly, said the woman, but I used to. I hain't been thar for more'n thirty year tho'. Thought I'd like to go back and see the folks.

Well, now, said Gurlie, that's interesting. Are they all still alive there?

Were last time I heard of them, laughed the woman, about two weeks ago. I bin livin' out near Chicago ever since I quit here right after the war. Wasn't more'n a girl.

You'll find the place changed, said Gurlie, remembering what she had heard from the fat auntie of the popularity of the pretty village as a summer resort since the narrow gauge road had been built to it in recent times.

'Spect I will, said the woman.

Did you bring those apples from the west? asked Gurlie in her usual outspoken manner. That's quite a big bag to carry all that distance.

Yes, 'twas pretty heavy at first. But we et 'em pretty fast. Most gone now. Don't take three young uns long to finish a bag of apples on a trip like this. Like to have one? asked the woman.

No thanks, said Gurlie, you keep them for the children.

Like the big girl to have one?

Yes, said Gurlie.

They're baldwins, said the woman. Grew them on our own place. She your daughter? Here you are, sis, try one of these. And she rubbed the apple up in the palm of her hand before handing it to Lottie who took it shyly. Pretty head of hair she has, them black curls. Must be from her father. You stayin' in Westminster long?

Just for the summer, said Gurlie. I wish to heaven that train would get here. You'd think they'd plan to make better connections.

Guess it don't pay 'em much to bother about it, said the woman in her practical voice.

Then in another half hour Gurlie heard the far whistle and finally the approaching noise of the narrow gauge train.

The ticket window opened with a snap and everybody came to purchase their passes.

There was the engine, then, after it, its tender, next a freight car, then the baggage car and finally at the end, a passenger coach with the name Hoosack Tunnel and Westminster R. R. painted in gold letters in full on it and the initials only, H. T. & W. on the tender — the Hoot, Toot, and Whistle as some local wag had nicknamed it.

There was quite a bit of backing, to get the engine shunted around. Then the passengers got in. The freight was loaded — with a laugh for the spilled whisky — and finally they got off.

To Gurlie it was at first a relief, then a source of alarm. The whole thing rocked so, and what curves! And what grades! It wasn't more than a twenty mile run up the Deerfield Valley but at places Gurlie thought it more a goat than a railroad train she was riding. Directly below she could see the river and that's all she could see. This is awful! she cried half aloud fearful lest the movement of her body in the thing would tip it over. But nobody else seemed disturbed so when the little train went scuttling across fields again, she relaxed and thought, at last, we are there.

The engine gave a sigh of relief after the two hour ramble and went to sleep breathing quietly on the dead end track in the middle of rows of piled up cordwood — until tomorrow. Railroad men became country men again as soon as they'd taken off their cloth caps and put on their ordinary coats. Several tall middle aged farmer types came over to the baggage car and leaning their arms on the door edge, looked in. Another group, men mostly, quietly watched the passengers alighting, waving a hand occasionally to someone and coming forward. There was no hurry. How are you? They seemed shy, not wanting to make a show of their emotions. Someone took the mail bag and went off with it on his shoulder to the village.

There was no one to meet Gurlie. No one paid any attention to her with the baby and small child. But she was content for the moment — the very air was different — you could feel it at once. She saw a young man with a horse and carriage over by the side of the station and asked him if he knew where the Paysons lived.

No, he didn't know that but, if she wanted someone to take her up there, he thought she'd find a young man around behind the station would do it for a dollar. There's usually a carriage you can hire if someone else doesn't get it first.

Yes, I know where 'tis. Over past Ray Pond. I'm driving up that way in about ten or fifteen minutes. I'll come back and pick you up. I got these things to take in to the town first.

In an amazingly short time, in spite of their slow movements, everyone had disappeared, even the engineer and the rest of the crew were gone, the baggage had been carted off and not a soul could be seen but one man in a blue striped denim suit.

Gurlie was worried. Oh, he'll be along after a while, the man assured her. If he said he'd do it, he'll be back. You don't need to worry. Stay right where you are.

So there Gurlie stayed, on that beautiful afternoon, waiting with her children. Just back of the station was a low whitepainted wooden house with a shed stretching off behind the kitchen connecting it with the barn. Back of that again she could see that the ground dipped down suddenly to a small stream and in the front yard, a lawn of deep, bright green grass, was a profusion of flowers. Gurlie felt the peace of the place already a benediction.

The carriage came. Gurlie and the children climbed into the back seat. The trunk was loaded up beside the driver and they were off, a little brown mare turning and trotting down the steep hill from the station, across the bridge and into the village at a round clip. It was a smooth dirt road. They turned right at the crossroads in the center of the town and now on the upgrade the carriage went more slowly.

Is this Westminster? said Gurlie.

Yes, ma'm.

Just this?

Well there are a good many farms around here but this is what we call town.

On both sides were the low, whitepainted Vermont houses of those who had made enough money to come and live by their neighbors. Back of this narrow fringe on the two main streets whose crossing made the business section of the town with its post office, drug store, bank, and general supply store, the rolling fields stretched out again rising to the near hills with other farther hills behind them — a house here, another there in the distance, cattle feeding — and dark heavily wooded hills beyond.

Peaceful it was and the air magnificent. So this was Vermont of which she had heard so much from her Scandinavian friends.

How far is the Payson farm?

Oh, about three miles, I guess.

What's happened to all the people around here? asked Gurlie. Where are they? She had hardly seen a soul since they started out, just a few shabby children chasing a dog, barefooted and bareheaded, near an unpainted house on the outskirts of the village.

Working I guess. They're around.

What do they do? Farm, I suppose.

No, not much. Most work in the pulp mill. Farming doesn't pay much around here. Some farms though. No money in it these days.

Gurlie couldn't believe it, for there was nothing but grassy pastureland and cultivated fields on all sides of them. And they looked to be thriving too.

I should think it would be wonderful grazing country, she said. I see some cows over there on the hill.

Yes, most places keep a few cows. Can't get along without cows in the country. Cows and chickens.

But isn't there a creamery here?

Yes, there's a creamery but it don't amount to much with the hauling and feed costing what it does today.

I should think you'd raise your own feed. I see most of the farms here have silos on them.

The boy looked sideways at her wondering how much she knew. Can't feed more'n a few cows through the winters here on the silage they keep.

Don't they raise beef?

Most people around here eats western beef. It's cheaper.

But it can't be as good as local beef with this beautiful grass to feed on.

No, it isn't as good but it's cheaper.

Isn't there any prize stock?

Not much.

What about sheep?

Costs too much for fences. I've heard say there used to be money in sheep up here but nobody but a few can make anything on them now and they can't make much. A few raise some prize sheep. Not many though.

What about horses? Don't you need horses? Somebody has to sell them.

There's a few good horses but they got better ones up in New Hampshire. The Morgan horses. You've heard of them.

But isn't there any industry, don't any of the farms pay? Doesn't anybody make any money?

Oh yes, a few make money but they ain't making it today. Most leave and go to the city when they get a chance.

What about maple syrup?

Don't amount to much.

Now, there's a lovely place, said Gurlie pointing to a rambling white house on a hill surrounded by big maple trees.

Yes'm, but he didn't make his money in this place. He's a lawyer down in Boston. Had the place made over last year. Comes up here mostly in summer now. Maybe around Christmas sometimes for the children.

A lovely place, said Gurlie, all admiration.

It costs him plenty to keep it up. Those were his cows you saw back on the hill. Fancy stock.

But didn't I see a factory of some sort down in the town? said Gurlie.

That's the mill. They been laying off men this spring already. They do pretty well when they're busy. It's the only place aside from the lumbering you can make anything at.

What about lumber? Gurlie asked.

Pulpwood. Most of it's been bought up though by the big companies.

What about real estate?

Are you interested in buying a place? asked the young man.

Oh, no, no, said Gurlie. Everything is so peaceful. Why do people live in cities when there are beautiful places like this in the world?

Got to have money to live, said the young man. Can't make money up here unless you got it to start with.

Oh, I don't think you know anything about it, said Gurlie finally, laughing. There must be some way to live up here.

Get up, said the young man to the mare as he flicked her lightly with the end of the whip. She shook her head slightly and Gurlie's head went back as the carriage started more rapidly forward.

Where does that road go to? Gurlie spoke again after a moment.

Down through Jacksonville and Colerain to Greenfield, about twenty miles.

And where does this road take you?

Brattleboro. This is what they call the Molly Stark trail. Starts at Bennington about twenty miles west.

And how far is Brattleboro?

About eighteen to twenty miles.

It was an enchanting spectacle to Gurlie, rolling hills, then as the road took a turn they entered a little glen, almost a tunnel of leaves, with a steep embankment to the left made up of small balsams and heavy underbrush while to the right went off sharply a stony bank to a tumbling stream churning itself white over large rocks. A cooling air came up from this small chasm.

The little mare trotted steadily on past several other forks in the road then fell into a walk. They were going sharply uphill now.

It seems quite a distance, said Gurlie.

Not much further, said the boy. I thought at first you might be going down to the lake. They got a fine new place down there. Regular hotel. Worth seeing if you have the time some day. Lots of city people come up here during the summer now.

They can have it, said Gurlie. I can imagine.

Then, unexpectedly, the horse turned to the right, leaving the highway, and began to climb a side road all grown with grass down the center. Just two tracks for the wheels either side. They bumped over several large rocks.

Is this it? said Gurlie.

Well, it's up this way. I think we can make it.

What!

It's pretty bad up a little further, I haven't been up here this year but, if it hasn't been washed out, I guess we'll get through.

Oh, said Gurlie as they heaved to one side going over a large flat rock in the road, be careful.

You don't need to worry, ma'm.

The road took a steady turn for a few hundred feet then entered a grassy cleared place. Across from it was a small barn. The horse was a little out of wind so the boy stopped for a moment.

Is this it? said Gurlie.

No, ma'm. This is the Conway place. Where you want to go is right up the hill there. You can't see it from here.

You mean we have to go up through those bushes and trees. Why I don't see any road at all.

It's there, all right. Come on, Sally.

Gurlie was straining nervously ahead as the carriage lurched from side to side. The road seemed to go almost straight up through heavy brush which switched against the sides of the carriage as they went through. The road was pretty badly washed out. Finally the underbrush ended. They came into a field where the horses' hoofs sounded soft and muffled. Ahead was the house, quite on the hilltop and, looking back, half frightened, Gurlie saw off to the north, a wide panorama of down-sloping field, undulating wooded eminences, the corner of a glinting lake and, beyond that, hill after hill and mountain after mountain as far as the eye would take her. The sky was blue, clouds hung in white patches . . .

Here y'are, said the man. He had driven over the thick grassy lawn right around back to the house itself. A handful of cats flew before the equipage, turning, half way to the barn, to look back, then walking on slowly and disappearing.

So Gurlie had brought the baby to the country.

The little thing was fast asleep now in her arms, her head thrown back showing the frail neck, her hat awry but, anyway, here she was.

She had seemed especially happy in the carriage — freed from the small spaces and reflected sounds, the shudder of the boat, the unrelenting clatter and shivering of the train — in the open air to the easy rocking as they went over the soft dirt road. The occasional bumps and jerkings left her unaffected. Now everything was quiet. She opened her eyes.

CHAPTER XVIII

The Payson Place

NOBODY SAID ANYTHING. The driver had jumped to the ground and was hitching his horse to an old post in the grass at the back of the house. There was the usual woodshed, nearly empty and further on some unpainted barns. A few chickens were pecking around in the sunny place in front of the woodshed.

Nobody appeared. The man began to lift the trunk off the carriage.

Well, said Gurlie, they must be out. Then, to Lottie, be careful. The man came and took the children lifting them to the ground also. Both of them stood there as if made of wood, looking at the soft grass where they were standing. Then the baby's legs wobbled and she sat down. Gurlie got down also and picked up the baby.

Whoo hoo! she called out loudly. Anybody home?

An old man with a bucket in his hand came out slowly from the barn and stood looking at them. He came slowly up the path. Gurlie waved her hand to him. He took off his hat, putting the bucket down at the same time and moved a little faster as he came toward them. Lottie got behind her mother. The driver had the trunk down now and was lifting off the smaller bundles.

Is this Mr. Payson? said Gurlie to the old man, speaking in Norwegian.

Yes, he answered, and whom have I the pleasure of addressing?

Didn't Gudrun write you?

No, was the answer as he shook his head slowly.

What! said Gurlie. Anyhow, they had arrived, letter or no letter. So Gurlie paid the boy who had brought them his dollar. He thanked her, tipped his hat, and drove off, backing and turning the carriage with much stamping and cutting of the turf as he did so. Well, here they were.

Why, you're entirely alone here, said Gurlie feeling as if she had been dropped from the sky into some inaccessible wilderness. She looked at the carriage retreating and for a moment seemed as if about to call it back.

No, we're not alone, said Mr. Payson, we have neighbors. Let's go inside. They went in by the kitchen way over a big slab of grey stone which seemed as if the house had started from that point in its building. On opening the door, they caused a little old lady to look up and to start hurriedly putting the work she was doing out of her lap. Gurlie went to her and kissed her.

She's deaf as a post, said Mr. Payson coming near. Then he shouted close to his wife's ear as she leaned to understand him. This is Mrs. Stecher. You know, the one Gudrun wrote to us about in the winter.

Oh, said the old lady, smiling sweetly and taking Gurlie's hands in hers. I'm so glad to see you. When did you come?

They are going to stay with us, shouted her husband.

The old lady looked at him, startled and serious. Why didn't Gudrun tell us? But then she took notice of the children and seemed very pleased. Come, come in here, she said and took them up two steps into the cozy, sunny parlor with its smell of disuse and old furniture.

Come said Mr. Payson coaxingly to Lottie who was a little bashful. Come, let us see if we can find any eggs. So shyly at first, laying off her coat and hat, she finally went off with him hand in hand while Gurlie, the baby and the little deaf old lady went upstairs where the young man who had brought them had taken the trunk.

It was a larger house than you'd think on first seeing it, as it had been built close down in a little dip of the land on the hilltop. Downstairs was the parlor, a dining room, the ample kitchen and beyond that a bedroom where the mistress, now in New York City, stayed when she was there. Then of course, by a passage which served as a sort of cold pantry, came the woodshed and so to the barns. Upstairs were five bedrooms, making six in all, two large ones and three small with low ceilings and all of them, with beds made, carpet on the floor and ready for service.

Gurlie took it all in at a glance. She'd already noticed the handpump beside the sink in the kitchen. There were wash basins and a large water pitcher in each room with a porcelain slop receiver beside them. But the air was magnificent. You could sense it even here indoors. She looked from each window she passed, the valley opened out beyond a straggling orchard to the north while southward a newly planted field, which she could see now from the second story occupied the top of the hill on a little higher level than the house itself. Mr. Payson and Lottie appeared for a moment in the barnyard and disappeared again into another enclosure.

Well, here they were sure enough. They'd have to make the best of it now.

The old lady was smiling as if she thought something had been said to her.

No, Gurlie said, shaking her head, I didn't say anything. The old lady leaned closer and put up her hand. What was that? That will do, said Gurlie shouting. I want to go outside and look around. This deafness was going to be the end of her if she had to yell like that all summer. She felt that she was running away. She had to. Maybe if she could once get a little used to it.

Let me take care of the baby? said the old lady.

Yes, said Gurlie, with relief. She should be fed now. Come, she beckoned and they went down to the kitchen. With hot water that was on the fire Gurlie mixed up a bottle of condensed milk, which she had brought with her fortunately, put it into the old lady's hand, motioned to her to take the baby and went out. Whew!

Gurlie loved the feel of a farm as she hated restraint of all sorts. She had been almost ready to scream with irritation at the smiling woman before her in the house. But the minute she walked out on the grass and had a chance, alone, unconstrained to look around, she was satisfied. She knew she could make a go of it. She took deep, repeated breaths of the sweet air and went off for a few rods walking on the soft grass along the bank west of the house. There after a moment she sat down facing again the magnificent view, northward, which she had first seen on arriving.

She laid her bare hands on the grass, then she lay back in it stretching out her arms, resting her head on the soft turf. But, unsatisfied, she sat up again, took off her shoes and stockings and stood there wiggling her toes, moving her feet up and down. Way below her now she could see the corner of what seemed to be a lake. Her twitching nerves were growing quieter. She sat down again, beginning to rest, the grass was thick, thick and full of all sorts of other leafy growing things which didn't seem to kill it, strange to say, up here. So this is Vermont. With her mouth closed, as children had been taught to breathe in her day, she deeply drew the deliciously scented air of the place into her lungs. This is what I need! Probably it wouldn't be any trouble in such a place to get some pine tar water to drink. Rested, she fell to thinking. After all, the old lady might be very useful, as she was this moment. It wasn't Gurlie that was going to sit still on that hilltop all summer and be tied by small children.

The ground when she stamped on it sounded hollow, compact, resilient. Where it was turned over nearby, it looked like some sort of rich cake. These pockets of locked-in loam in the hollows of old mountains reminded her of all that she remembered of Norway.

There were a number of Scandinavian families about there, she had heard. Fun to hunt them out. Some years before, there had been a land development company which had bought up a number of the abandoned farms in this region, on speculation. Good small farms with serviceable houses and barns on them, the soil rich and productive but — the people had left them to go west or nearer to a money market. The company had made a play of advertising what they had in the shipping cities of Sweden, the Swedes being a thrifty, desirable race who were migrating heavily to America at that time. The thing never caught on too well but the low prices asked did bring on a few families. Some even came east from as far off as Wisconsin. Emma P had been one of these. She wanted to be nearer New York.

As a girl her family had been well to do. She was a sturdy sort and had gone to college, taking the agricultural course, farm management. Then the family went broke.

Emma never quite forgave the old people. But having plenty of determination, she came to America, set herself up at what she could do, married, unhappily, returned from the west to the big city and then, when her old parents arrived in America, sent them up there.

Leaning back in the grass, Gurlie put her hand on some chicken dirt and, feeling besides a sort of dampness in the air, decided to put on her shoes and stockings again and go back to the house. But seeing the old man heading toward the barn once more with Lottie close behind him, she thought she'd take a look there herself first.

He was getting ready to milk.

Have you a horse here? asked Gurlie sticking her head in at the shed door.

No, said the old man looking up.

What! why how do you get to town?

We don't go very often. We don't need many things. We have milk and eggs and . . .

Gurlie had turned and started for the house. There she found old Mrs. Payson sitting by the window which overlooked the valley holding the baby in her arms and talking to it softly as she rocked back and forth before the window, singing very quietly.

It's getting late, shouted Gurlie at her. Yes, nodded the old woman. Can't I help you get supper ready? At this, the old lady stood up, placed the baby on a blanket on the floor, and turned with a rather serious face to Gurlie.

We haven't very much for supper tonight, she said, I meant to tell you. We eat so little. We have six eggs and plenty of milk . . .

You have some bread, said Gurlie, that's all we need.

Oh yes, the old lady smiled back at her. So she went to a cupboard in the passage leading to the woodshed and brought out a third of a loaf of white bread which, before she could wipe it off, Gurlie saw was all mouldy on the cut end.

Oh! said Gurlie.

The old lady was very much confused.

Gurlie patted her on the back and laughed. That's nothing, she said, cut that end off and we'll have toast.

Oh, we have a little butter, the old lady went on. And there is a jar of preserve.

The truth was, as Gurlie soon discovered, that there wasn't another thing in the house. Why, what can Gudrun be thinking of, she said to herself aloud, why they're starving to death. And she began to take things into her hands forthwith.

That's all right, she reassured the old lady. I'll take care of everything. You have plenty of wood left. Put some water on to boil again. We'll have eggs and milk. You have some salt, haven't you?

The old lady laughed at such a silly question. Of course, there was salt.

Then everything is all right. I have brought con-

densed milk for the baby. Everything is all right. And
out she went top speed to talk to the old man. She had
to get to town.

No, he didn't think he'd like to ask Mr. Pike for his
horse tonight. He was very helpful, very kind. But it
wouldn't be wise to take advantage of him. He lived
down the hill, right where the side road turned off,
the small house to the left — but.

Gurlie was gone.

The first thing she did was to borrow a piece of
writing paper from Mrs. Payson and compose a letter
to her hostess. Gudrun: You come up here right away,
she said to that person, in her decided manner. Why,
these old people are starving to death. What do you
mean, leaving them up here this way without a horse
and not even a piece of bread in the house? Get somebody to take your place if you have to, but come. I
can't stay here this way.

Then she took money from her purse, took the
addressed letter in her hand and waving as much as to
say, don't concern yourself with me, started down the
overgrown carriage way down the hill to find Pike's
farm.

Half way down, she came to the Conways where
she stopped and spoke to a woman she saw there, who
happened to be Mrs. Conway, and asked her where she
could find the Pike place.

Why, it's terrible, said Gurlie to the woman, to leave
those two old people up there that way. I can't understand it.

No, Mrs. Conway agreed, it's been pretty hard on
them, I guess. We do what we can for them but they
won't take anything and, being foreigners, we have a
hard time to find out just how things are. We look up

every night to see if the light's burning and, as long as it is, we feel they must be all right.

I don't see how they can possibly live there in winter, said Gurlie.

Well, they did have a man up there last fall who filled their woodbin for them and put hay into the barn. But I guess things have been getting pretty low recently. You'll find Mr. Pike's place down at the bottom of the road. Doubt if he'll be going in to town tonight though.

Gurlie got a promise that her letter would be mailed early next morning. No use taking it down there tonight, Mr. Pike told her. It won't go out till nine o'clock anyway you put it. Why, yes, if you can get down here early enough, the boy can take you down when he goes. Glad to have met you. You folks up here for the summer? Guess they'll be glad to have company up there.

Supper turned out better than Gurlie had thought. Lottie who didn't like eggs, ate one fried — as she was never allowed to have them at home — nevertheless. Even asked for another, fixed so there was nothing runny about it and not greasy either as the old lady knew wisely how to prepare them.

Really it was wonderfully cozy there in the kitchen where the old people were accustomed to take their repasts, the oil lamp burning, leaving the corners in dark shadows. All this we lose, said Gurlie to the old fellow, as she felt again the closeness, the intimacy, of such life in the country. Soothed, quieted, the whole small company sat and ate, the baby along with them. There was bread, too, since Gurlie brought out the lunch her sister had over-abundantly prepared the day before.

They even laughed. The cats wove under their legs after they had got used to the newcomers, but you couldn't catch them. The cow mooed distantly in her stall. But the sense of isolation, of peace, of satisfaction, kept them mostly silent. Just the click of forks, the movements of chairs.

What a beautiful country, said Gurlie once again when they had finished their simple meal. I wonder if all those people we see in New York know what is here.

The old man nodded his head, doubtfully. If we could be rich it would be fine to have a place here in summer.

Rich! Yes, that would be something. Oh, how I should like to be rich! That's why we come here, isn't it? Would we have come here otherwise.

With only a little money, I could be happy here, said the old man.

But you must have money, said Gurlie. We are all the same, we that come from the other side. We didn't come here for love of the country, but to better ourselves. How can we love this country? We are from Europe. That's our country. That old love of home sticks to the second and third generation. That's why America is all for greed. This wasn't our land. It belonged to the Indians. It will take a long time to get a love for it like we had on the other side.

I think it is not so strong there either in these days, said the old man. There is too much injustice.

Yes, but there it's a different feeling anyhow. Here, we don't care. Nobody cares. If you go to jail and you make money anyhow, who cares? But when we lost everything in Norway, and my father wanted me to work, do you think I would do it? I should say not.

Do you think I would take a job in a house or a store? I was too proud. But when I came here, what difference did it make? I didn't care any more.

That was because nobody knew you, said the old man.

No, said Gurlie. It wasn't that. I saw everybody doing the same so I wanted money too. In Europe when there was no longer a place for us, we came to America. When a young man would do something he shouldn't have done, send him to America. America took the place of the convent. If a girl would forget herself, to America. Then it's natural that they are the people who make the country.

Sometimes it was the best people in the village who would have to go away, said the old man.

But we should be fair, Gurlie went on, I never liked this country, except for the one thing. But now that I see this place, I think I could be happy here too. I suppose if we should go back there, after being here, we wouldn't like it. It's too slow. Everything is embroidered. I think now it would make me crazy. I should want to push them. Everything is set. Everyone stays in his own class. Here it is wider, bigger, everyone is the same — unless you have money. There is more opportunity to expand. I don't think you could live over there after you get used to here — except when you are already old.

The old man tried to make clear to his wife what they had been talking about. She smiled and nodded without making any comment.

But I hate the city, said Gurlie. To me a tree and a bush can talk. I love nature.

When the children were asleep and the old people about to retire, Gurlie determined on her part to go out for a lonely walk. The night seemed to fly at her as she left the kitchen door. Her head somewhat bowed, watching her step at the doorway, she could see absolutely nothing. She stood still. Not a sound. As she moved shuffling, feeling her way to the edge of the big stone step — things began to grow a little clearer.

Quickly as her eyes grew accustomed to it, she saw an absolutely cloudless night without a moon. She felt a coldish wind blowing from around the house's western corner. She went in that direction, silently, on the grass, to stand looking away down the hill again where she had stood in the afternoon.

A blue white mist lay heavily in the valley whose black outlines of trees and low bushes along a serpentine brook stood out here and there in the patches of mist between them.

But it was the absolute silence that held Gurlie in a kind of awe. Not a sound, not even an insect sound could she discover. She put her hand up to her ears as if to clear them and heard only the brushing of her fingers against the flesh.

She did not move after that but stood there listening. Then far off in the darkness toward the heavily wooded mountain, there sounded a hollow but clear trumpeting, who, who, who, who! each syllable distinct, softened by distance. Who, who, who, who! Again. Again.

Gurlie shivered and went back into the house.

CHAPTER XIX

Country Rain

The next day it rained, as it can rain in the country — in Vermont! To Lottie who was up early and had dressed herself it could be seen, from her low bedroom window, raining still far off into the distance, curtains of it drifting and falling.

Tip-toeing into the hall she got safely past her mother's door and started timidly down the dark stairs. Suddenly a door at the bottom opened taking away her breath and letting in the head of the old man. What's this! up so early. She stopped abashed. Why if it isn't my little friend! the old man's reassuring voice lifted her again to happiness. Be careful now, he said. Here. And he gave her his hand.

Arrived on the ground floor Lottie breathed again, smiled and went a little shyly to the window to hide her embarrassment. But as she looked a big cat came running toward the house, swinging right and left with his tail held high. Swerving toward the woodshed, before which three bedraggled hens and a tall rooster stretched their necks as he passed, he was soon under cover while they settled down again disconsolately. Sitting, the cat began licking his sides but seemed to hear something then and trotted off out of sight.

Lottie kept looking, watching the chickens who did not move thereafter.

Why don't they go into the barn? said she to the old man who was putting wood into the stove. They're getting all wet.

That's why they have feathers, he replied. She just looked at him not knowing what he meant.

Hardly had the others dressed and come downstairs also when from different windows they saw a horse and buggy arriving, coming noiselessly over the streaming grassy drive to the house.

It was Mr. Pike's boy with whom Gurlie had arranged the night before to drive to town. When they opened the door, he was already standing there under a big flat umbrella. Come in, come in, Charlie, said Mr. Payson. Whew! pretty wet, eh, today?

Gurlie began at once bustling around to get herself ready. You must have your breakfast, said Mr. Payson. Nonsense, I never eat breakfast. Just pour me a cup of coffee. Then for the first time she took a good look at the boy standing there waiting for her. He had a long narrow face with pale blue eyes and could not have been more than ten years of age. But he's only a child, turning to the others. Then she thought of the steep hill just beyond the house. Do we have to drive down that steep hill in this rain? The boy just looked at her.

You could hear Gurlie admonishing him as they drove away. Now, now, do be careful. Be careful now. But after another moment they were out of earshot and soon disappeared from view through the bushes at the top of the hill.

When he returned to the house after seeing them off Mr. Payson saw his wife shaking her head dubiously. Whew! said the old man, what a whirlwind. What do you think of her? he shouted close to his wife's head. Such energy, she replied. She must be very strong and healthy. But is she a good woman? I wonder. There was nothing malicious in the old lady's voice or, if so, only in a general way.

Her husband laughed out loud. What an idea! he said.

She is real Norsk, his wife went on. Some of them are very fine.

Do you think the children will tire you too much, he asked her then.

No, no! the poor things. The baby is so cute. And she has a will of her own, do you know that? I must try to feed her till she is big and strong while I have her here this summer. I am so happy to have a baby near me again. They need so much. I see so many things already to do for her.

Would you look at that, said the old man suddenly changing his voice.

There was Lottie down on the floor just finishing taking off her second shoe and beginning on the last stocking. Look at that. She saw Charlie barefooted and now she wants to be the same. And the baby clinging to Mrs. Payson was holding up one of her feet also saying, shoe, shoe.

Not on your life. Not till you've been here a while anyhow. You're coming to the barn with me, young lady, but I'm going to carry you. Put those shoes on again right away — and he did it for her, leaning down slowly to do so.

The rain had stopped a little now so they merely threw part of an old blanket over the child's shoulders and off he went carrying her, slopping through the wet.

As they entered the barn door, it was very dark at first and the rain drummed loudly on the high roof.

Then a hen burst forth into a wild cackling near them and flew madly through the open door. Mr. Payson took Lottie to the nest at the edge of the hay and let her gather the two eggs, still warm.

Downstairs they could hear the calf jerking at his chain.

When Gurlie returned from her shopping an hour or two later, she saw the old lady, out of the corner of her eye, putting a little stocking down quickly into her sewing basket. Gurlie had brought everything they would need for the next few days, a leg of lamb, some carrots . . .

We have carrots.

And all sorts of other things — bacon, sugar, bread both white and rye, all things that had been lacking. The old lady watched her lay them out one by one on the table. But no newspaper! She was disappointed in that. Oh well . . .

As the old lady had been almost ready with the children's lunch anyhow by that time, she went on with it while Gurlie got herself straightened out after her morning's jaunt and sat down to talk a little with the old man.

I grabbed the lines, she was saying in reply to one of his questions, I thought sure we were going over. You couldn't see the road at all, only the back of the horse and branches swishing in front of us all the time.

What did you do then?

She is so little, the old lady broke in turning to them innocently — not realizing that they had been talking. But a little baby is much closer to the heart. They had to stop and wait for her to finish, the baby also stopped drinking and looked up at her. But she is smart! And the old lady smiled, leaning down to pinch the baby's cheeks.

What did you do then, repeated Mr. Payson. But before they could say anything further they had to wait once more. Such pretty teeth. What does she say? turning to Gurlie. Does she know many words?

She knows words like mama, shouted Gurlie, papa, baby, book, hat, hot — and like that. But she talks a lot of foolishness too that nobody can understand.

No, said the baby, seeing they were looking at her, shaking her head hard from side to side.

That's her new word, no, said Gurlie.

Yes, yes, the old lady nodded without hearing anything. I think she will talk before she walks. The baby had finished the milk and lay back smiling. Then, feeling the round glass buttons down the front of the old lady's dress, she turned sidewise to touch them.

I'm so sorry you were interrupted, said Mr. Payson to Gurlie apologetically.

Let me take the baby, she answered, your wife has many things to do.

No, no. You were saying, you grabbed the lines . . . what did he do then?

He looked at me with his mouth open as if I was crazy. So I let go and after that it was all right. The horse would almost sit down sometimes it was so steep and wet. And she laughed to think of it. But it didn't take long. Then changing her voice, Gurlie added, Pay no attention but listen to her, nodding toward the baby.

The infant was talking right along with her mother at the top of her voice, a lively chatter. When her mother stopped suddenly she stopped too and looked around smiling.

Fine! said the old man, only it's all in Norwegian — nobody will understand you. And he laughed.

His wife had something in a pan stewing over the

fire. She put the baby down. Gurlie was curious. What's that? she asked and got up to see. It looks like what we used to call *portulak* in the old country. *Portulak,* she shouted in the old lady's ear.

Yes, that's right. Here they call it pussley. It's a weed but we like it very much when it's young and fresh.

What do you think of that! said Gurlie. Why everything we need grows in the ground if we knew it. Everything. That's what I like about the country. We don't need much either. All my life I have prayed to God that I could have a farm.

The old man shook his head. You don't think I could run it? Maybe, said the old man. You have plenty of courage. But not up here. Of course not, said Gurlie, but even here if I had to.

Better stick to the city. How is New York? A wonderful place. We saw it for three days when we first came here.

Agh, I hate New York. You don't know how lucky you are up here. There's air. You can breathe.

They say there's a lot of poverty there still.

The stores are full of people buying trash. I can't see that there's any want. But I'm not interested in that place. How many cows have you here?

Two, said Mr. Payson. One is no good though.

What do you mean, no good?

She is very pretty. We have been feeding her for a year but she refuses to have a calf. I thought she was going to be wonderful.

Are you telling her about the cows? asked the old lady of her husband.

Yes, said he, I'm telling her about that good-for-nothing Bessie. The old lady was interested. Yes, she said, my daughter bought her at the fair. She won a blue ribbon. She was so pretty. But she won't have a calf. They tried three bulls. They even left her in a field with a good bull for three months but it was no good. And she is so pretty. Such a nice face, like a deer. What a pity.

Gurlie let out a whoop of laughter. Why don't you kill her, then?

No, no, the old man shook his head seriously. I wish we could do it but nobody wants even to sell her to the butcher.

You're fine farmers, said Gurlie. You know I think your wife is a faker. She can hear all right. Can you hear what I say? she shouted at the old lady.

Yes, I hear pretty well, Mrs. Payson answered her.

Well, she hears all right sometimes, in the morning especially, her husband said. And if it's about babies or some gossip they have. That's her specialty. She has a friend who comes here sometimes and talks to her. You'd be surprised what she knows.

I'll bet, said Gurlie.

Some scandal, you know, something good and salty, somebody's wife run away, some baby without a father . . . you bet she finds it out.

Smart woman, said Gurlie.

She's not a true Scandinavian, is she? to the old man in a lower voice.

Yes, her mother was a Jacobson. But her father was a sea captain and his father's people came from Scotland, I think — like your Ibsen.

You see, said Gurlie, you see. I knew it. You are Celtic, she called out loudly to Mrs. Payson. You came from Asia. She is not a true Norsk. She added again to the old man, like we Norwegians.

The baby was at his wife's skirts, having pulled herself up from the floor, to stand there unsteadily.

Ha, ha! laughed Mr. Payson and chanted heartily, Ten thousand Swedes ran through the weeds, chased by one Norwegian.

What's that! said Gurlie, What's that? I shouldn't think you'd sing a thing like that, when you're a Swede yourself, mister.

Oh, said the old man, still laughing, when I was a young man, there was nothing that used to make me madder than that poem. But now that I am old I can laugh at it — too.

And so they sat down to a modest lunch which the old lady had prepared for them. Rain. Rain. Rain. The long grass outside the window was bent down and still running with water drops.

In the afternoon the rain had gathered new violence just when they thought it was over and now almost supper and no sign of a let-up. The old lady had the baby on her lap at the table once more.

The infant reached for its cup and began to drink milk from it. She had it between her hands, the fingers of one of them over the cup edge dabbling a little into the milk as she drank. The old lady had her own hand underneath supporting the cup from the bottom. Mr. Payson was crouched down at the hearth rubbing a small knife on the stone and Lottie beside him crouched down too, all attention.

Well, it looks to me as if everything is settled here for the summer, said Gurlie, I might just as well go back to New York.

Oh, don't say that, said Mr. Payson looking up. We want you to be happy too.

I am happy, said Gurlie, I'm always happy if the sun will come out. It was raining steadily now with a sea-like roar on the roof above them. Occasionally there would be a flash followed at a long interval by mild thunder, hollow and far away. The rain would diminish at such times then begin again heavily in reply. It died once more and there was a hush followed by a flash and deafening crash. Whee! said Gurlie as the children looked around in uncomprehending amazement.

Quick! said the old man, see if you can see any smoke anywhere. Gurlie went to one window, he to another. But it had grown almost night and they could see nothing.

Three barns have already been struck around here this month, said he, and one of them burned down. Some cows too have been killed under trees.

There was a tap at the door. Everyone but the old woman turned to look. When they went, they found it to be two children, a lank girl of about thirteen years in a colorless dress and a milk pail in her hand. She was barefoot and had a man's coat over her head and shoulders. Her small brother was behind her, grinning, his hair plastered to his head. They waited where they were. Till Gurlie took the girl by the shoulder and whisked her inside. The boy followed. You get in here, she said. Go stand there by the stove, to the boy, till I wipe your head. Both did as they were told leaving wet footprints on the floor. Lottie and the baby gazed at them entranced.

What in the world is this? said Gurlie. Where do these things come from?

They've come for milk, said Mr. Payson.

But what a time to come for milk, in this rain. All up that road? You ought to have better sense, said Gurlie.

We been coming all day, waiting for it to clear, spoke up the girl. Ma said if we didn't make up our minds pretty soon it'd be dark before we got here. She spoke slowly in a low voice. Just like us to come through the worst of it, piped up the boy looking directly at Mr. Payson. Didn't expect no such lightning as that, though.

Pretty sharp, wasn't it?

Scared the life out of sis, he replied. We wasn't looking for it just then. Think we'll get any more?

No, no, said Mr. Payson. That's the end of the storm. I'm an old sailor, you can count on that.

The little fellow seemed pleased and began to look at Gurlie and the children with a new interest.

As a matter of fact, with that final thunder clap, the worst of the storm did seem to be past. And now from under the edge of the heavy clouds in the west, though a little rain was still falling, the sun actually appeared for the first time that day almost on the horizon. It cast forth a strange level beam of light which struck the trees all up the adjacent hillside till they stood out against the dark slate of the sky to the north. It was very pretty but awe-inspiring to the little group who all turned instinctively to the window.

How is it? said Gurlie when the children had gone again, that you give those farmers milk? Haven't they a cow? How much do you charge them for it?

They don't pay anything. What! said Gurlie. You see, went on Mr. Payson, sometimes they bring us what they have growing. Or they take letters down to town for us. It doesn't cost us anything. What's a little milk? And it won't be for long. They have a good cow coming in next week.

You can't beat a yankee, said Gurlie.

No, no. They are good people. They help us a lot. And it's so nice to see the children coming every day.

But you can't afford it.

We have sometimes thirty quarts a day. As much as that? Gurlie grew serious at once. Yes, and sometimes more. We can't use all that.

What do you do with it then?

We feed it to the calf. We get them for two dollars up here. He takes from five to eight quarts a meal. The rest we use for a little cream — as much as we need. What is left over we put in a pan for the chickens.

It was beginning to get really dark in the rooms by now.

We should do like they do in the old country, in the mountains, said the old man, with his ever ready smile. In winter they have what they call " cellar milk." Yes? said Gurlie. They put maybe five gallons, maybe fifteen gallons, of fresh milk in a tub in the cellar and there it stands.

But doesn't it get sour?

Yes, a little, but it is good.

I should think it would rot, said Gurlie.

No, it forms a coating of mould on the top that is green sometimes, like a blanket. You lift that up and underneath the milk is good to drink. You can keep it that way all winter, they say — till it is used up.

That's wonderful, said Gurlie. I must remember that.

But you have to have a cool cellar, said the old man, or so I am told. I never saw it myself.

You know, I remember now, Gurlie took up the burden, tetter milk, did you ever hear of that? Yes, I think so, said Mr. Payson. I think they make it from a little plant, Gurlie went on. They take some of the leaves and put them in the milk. Yes, that's right, said Mr. Payson. Then they beat it and beat it until it gets sort of stringy. I never liked that.

Then when you want to make more, the old man continued, you take a tablespoon of it and add to the fresh milk and it gets the same way. In Wisconsin, my daughter told me, they sent to the old country. Some friends soaked a piece of cloth in it, then they dried it out and sent it in a letter. It worked fine. I guess I'd better light the lamp before I go down to the barn now.

No, not yet, said Gurlie, it's so nice to sit this way. The children have been fed, we'll just sit here and wait for you.

Light the lamp, Emil, said Mrs. Payson to her husband. Here is a little sleepyhead I want to put to bed. So the old man lighted the lamp on the table while the children watched him.

Give me the baby. I'll fix her for bed. You have work to do, Gurlie shouted, leaning toward Mrs. Payson. But, as Gurlie picked up the child to take her on her lap, the little thing struggled, twisting herself around in her mother's arms to look back at the old lady.

And now the other started. The old man had taken the lantern and gone to the barn when Lottie was discovered there half-sobbing, her finger in her mouth, looking at the blank door.

What's the matter? asked her mother. He's not

going away. But Lottie was not to be consoled. She walked waveringly to one of the front windows but did not look out, knowing it was night. Then she turned round with tears in her eyes, choking back the beginning sobs. When they spoke to her, she began sobbing as if her heart would break. But he's coming back in a few minutes, said Gurlie. He's only gone to the barn. Agh, children are unreasonable, she added looking at the old lady. Leave her alone.

Gurlie sat holding the baby, making no attempt to undress her.

You should not have bought that big leg of lamb, said Mrs. Payson, you are too good. If we had known even one day ahead that you were coming — She was beginning it again. But Gurlie just laughed.

By the time Mr. Payson was back with the milk everything was ready and they all sat down once again at the table, the children also, as Lottie was afraid to be put upstairs alone and the baby lingered on with her. Being hungry everyone set at once to eating so that for a while silence prevailed in the room. The rain had stopped entirely now and a light wind had come up. Suddenly everyone seemed wrapped in his own thoughts as if the accustomed loneliness of the house had come out of the room's corners and possessed them all. Gurlie felt it and turned her head quickly as though someone were approaching on tiptoe behind her. Brr! she shivered and laughed.

What in the world do you do with yourselves in the evenings?

We go to bed, said the old man. There is nothing to do and we are tired. We read a little sometimes but we have only two or three books.

I should think you would play cards.

Listen! said Lottie. It was a cricket which had started to chirrup near the door.

Let him stay out, said the old man, they do more damage than moths.

I never heard that, said Gurlie.

Isn't it true, mother, that crickets do more damage than moths? Yes, yes, said the old lady, I have seen big holes, like that, in a coat they have eaten. Is there a cricket here? Her husband told her that there was. Let me take the baby so that you can eat now, she added addressing herself to Gurlie. No, said Gurlie, you eat yourself. And she signaled with one hand for Mrs. Payson to stay where she was.

Strange to say, the baby wasn't at all sleepy but sat quite placidly on her mother's knee slapping her hands on the table now and then, completely at ease. But at this point she began pushing and straightening herself out to get down on the floor.

It's such a pleasure for me to have her, the old lady pleaded, I haven't put a baby to bed for so many years.

All right, said Gurlie. So Mr. Payson picked Flossie up and carried her round the table to put her in his wife's arms. The infant looked up at the old lady, then back at her mother, with a curious expression on her face.

I think she already likes her better than she does me, said Gurlie to the old man.

Oh, you mustn't say that, answered he. Yes, she does, said Gurlie, I'm jealous. And she pouted.

The old lady began to unbutton the baby's dress. Now, up with your arms. But the dress had a very small neck which stuck about the little head so that she had a job getting it off. It was quite a struggle.

The baby put her hands up to push as she could but finally the old lady just had to drag the garment clear. The baby frowned a moment when it was all over and scratched her head.

That's that tight dress, said Gurlie.

I remember, said the old woman, how I used to amuse Astrid when she was a child. I would take off her shoes and then hand them back to her. That would keep her busy for an hour or more sometimes.

The room had grown very warm by now with them all sitting in it and the fire going so the old man went to open the door for a moment. As he did so, a half grown kitten came running in from the night, his tail straight in the air. The older cats had been in all afternoon but they were shy. This one, however, went straight to Gurlie who leaned and picked her up. Prrrr! Prrrr! Sweet! said Gurlie. You're not pretty but you're black. That's good luck. And did you see that, he came right to me?

Good luck to him, I guess, being black, said Mr. Payson, maybe that's what saved him.

What's that? said Gurlie. Lottie had come around to pat the kitty in her mother's lap.

We had two of them, the old man explained. She had them in the barn. When I went there the other day, Pilka, that's the mother, followed me asking for milk. As I opened the door, she went in with me when — Zip! Smash! Such a screaming and spitting! I didn't know what had happened. She flew at something under the old carriage. It was all over in a second. Such a racket you never heard. I turned just in time to see her chasing a big black away off down through the fields bouncing away, he running and she after him, over the high grass until they disappeared.

We found the little gray kitten in a pile of rubbish with her neck all chewed but Billie we couldn't find anywhere. I thought he was dead too. But he came crawling out from somewhere in the afternoon.

What is that? asked the old lady. Are you telling her about the cats?

Yes, nodded her husband.

And what do you think? the old lady took up the story as if she had heard it all. The beast had the courage to come and sit here the next day and try to make love to her.

What do you think of that! said Gurlie, Did she take him?

I don't know, said Mrs. Payson. I think so. I don't know where he came from but maybe he has the virile strain in him. What can you do? She has another cat here, and they are good friends, but she lets the one that killed her kitten visit her too.

Can I have another cup of coffee, asked Gurlie. Everything tastes so good tonight. A fine supper, she shouted to Mrs. Payson. You're a smart cook. So quick, too.

Just scraps, said the old lady, except the things that you bought yourself.

Scraps at home are better than the finest food served in a restaurant.

Maybe, said the old man, but I know a restaurant in Stockholm I wish I was in right now. Do you know fish pudding when it is good? he asked Gurlie.

She let out her big wild laugh. Don't try to tell me about that. That's a Norwegian dish, we had it at home every week in the season. I bet you never tasted anything like that.

There, broke in the old lady, pointing toward the

window ledge. Don't they look like husband and wife? The two home cats, the black mother and the grey male, were sitting facing each other, half asleep, their noses almost touching.

Ya, ya, said Gurlie, apropos of nothing. If all the people in the world were like us, what a fine place it would be.

Yes, I could never understand why men cannot be good, said Mr. Payson, I guess it's because of the original sin, like the good book says. Men have always been evil, it's the only way they could get what they want. So it's become a habit. I'd rather have nothing. But I know everybody isn't like me.

Well, said Gurlie, I'm proud of my ancestors. I like to think that I come from a line of strong, healthy people. What would we be if we didn't sometimes think of those who are gone? They are more important than we are — because they made for us everything we have.

Yes, and they made us big fools too. If we could all be smart and healthy — and good looking, then we should have something to talk about.

Ancestors make us proud, said Gurlie. Pride of race is what makes us go ahead.

Everybody is proud of his race. I think of my father and my grandfather sometimes, but that's all. After that it mixes into the race — like everybody else. He reached into his waistcoat pocket and took out a little box.

What's that? said Gurlie.

Snuff, said the old man. I use a little sometimes. It is very good and cheap too in this country.

Let me see, said Gurlie taking the circular tin box out of his hand. Yes, it's snuff, sure enough, said she.

I didn't think they had it in this country. I thought that was only our own bad habit. The baby reached for the snuff box but Gurlie held it away from her. Come now, said Mrs. Payson approaching and taking the baby into her arms. It's time someone should be put to bed. You too Lottie. I'll go up with you. No, no, said Gurlie, I can take care of that.

Let her do it, spoke up the old man. Or why don't you both go? Get out of here and let me wash the dishes in peace. Lottie was yawning at her mother's knee. So the two women, each with a child, went upstairs.

CHAPTER XX

The Soundout

M<small>R</small>. L<small>EMON</small> held back a curtain for him to go into an adjoining room. It was arranged as a library and lounge with a large, somewhat ornate, walnut desk by the window. Sit down, won't you. Joe went toward a straight chair by the desk, but Mr. Lemon wouldn't let him take it. No, no. Over here on the lounge — a red leather one — you'll be more comfortable. I was just ordering a little drink when you came in. Won't you join me? Joe hesitated a moment. Or perhaps something stronger? No thanks, said Joe. Can't persuade you? No thanks, but go ahead yourself if you want to.

Sorry to disturb you on a Sunday evening this way.

It's all right, said Joe.

Really hot tonight, though. Isn't it? How did you come?

I had plenty of time, said Joe, so I took it easy and walked.

That's too bad. You wouldn't really care for a drink? Something cool?

I wouldn't mind a glass of water, said Joe.

Nothing stronger? A gin rickey is very pleasant on a night like this.

I'll stick to water, said Joe. So Mr. Lemon had a pitcher of ice water, a thing Joe never could tolerate, brought in and placed on the table. I'm taking off my coat, said he. He had on a belt and no vest. Yes, that's a good idea, said Joe. But he had on a vest and didn't want to remove it because of his suspenders. Nothing could make him. So they began to talk.

Now, I tell you, Stecher, let's get down to business without too much shinanigan. You know why I asked you to come here today and all that. A certain amount of secrecy is absolutely essential to our success. So just bear this in mind, agree or not, whatever we say here tonight is strictly between ourselves.

Joe nodded. Yes, of course.

As I understand it, you like our product. You think it's pretty good, don't you?

Yes, said Joe candidly and at once, no question about that.

That was the impression I had. And if we're to make a bid, that's the paper you'd use — I mean, as a practical man. There wouldn't be any question about that, would there? You think it's the best.

I know it's the best, said Joe.

How much do you think this whole thing is going to cost us? To get the plant set up, that is, and be turning out orders?

That's what I came here to talk about tonight, isn't it? said Joe.

Lemon took up a box of cigars from the desk and handed it toward Joe.

Thanks, I'll smoke one of my own, if you don't mind. I'm more used to them.

Lemon put the box back on his desk, took a cigar, bit off the end and lighted it. As he did so he paused long enough, looking through the smoke, to say, You married, Stecher?

Yes, said Joe. I'm married.

Children? Yes, said Joe. That's fine. By the way,

Stecher, are you a member of any fraternal organizations? No, said Joe. Interested at all in churches? We go sometimes to the Lutheran church, said Joe.

You've got a record, Stecher, as a labor organizer that's rather impressive, you know. Would you object if I asked you a few direct questions along that line? I'm interested.

No. Go ahead, said Joe.

How old were you when you came to this country? Nineteen.

Could you speak English?

I could speak a little from what I learned in the *Gymnasium*.

So you did have some secondary school education.

My family wanted to make me a professor, said Joe smiling, but I had to make money.

Quite an orator and special pleader, I'm told. How did you manage all this in such a short time?

Joe smiled again. Conditions in the printing trade were pretty bad when I came here. Somebody had to do it.

So you did it, laughed Mr. Lemon. Sounds pretty easy. But then you quit all that.

Yes, said Joe, I'm not interested in politics.

Politics, eh? Don't think much of it. Well, I'm afraid you're wrong, Stecher — though I can understand very well what you mean. Unfortunately, we've got to have the machinery of politics for government, unless we surrender the whole affair and it comes to a bloody anarchy.

That's what you've got now, in politics, said Joe.

Very good. Yes, no doubt. Labor politics, you mean.

Amounts to the same thing, said Joe.

But unhygienic shops, dangerous working conditions, starvation wages — don't you think that politics can better such things?

Not the kind of politics I've seen, said Joe.

So you quit.

No, I'm still a printer, said Joe.

But you quit taking an active part in the organization of labor. I'm curious. I'd really like to know why.

The unions are dishonest, just as dishonest as the bosses, said Joe.

Yes, but you're honest. Isn't it just such men as you that they need in there, then?

I was in there — for seven years, said Joe.

Ah, I see. Sorry to press you this way, Stecher, but I feel that we have to be on a perfectly candid footing if we're going to do any work together later on. I hope you don't mind.

Not at all, said Joe.

You see, the thing is this. It's men like you who are needed in both business and labor organization. Really able and disinterested men, sufficiently disinterested to take hold of a major investment and see both sides of the questions involved — and deal with them intelligently. Believe me, they're hard to find.

Joe put his cigar gently to his lips and puffed it without further comment.

You've never been in business for yourself before, have you, Stecher?

Not for myself, said Joe.

The men smoked silently for a moment. Lemon got up from his chair and walked up and down the room. The only question's going to be you'll have to handle the entire situation yourself — without assistance —

especially at the beginning. We can't for obvious reasons have my name appear in it just now. It's something more than an ordinary man's job, I tell you. Especially if they get the jump on us. Think you can swing it?

I think so.

You say that very calmly. What makes you think so?

What part of it do you think I won't be able to handle? said Joe.

Well, you're going to have to spend a lot of money. I'm just wondering if you know what that involves.

I think I do.

The people down there are going to raise hell. And labor.

I'll take the whole department with me when I leave.

Whew! Listen, Stecher, we're not starting a war, you know.

I think we are, Mr. Lemon.

You do, eh? Well. That's different. And you think you can keep them satisfied?

Why not, if we pay them decent wages?

All right, man, if you think you can do it. Now what about money? Let me ask you a hypothetical question. You know money's a funny thing. People have crazy ideas about it, they don't know what they're talking about. Now suppose, just suppose, that by giving you certain information I made it possible for you to clean up a hundred thousand dollars in the market tomorrow morning. What would you say?

No thanks, said Joe.

What do you mean, no thanks?

I wouldn't want it that way.

You wouldn't? Why not?

Joe shook his head. There's only one way to get money honestly, said Joe, and that's to work for it. If you don't it has to come out of some other poor sucker's pocket. That's why I don't like the stock market. It's a swindle.

Mr. Lemon looked serious. Just a minute, now, Stecher. I have money and I didn't work for it — not all of it. Some of it I made in the stock market. And I think I made it honestly — and it's this money I'm lending you.

I expect to work for it if I get any of it, said Joe.

Just a minute, now, Stecher. This is the same viewpoint that took you out of labor organization and there's a danger in it. After all, you know, the whole world isn't dishonest. The danger is this — what you evidence is a moral viewpoint. A stern one. Something centered in your own, shall I say — Calvinistic — nature. I have every sympathy with such a viewpoint, Stecher, as far as it relates to a man's private character. But it has nothing to do with business.

I think it does, said Joe.

Damn it, Stecher, I disagree with you. You're heading straight for trouble if you don't get those notions out of your mind here and now. Don't misunderstand me, I've got nothing to sell — or if I have that's entirely secondary. But you can't go into business that way. Money can be made, big money, quickly and with complete honesty, in this country and you might as well understand it. This is America. We're not talking of a young emigrant from East Prussia any more . . .

Joe flushed in spite of himself.

We're talking of an American with all the towering resources of this extremely active and wealthy society at his elbow. Fortunes can be made here today as always with no more capital to begin with than would buy a dozen bags of peanuts. A society ready and eager to reward you richly for genius and industry. Sounds like a 4th of July oration — but it's the truth, anyhow.

Get the money! That's all that seems to count here, said Joe.

But Stecher, take it easy. Take it easy. Don't you see? Don't you see what money really is? It's power. I'm trying to work around you, as you'll realize in a moment. And power, especially in this country, is men, like yourself, who have the character to administrate it. That's all that money means — here.

I don't care what economic phase you accept. I don't care anything about that. Man is money and it's got to be passed on to men. And those men usually come up from the bottom — through trial by fire. Say what you please, it is an attractive conception of who shall have the responsibility for the possession of money and its management today. And the winnings are theirs. Don't go in there thinking you're going to have to deal with a lot of acknowledged crooks. They may be — but you've got to do business with them — and you're not going to show it.

We're up against a lot of dirty crooks, just the same, said Joe.

And how do you think you're going to beat 'em. You're speaking out of your own somewhat bitter personal experience.

By being honest.

You're a rank conservative, old man. You'll have to do better than that. You want to make money, don't you?

Yes, said Joe. I want to make money honestly.

Then you'll have to eat it and drink it and wake
with it and sleep with it — and dream of it, day and
night — if you're going to go through with this proposition. Take my advice, Stecher, don't let your morals
get too much mixed up in it — watch 'm, but they're
all good fellows after all. Anyhow, you've got to do
business with them. The same for the help, don't be
too soft. We've got to make this thing pay.

I've got some figures here might interest you, said
Joe.

I'm leaving that to you. Would twenty-five thousand cover the initial costs?

It might do that, said Joe.

How far would fifty thousand take you?

Fifty thousand would do.

More?

No.

It'll be to your account at the Close National Bank
tomorrow noon. I tell you, Stecher, said Mr. Lemon
finally, leaning over and putting his hand on the arm
of Joe's chair, it just comes down to one thing. You're
young, in good health. Courage you definitely have —
and ability, that goes without saying. And now I've
given you the money. Will you fight? That's what it
amounts to. Because you'll have to fight, don't make
any mistake about that. Will you join me and fight
them? Fight! That's what it takes. Fight! And it will
be a hell of a fight before we get through with it.
Will you?

Joe felt the blood burn in his cheeks. What do you
say, Stecher, are you on?

I'll be ready to start in about a month, said Joe.

A month!?

I'd like to talk it over with my wife first, as soon as

she gets back from the country. And do a little more figuring before I'm ready.

Oh. Well then, I think the conspirators ought to rest. Look, it's beginning to cloud over a bit outside. Is that thunder?

Yes, I think I'd better be getting home.

Home? At this time? I should say not. You got nothing to do. Come now, let's really make it a drink this time. Come on, change your mind, Stecher. After all, you're a good Dutchman. To start us off right. What do you say? Success to the new firm.

Yes, said Joe. I wouldn't mind a nice cool drink right now.

Good. And he called the butler. What kind of a shop are you going to run, Stecher? Union?

Open shop, said Joe. Good pay — as much as the business can stand, decent appointments, protect the machinery — give them everything they need to do good work. And stick to them as long as they stick to me.

And if they turn out no good?

Fire 'em, said Joe.

Well, if anybody can do it, you can, said his host.

I wouldn't have a shop under any other conditions, said Joe.

And tell me, Stecher, what do you really think of the American Federation of Labor? I want to get back to that before we're through.

Joe looked at his host and smiled broadly.

Yes, I understand all that but specifically what?

It's a business, said Joe, like any other business.

You think so?

No, said Joe. I never think much about it any more. But it's a good business. If you like it.

What do you mean? Come on, come on, let's have it.

Well, said Joe, holding his glass in both hands, if you're going to make deals with employers and sell the suckers out — somebody has to do it.

That isn't the way you yourself started, is it?

Oh, when I started it was all right, said Joe, only the suckers were too easy to skin. They never know when they have it good. They've got to be hogs. Somebody's got to put sense back into them when they act like that or they'll wreck the best business in the world.

But suppose, as the radicals say, there's something fundamentally wrong in the capitalistic system itself. What then? Have you ever thought of that?

Yes, I've thought of it. They'll always be the same. I don't want to be one of the smart grafters that suck them in — because there's always a few good ones among the others and they have to suffer too.

There you go again, said Mr. Lemon. You carry water on both shoulders. You can't be humane in business, Stecher — without sacrificing the business.

No, said Joe, I've noticed that.

Well, said Lemon opening his hands, anyway — your credit is unlimited. You'll have to fight but you'll win. It'll be a dirty fight too. But you'll win it anyway. And when you have won and when you have made money . . . you're going to make plenty of money, mark my word.

I think I can wait a while for that, said Joe.

You may be surprised. You intend to remain in New York the rest of the summer?

Yes, I think so.

Have you looked up a loft? Have you a building in mind?

I think so, said Joe.

I'll bet you even have the presses ordered, laughed his host.

Joe laughed too, loudly.

Don't let them get so much as a smell of it. Do everything under an assumed name if you can.

They finished their drinks and Joe got up. As he was shaking hands at the door Mrs. Lemon and her sister came in and were introduced. Good night. Good bye.

Well, what do you think of him? asked Mr. Lemon of his wife as he turned back into the hall.

Good heavens, he's handsome! with his wavy black hair and those fine grey eyes with such a direct look in them. And what a lovely voice and smile.

And a good head for business, I think. A first rate mind. Really great possibilities in that man.

I noticed his small feet. Well, what's the trouble now?

Just wondering. Too decent perhaps. Certainly too intelligent and able to be working for a lot of cut-throats such as those who have him tied down there today.

What's all this about? Something new?

I don't know. Perhaps, who can tell.

Stuck?

No. Far from that. Just interested, I guess.

CHAPTER XXI

Fourth of July Doubleheader

THE GIANTS were in second place, one game behind the leading Cards. If they won both today the standings would be reversed and they would go into first position. It meant a lot to both teams. Every now and then a loud boom could be heard coming from the streets or the rat-a-tat-tat of a handful of firecrackers exploding somewhere to remind you of what was going on outside. But inside the park it was another world.

But it hadn't started too well for George Wiltze, McGraw's lanky right hander. Bauer, the Cards' lead-off man, scratched an infield hit on a slow bounder toward second. Then Johnson, the second man up, drove a hot one past third, Bauer stopping at second. Not so good. And with two on and nobody out Archer, the Cards' big first sacker, drove the first ball on a line between center and left for two bases. It looked like curtains for Wiltze.

Six weeks from today bids will be opened . . . It'll be a dirty fight. But we'll lick 'em because they're guilty and they know it and we're . . .

Take him out! Take him out! yelled a fan sitting immediately in front of Joe. What is this, a procession?

But I got 'em when it comes to the paper — I got 'em there. That's what's going to hurt. Can't get around that. Must sleep more though, can't afford to get sick now. Take it easy because that's only going to be the beginning. Only the start . . .

Time was called while the Giants' infield gathered around Wiltze near the pitcher's box, looking down and kicking imaginary pebbles in the dirt for the most part. But after a couple of minutes they ran back to their positions and the tall right hander got a cheer as he pulled his cap down and took his stand once more.

Better tell 'em tomorrow I'll be quitting at the end of the week. Need a rest. No. Just quitting, that's all. Give 'em no reason. No, that'll make them suspicious. Can't afford that right now. Stick it out for the month. Looks nasty staying in and plotting to take away their business. Not though. What must I do? Cut my throat to do them a favor. Bid's 'r open to the public. Would they consider me? Should say not. A fair bid's a fair bid. They never made a fair bid in their existence. Got to play safe, that's all. Got to out-guess 'em. No other way. Got to stick it out and fool 'em. They'll make it plenty hot anyway when they find out — sooner or later.

Two in and nobody out with a man on second waiting to go. Strike one! Yeay! yelled Joe in his gruff laughing voice, that's the stuff. Give him another in the same place. Strike two!

Then it happened again. The same queer feeling. Wiltze leaned far forward, recovered, took a slow look toward second, then whipped over a third strike while the crowd howled. Joe recognized every move as it happened. That'd happened before, just the way Wiltze had gone through it now. Not another play like it but the *same play*. Twice. Every move. From the time Wiltze had first leaned forward until the pitch had been delivered Joe's mind had preceded every move an instant before, action for action. He'd seen that play before, at some other time, in some other place. That identical play. Twice during the last half hour he'd had that same strange feeling. Agh, he said aloud and took out a cigar. But he didn't light it and after a moment put it back into his pocket.

One down. The next two men were retired on easy ground balls and the inning was over. That's pitching, said Joe. But his eyes were bothering him a little and he rubbed them with both hands.

Wonder when Gurlie will be wanting to come home.

In their half of the first the Giants got one back. Fletcher started it with a clean single and promptly stole second. A very close play. The Cards swarmed around the ump but Fletcher stayed where he was and advanced to third a moment later on an infield out, scoring when Merkle, on a well executed squeeze play, tapped along the first base line. It was smart base-ball, just the stuff Joe delighted to see, the sort of ball McGraw taught his boys. A great afternoon.

Everything has to be thought of. Can't trust anybody. Too bad but can't help it. Every smallest detail down in black and white — perfect, to the last penny, minute detail. Counting devices for each press, every sheet numbered serially — every coupon, in fact. Even after they come off the presses, still danger — greatest danger of all in fact. Wears you out. Can't help it. Got to think of everything. Got to play safe. McGraw thinks of everything. Just the same a man might slip . . .

The fourth inning now coming up. Joe in his favorite position back of first base, his coat off, men all around him smoking and fanning themselves with their hats, entirely at home. Knock him out of the box! yelled the man in front. Send him to the showers. Get that big stiff.

Not today, said Joe. They had their chance. Too late now. Knock him out of the box, yelled the man addressing himself to the field in general. He's got nothing on the ball.

They'll ask plenty questions. Not so dumb. Tell 'em I'm going back to Buffalo. More money. Bet they double me. Too late now, boys. No, tell 'em nothing. They'll have me watched. Won't be able to go anywhere after that. Can't quit till everything's settled — then I'll take them fishing. Got to work through someone else after that. Gurlie can help.

Wham! the first man up in the Cardinal's half of the fourth poled a triple to deep right. There they go! What'd I tell you he was no good? Take him out! Take that big bum out of there. Joe couldn't tell which side the man was rooting for — if it wasn't a grudge against Wiltze himself, maybe. But the next batter, trying to put it into the stands, went down swinging, Wiltze making it two in a row on the next and knocking down a smash through the box with his bare hand and tossing easily to first for the final out. What a man! Joe was delighted.

Up to now the Giants had seemed small and at a disadvantage and the St. Louis team much abler and more rugged. But now it began to change. Last half of the fourth, St. Louis still leading 2 to 1. Wiltze himself at the plate. One to tie and two to win. Wiltze swung viciously but only succeeded in knocking three fouls into the stands, one after the other. Then he watched a third strike go by, waist high, and retired to the dugout with bowed head.

The next man followed with a hard smash to short and was thrown out on a fast play by Clancy of the Cards. Good work Clancy. The Giants were meeting the ball but couldn't seem to drop them safe. Two out. So that when Magee, reaching for a wide one, managed to tap a short fly safe behind first nobody thought anything of it, Joe along with the others. But the next man singled and the next after that and before you knew it two runs were in and . . .

Looked all right, ought to hold anything I want to put on it. That's something they'd like to know — 28 Center St. Right across from the jail. Better get building inspector to look it over before presses begin to move. G. W. Hoe and Co. Three lithographic presses. That's what costs. Never thought I'd have the cash to buy those. They'll be watching.

Pandemonium broke loose as the second run crossed the plate. The stands which had been mainly quiet hitherto, morose as a child, were screaming now, yelling their heads off. Joe bit the end of his cigar and lit it, smiling to himself with satisfaction.

That's something like it he said to himself grimly, absorbed and amused. Yes, that looks a little better, answered a voice from the seat to his left. A little startled Joe turned slightly and saw a straight-shouldered man of about fifty, red faced and wearing a striped blue suit, white shirt, black cross tie and a cloth cap. He did not return Joe's look but remained with his face unemotionally fixed toward the diamond.

With two runs already in, two out and a man on first Jansen, for the Cards, lost his steadiness, passed

two and was yanked unceremoniously from the scene
of action. Well, well. It happens to the best of them,
thought Joe. But that's baseball. The game was
stopped while the new pitcher strolled in slowly from
the St. Louis bullpen and the twenty or thirty thousand waited.

That'll be the big day — when the contracts are
opened. They'll have two bids in as usual, one high
and one — cut-throat, to kill off all competition if
necessary. Do it at a loss to hold it. They'll be watching. Mustn't even be in Washington. Stay home. Go
fishing, really. All through some inconspicuous . . .

Nobody can underbid my figures — if it's a fair bid.
Unless it's crooked. Unless they've got it fixed, in ways
I don't know, in the post office department itself. Page
has always been honest though. Never can tell. But
I'll fight it if it takes me to the very White House.
I'll show 'em up in the papers. I'll bust the whole
crooked business wide open. I will. I will. Family or
no family. Building, presses, ink . . . payroll

Nobody scored in the sixth. The seventh inning
now coming up. The lucky seventh. Peanuts. Here
y'are, get your fresh roasted peanuts. Fi' cents a bag.
Sasprilla. Ginger ale. Pass it in, will ya Buddy? Joe
took the bottle gingerly and handed it down the line.
Then he passed back the nickel. Wonder what some
people come to a ball game for anyway, said the man
in the next seat. Joe looked again. A tall, deep-
chested man looking straight ahead at the playing
field as before.

Just enough breeze to lift the flags along the upper
edge of the north stands and let them fall again lazily.
The diamond and outfield, sharply cut, were a bright
velvet carpet to Joe's eyes. As the players ran back and

forth on it he could feel with envy its turfy spring and wished for — something, nearer definition now than ever before in his life.

Wonder how they're making out in the country up there. Some day, some day — pretty soon, maybe.

The Cards were unable to score in their half of the seventh. And now it was the Giants' turn. Everybody up! It felt good to stand and stretch once more. But the Cards' new pitcher, a bespectacled rookie named Williams, let our Giants down one, two three without a man reaching first. And so it ran into the eighth frame, New York still leading by the slim margin of one run. Archer up for the Cards, the man who had poled out the long double in the first scoring his team's only runs so far.

With two balls and one strike on him the hefty first baseman caught the next one on the end of his bat and sent it high toward the left field stands. Going! Going! It seemed to take minutes as Joe watched it ride, clear over the top of the stands and bounce way up onto the elevated tracks beyond them — outside the park. Gone! Wow! What a hit — tying the score.

That's the stuff, said Joe in spite of himself. Knock it out of the park.

The man in front was on his feet at the crack of the bat. There it goes! There goes your old ball game. What'd I tell you? As the big runner ambled around the bases the crowd sat stunned.

That don't mean a thing, said Joe's neighbor. That can happen to anybody. They'll get that back. Wait and see.

Put in Mathewson! yelled the wild-eyed rooter in front. Put in a pitcher. Hey you, McGraw! why don't you put in a pitcher and give us a break for our money?

Guys like that ought to be put in cages, said Joe's neighbor out of the corner of his mouth. Mathewson! he added with contempt. All you hear now is Mathewson. I'll admit he's a good ball player but you'd think to hear some of them talk it was him invented the game. I been waiting for that.

As Wiltze still remained on the mound the man in the front row made a great show of slumping back in his seat. Good *night!* There was however no more scoring in that frame and it went into the ninth still tied up, 3 to 3.

High over the field a flock of pigeons wheeled into sight — swooping suddenly in a swift flow of wings. Joe watched them and tried to count them as they rose again, circling back over the field. Pretty though, pigeons, flying that way in the sunlight and fresh air — cleaner up there than down here, like on a mountain.

And in the ninth the Cards broke loose again, pushed over another run on a free pass, a wild pitch, an infield out and a long fly to center. So that when Bresnahan faced the St. Louis hurler in the last half of the ninth, the Giants were trailing again by one run.

Hit that ball! Hit it! Joe implored. And that's just what Bresnahan did, a smashing single straight over second. He was advanced, following McGraw's usual strategy, on a sacrifice bunt. Then Wiltze himself shot an unexpected safety along the first base line just out of Archer's straining grasp. One away with a run needed to tie and two to win, both of them now on the bags. Looks good, said Joe's neighbor. Thought he might put in a pinch hitter that time but I guess it worked out all right at that.

Better take out some more insurance, thought Joe, while I have the chance. You never can tell.

But Fletcher popped out, close to the stands, and the Giants were two down and it was up to Donlin, now or never, to bring home the bacon. The stands were absolutely still as the New York second baseman walked to the plate, knocked the dirt from his cleats with his bat handle and faced the mound.

The first pitch drove him back in a hurry. The next clipped the outside corner. The next was high. But on the next the big Irishman swung with everything he had and met the ball square, a beautiful drive between first and second. Bresnahan was already at the plate when Wiltze, legging it for second, saw the ball coming, tried to dodge but it hit him in the side of the foot — and the game was over. St. Louis 4, New York 3.

Well, there it is, said Joe's friend on the left straightening his back and stretching. Nice game, barring a few accidents. I used to play with this outfit myself, twenty years ago. Tip Meehan. Ever hear the name? No, Joe couldn't remember that he had. Yes, I've caught 'em all, from Amos Rusie right on down the line.

Joe wanted to ask him what he was doing now.

I still like to watch 'em. You wouldn't take me for a man of sixty, would you? I should say not, said Joe. Well, that's what I am. Sixty-one at my next birthday. Coming up? said he, rising.

No, said Joe. Not just now. Well, take care of yourself. Do my best, said Joe.

Rush, rush, rush! For what, my God? For what? Money, that's all. And when you've got it, what?

A small place in the suburbs, not too far from the city — with a green, well-kept lawn. Flowers, a few trees about it. *Ein Obstgarten.* Blue, red and white grapes on an arbor. A tree of good late apples. A plum tree. Greengages, they're the best. He remembered being told — no, he'd seen it himself — that if a tree won't bear fruit you drive eight or ten good iron nails into it. Good strong nails. Take an apple tree or a plum tree, for instance. Pick a good spot and drive in enough iron nails. Next year you'll see fruit. Doesn't seem to hurt the tree either. But a lawn, that's something else again. Requires a lot of care. Pretty hard to have a really good lawn, moles get into it, weeds — like this playing field for instance, without a man to care for it every day. Nothing finer though than a fine green lawn. Nothing finer. But is it worth it?

Batteries for the second game! For St. Louis, Slezak and Meyer. For New York, Mathewson and . . . Shut up! Shut up! shouted Joe. But it was no use. At the mere mention of Mathewson's name the crowd burst into an uproar. Joe looked instinctively to his companion on the left — but that notable had not returned for the second game. In fact there wasn't much to it. Matty proved to be in such fine form that all the Giants needed was the one run they picked up in the second — though they got a few more later — and that ended it. None of the excitement of the first encounter.

As the crowd filed out Joe followed those who were going down the aisle instead of up, toward the playing field. He had no place in particular to go, he might as well take his time.

A little self-consciously he wandered toward the pitcher's mound. He hadn't realized how much raised it was above the rest of the diamond. That's just it, he said, when you really get up close to a thing . . . And the way they whip that ball in! Walking in toward the plate he looked back to where Wiltze had stood. But when several fourteen to sixteen year old boys approached he turned and walked back across the infield, past second base out into the soft grass beyond. It was coarser than he had thought it to be from the stands, much more uneven and full of worm casts.

As he passed through the center gate with the other stragglers of the crowd he thought he saw, ahead of him, the old fellow who had sat beside him during the first game. Wonder where he's been. And so out into the dirty street under the elevated tracks. And home.

CHAPTER XXII

The Ferry Children

I BEEN THINKING maybe you'd come in sometime.

I would have come before, said Gurlie, but you know . . .

That's right, I guess, with the children and all that. But you could of left them here any time. We'd be glad to take care of them for you.

Gurlie thought she'd better change the subject. I think she's waking up, she said of the infant in the lopsided carriage backed against the porch support. Look, she's smiling.

She don't know what she laughs about sometime. She looks at the wall and she laughs, said Mrs. Ferry.

The hound stood up and shook himself, rattling his long chain, shiny from being dragged, day in, day out, over the porch boards. After he'd scratched himself he stood there a moment looking around. Then he let out a long meaningless bay at the romping children and turning, came up onto the porch. There he scratched himself, then went down where two of the boards had been pulled away from the porch floor disappearing underneath. His chain dragged behind him, the board was eaten and raw all along the edge from similar draggings of the chain since the beginning of hot weather.

Mrs. Ferry turned to the baby in its carriage and Gurlie leaned to look also. It was a white-faced little thing in a pale blue silk hat and enough covers on it to choke it in this weather.

Why don't you take all those things off it? said Gurlie. Look at how it's sweating. That can't be good for it.

She ain't more'n six weeks old, said Mrs. Ferry. Gets awful chilly up here toward night.

I'd take it out of that carriage and give it some sunlight, said Gurlie. I don't think that can hurt it.

Might get in her eyes, said Mrs. Ferry. Little babies like that has awful weak eyes.

But can't you cover its eyes? Gurlie persisted. Look how pale and white she looks.

I guess its being so high up here. The sun's awful hot in summer. It don't be good for them to have too much sun. My sister lost two of her'n that way. They sickened one night and the next day they was gone.

The flies were terrific, settling on one's shoes, preening themselves, running over the sunny boards of the porch, everywhere. Gurlie saw two or three on the baby's face moving toward its eyes and couldn't stand it any longer. She got up and shooed them off. The mother turned with mild interest and watched her.

Don't you have any screens on your windows? asked Gurlie.

No, said Mrs. Ferry, smiling her toothless smile, we ain't bothered much. Some has screens, but I guess we don't have flies up here like some has.

Gurlie just looked at her. There were six or seven children of various ages in groups of two or three about the yard, little girls with two older boys and a toddling child of about three, with powerful fat legs, who kept running back and forth and falling constantly. If anyone leaned to pick him up, he'd lie on

his back and kick, then laugh and roll over, get up
and run again.

It was a triangular piece where the children were
playing between the road and the brook with a
kitchen garden along the path to the privy and a
number of fruit trees. Near the brook, in fact leaning
over it at the top of a low bank, was one old apple tree
that had been very nearly split in half some years previously leaving only three branches, all on one side.
It was full of green fruit.

The grass everywhere was brilliant green and soft
as it always seems to be in Vermont. A cow was wander-
ing loose on the bank over near the small bridge by
the road. Once it got into the road and the children
chased it back again. It went on winding its tongue
round the lush grass and tearing it off with a quick
side movement of its head as before.

Lottie was making mudpies with one of the little
girls of her age while the older one was fetching water,
taking an old can that leaked and going back and forth
with it between the brook and their play corner under
one of the old fruit trees.

About a half mile to the east just before the road
took a turn back of the hill, two men were taking in
hay on a sloping field.

Is that your husband over there? asked Gurlie
pointing.

Yes, him and his brother. They'll be coming in
pretty soon. Had to kill the old sow this morning and
he'll have to finish dressing it.

Why, what happened? said Gurlie.

Broke her leg, caught it in the old trough and fell
on it, Charlie says.

It was toward the end of August. Already the days

were growing shorter and the evenings cool. In fact, there had been frost in the valley on the way to town and the tops of the standing corn looked dead there.

Expect to be coming up here again next year? asked Mrs. Ferry of Gurlie.

Lottie! called out the latter. No. No. Lottie stopped with the can in her hand, hesitated and came back from where she had been on the way to the brook for water. The older girls took the can and ran off instead.

Yes, I'd like to come back again, said Gurlie. But not the way it's been this year.

Seems to done the young 'un a heap of good, ventured Mrs. Ferry. She didn't look like she was good for much when you come here in June.

Gurlie looked at her smaller daughter standing at her knee as if, yes, for the first time she did realize what a remarkable change had been wrought in her. The thing was really beginning to be attractive. Her hair especially had grown and was in blond ringlets tho' small ones, about her temples and right on top of her head.

Can I please take her, asked the older of the girls who had come up now. She wants to come. Don't you want to come with Eleanor? she asked putting out her hands to the baby.

Yes, yes. Flossie struggled with her feet to get them around that way and suddenly sat down, wham, on the floor.

Can she come with me, Mrs. Stecher? asked Eleanor. I'll watch her good.

Well, said Gurlie, all right. But be careful. Eleanor wanted to carry her but the child stiffened out and wanted to get down and walk. Eleanor had to hold with both hands from behind. The awkward feet went in all directions eagerly.

She's kind of slow walking ain't she? said Mrs. Ferry. Eleanor was delighted to play the little mother and sat on the grass holding Flossie, watching the pie-making. The other two girls, industriously had a row of eight hand-made mud dumplings on a piece of board under the tree.

Now and again Gurlie thought she could catch the odor of new-mown hay even from that distance. Certainly the brook could be heard at the rocky gorge back of the house splashing and rustling. The day was fairly hot but pleasant.

I didn't see you at old home week, said Gurlie to Mrs. Ferry who sat in an old rocker swaying slowly back and forth.

No, I ain't been but once. We don't come from around here. Charlie wanted to take me last time but with the haying and children and all that we never did get around to it. And the new baby too, you know, how it is. I don't feel so strong neither. Can't stand much no more the way I used to.

Yes, I wondered, said Gurlie thinking of the immaculate farms in the neighborhood, if you were from around here.

And you can't take children out like that without buying them things. I think maybe the boys did get down in the afternoon once but they said it wasn't much. Guess I'd better be peeling my potatoes, said Mrs. Ferry stirring her relaxed bulk heavily. She wasn't an old woman but she moved with difficulty, her big legs seeming to have little strength in them. There was a wad of old cloth flattened on the seat of the chair where she had been sitting. Won't you come in a little minute, she said to Gurlie politely. You're welcome if you want to. They'll take care of the children, you don't need to worry.

Gurlie was extremely anxious to see the inside of the house. All afternoon she had been looking at a cameo brooch Mrs. Ferry wore at her throat — wondering if it might be something old and of value. She thought there might be some old pieces of furniture about.

I ain't able to get around the way I used to, said Mrs. Ferry again as she led the way into the house. When Gurlie looked at her from behind, she remembered that some of the children were thin-legged and the others heavily fleshed, some like the father, some like the mother, about evenly divided. The back was broad and heavy. The skirt fell straight down to the floor.

The children played under the tree for awhile and the older girl never let little Flossie out of her reach for a minute. Pretty soon, though, the older boys came around and stood watching.

Go on, let her have it, said one of them to his sister as the baby tried to get at the working place where the two younger girls were busy. No, she can't, said their sister. Can't you see she has a clean dress on.

Go away, said the busy sister to them. Lottie looked up in surprise.

You're just trying to spoil their fun, said the older girl.

What's her name?

None of your business.

Yes it is. No it isn't. 'Tis so. No 'tisn't. Yes. No. Yes. No. Yes. No. Yes. No. Yes. No.

The little, intense child who had been working with Lottie then stood up, looked at her smeared hands a minute then ran at her brother. He held her away with his long arms and she tried to kick him.

Aren't you ashamed of yourself? said the girl who had been holding the baby going to help her sister. With that the baby got down and soon had her hands in the mud. Lottie was too amazed at the whole performance to resent anything.

Look, said the older of the two boys, then, pointing at the baby and as the others turned to look, he and his brother started to laugh.

Anna and the others then went down to the shallow stream to wash the baby's hands.

Want some apples? said the boy who had started the mischief in the first place.

No, said his sister. You know they ain't ripe.

I don't care, said he. I ain't afraid to eat one. This he proceeded to do but spit the mouthful he had taken quickly into the stream and they had a laugh on him that time.

Let's try to catch a fish. All right. All the children except the baby were barefoot. The boys had an old cooking pan with a handle and a hole in the bottom so with the others watching they started to maneuver in the shallow water. Anna took the baby to a good place on the bank and like a careful mother held her to watch the others.

It didn't take the boys long. With the pan half full of water a finger held over the hole in the bottom they came up on the bank and all the children gathered round to see. There were two greyish fish suffering in the shallow water. After a while the boys dumped them out on the grass being distracted by a green frog which had jumped into the water at their feet. Failing to catch him, they continued down the stream and disappeared.

When Gurlie entered the kitchen with Mrs. Ferry she found a long, bare room with a long, plain table along one wall of it and chairs, not one of them whole, ranged around it. On top of it were two pies, one almost gone and a big dish of doughnuts. Everything in the place looked as if an army had passed over it, the floor itself furrowed at the doorways, the door edges polished from handling. There was a cupboard at one side with plain dishes piled on it, the sink, with a small hand-pump, the range with wood piled behind it, a business-like rifle standing in one corner by the door, a very worn looking overcoat on a hook near the same door and that was all.

Mrs. Ferry started to make up a fire with kindling and light sticks.

Whew! said Gurlie, don't you open these windows?

I don't think you can open them, said Mrs. Ferry. Try if you want to, but Gurlie didn't try. Instead she sat watching the lady of the house take half a pail of potatoes from a closet and start to peel them dropping the white, smoothly whittled chunks into a pan of water and the peels back into the pail as she worked.

Can I help you? asked Gurlie. No, said Mrs. Ferry. It don't take long.

What are you going to have? said Gurlie fascinated.

Potatoes and cream gravy. That's what they like mostly for supper this time of year. Sometimes we have something from the green garden but mostly we have potatoes and coffee.

Gurlie was looking at the chairs and the dishes on the shelf to see if there was anything old there but she

couldn't detect a thing of value. All she found that
she hadn't seen at a first glance was a calendar beyond
the dish closet of Remington Firearms representing
a deer jumping over a fallen tree and, on a low table,
some old books, in very bad condition, one of them
the plays of Shakespeare in a single volume.

Oh them, laughed Mrs. Ferry. My husband bought
them for ten cents along with some dishes in an old
box at an auction.

Gurlie laughed and went over to sit by her hostess.

The boys came back along the edge of the brook
after a while with hands full of raspberries which they
proceeded to eat holding them up one at a time for
the others to see.

Stingy! Mean! said the girls. Come on, I know
where they grow, said the smaller of the farm girls.
But this time the boys relented and, in a nonchalant
manner dumped each a handful of the berries in
Anna's lap, who passed them around. Flossie got one
and sucked it seriously, smacking her lips and blinking her eyes. More! she said presently.

That made the boys go into stitches of laughter.
These city children appeared to be about the funniest
things on earth to them.

More, they said imitating the baby who paid no
attention whatever to them but smacked her lips
delightedly over another berry and blinked and
twisted her little face up in great earnestness.

That set the boys laughing again. They couldn't
contain themselves but rolled on the grass idiotically
and their little brother beside them in his turn imitating them.

All the berries were gone by this time and Flossie
still saying, more. Come on, said the older boy. We'll

show you where they grow. Come on, down back of the barn.

I don't think we better, said Anna. But the others had already started at a run, seeing which one would get there first, so she took the baby up and went after them, across the road and up the side road where among the stones of an embankment near the barn there was a thicket of wild berries. There weren't many left at this time of year so it was fun to hunt for them, only one at a time being found. But they were very sweet.

As the children were at this, down the road came the loaded hay wagon with the two men on top and a fine team of dapple grey horses drawing them, trying to break into a trot. Up the incline they went. The men had to lie flat on the hay as the wagon went with a swish through the high door. The horses' hoofs pounded on the wooden floor. Whoa! shouted Mr. Ferry. God damn you to hell, where the hell are you trying to take us, through the back of the barn into the sow pen? Whoa! what the hell's got into you? You hear me! Whoa! Unhitch 'em and let her stay here tonight, Jim.

The children came running. They had to go around another way to get where they could be ahead of the horses. The boys were in the lead. They ducked in around several obstacles and were gone. But as the girls and both Lottie and the baby in tow came around the barn's near corner, Lottie stopped suddenly and would go no further.

Trussed up by block and tackle just inside the door which they were in the act of entering was a newly slaughtered pig of a pink color, gutted and with a stick of wood springing the severed ribs apart. It won't hurt you. It's only a pig, said Anna. But Lottie was backing up in alarm and the baby, seeing her, began to whimper in sympathy so the smaller girl and her toddling brother went on anyway and Anna had to go back with them.

The potatoes were boiling now and Mrs. Ferry was showing Gurlie the front rooms of the house with its formal parlor very seldom entered. No, we don't come in here much. We don't know many people round here. Some times we have the school teacher call on us, but not often. What do you do in winter? said Gurlie. Oh we get along pretty good. He does some hauling . . . Then there was the crack of a heavy rifle. What's that? said Gurlie. Then another crack.

When they went out, Mr. Ferry, a lean sweaty man with a three days growth of beard on his face, was standing in the road with two rather well dressed men from the lake. A damned good shot, one of them was saying in a clear Boston accent.

Should have hit him the first time. That's too expensive shooting for me. Twenty-six cents for one woodchuck. Them shells cost thirteen cents apiece. The men laughed.

What in the world are you shooting at? said Gurlie at the door.

Mr. Ferry immediately took his seedy hat off and turned with a smile. Just fooling with the boys. Don't know your names, boys. This is the lady's been living up on the hill this summer, Mrs. Stecher. The children were standing back in a fascinated circle, the baby's face smeared with berry juice, her hands sooty, quite part of it all.

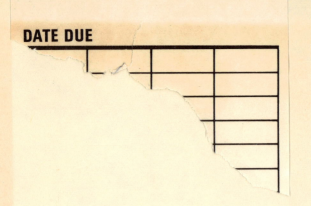

DATE DUE